Two Moon Princess

Carmen Ferreiro-Esteban

Tanglewood • Terre Haute, IN

Published by Tanglewood Press, LLC, 2007.

Cover illustration by Sarah Brennan
Cover and interior designed by Amy Alick Perich
Edited by Lisa Rojany Buccieri

Tanglewood Press, LLC
P. O. Box 3009
Terre Haute, IN 47803
www.tanglewoodbooks.com

Printed in the United States of America
10 9 8 7 6 5 4 3 2 1

ISBN-13 978-1-933718-12-5
ISBN-10 1-933718-12-9

Library of Congress Cataloging-in-Publication Data

Ferreiro-Esteban, Carmen.
  Two moon princess / by Carmen Ferreiro-Esteban.
    p. cm.
  Summary: Andrea, a reluctant, tomboyish princess from the Kingdom of Zeltia— a world resembling medieval Spain—is transported from a forbidden cave into modern California, and when she accidentally returns to her home with the wrong person, it sets off a chain reaction that threatens her family and their kingdom.
  ISBN-13: 978-1-933718-12-5
  ISBN-10: 1-933718-12-9
  [1. Time and space—Fiction. 2. Sex role—Fiction. 3. California—Fiction. 4. Fantasy.] I. Title.

PZ7.F367Tw 2007
[Fic]—dc22
                                2007009892

For Natalia, For Nicolás

My angel, my rebel

My love

ONE

A Broken Dream

"The arrow knows the way. Just let it free."

Burnt into my memory by endless repetition, the words came to my mind unbidden, with the soothing rhythm of a familiar song. But somehow this time, they were not just words: A tingling feeling ran through my fingers, and the bow became an extension of myself. I could feel the trembling of the string and the cold of the metal at the tip of the arrow as I felt the tension in my muscles and the pounding of my heart.

Then the arrow took flight. Like a falcon aiming at its prey, it went straight to the target drawn on the trunk of the distant oak. In the complete silence of the wait, I heard the vibration in the air and the thump of the tree hurting as it was hit in the center of the bull's eye.

All over the field, the roar of the multitude exploded like sudden thunder, breaking my concentration. Still holding the bow I no longer felt, I tore my eyes from the arrow trembling in the tree and walked back to my companions.

Don Gonzalo, our instructor, moved forward as I approached them. "Bravo, Princess Andrea!" he shouted. "A perfect shot!" His red hair a mane of fire in the midday sun, he crossed his right arm briefly over his chest before extending it toward me, his open hand facing the sky. The salute to an equal. I blushed with pleasure at his words and returned his salute while the pages surrounded me, screaming my name in victory.

I laughed with them and answered their calls. And for a moment, lost in the exhilarating feeling of belonging, I almost forgot the empty seat on the High Stand by the king's side. The empty seat that meant Tío Ramiro had not come to the Games. The empty seat that meant, despite my perfect shot, I had already lost.

"Andrea, I will try to be there," Tío had told me months ago before leaving for his manor. "But you know it doesn't depend only on me. I have other obligations."

It was not exactly a promise, but I had taken it as such because he was my only hope. Tío Ramiro, my mother's brother, was the only one who had shown any interest in my desire to be a knight. I knew that without his help, the king, my father, would not allow me to become a squire. He would send me to Mother instead to be made into a lady as he had promised her he would on my fourteenth birthday. And my fourteenth birthday was only months away.

A lady! I shook my head. As a lady, I would not be allowed to play in the courtyard or hunt in the woods. As a lady, I would have to stay inside the castle and do a lot of curtsying and smiling.

I shook my head again to get rid of the dreary thought, and closing my fingers around my lucky charm—a flat round pebble with four perfect holes I had found once in my uncle's room—I watched as the herald, magnificently attired in the blue and white colors of our kingdom, rode into the center of the field and in a clear voice announced the winners.

"Winner at the wrestling contest, Don Luis de Can. Winner at the sword competition: Don Enrique de Hul. Winner at archery: Princess Andrea de Montemaior."

The world around me disappeared in a cacophony of sounds, and I knew I was shouting, although I could not hear my voice. Moments later, and without any recollection of how I had gotten there, I found myself in front of the High Stand where my father was now standing. His eyes, bright and proud under his bushy eyebrows, met mine briefly as he offered me the prize: a golden arrow. One knee on the ground, my head bent in respect, I took it from his hand and went back to my comrades.

I could not stay long, though. After all, I was a princess and was expected to be with my family in the Great Hall. I would join the pages later and wait with them while the knights met to choose their squires. *While the knights* fought *to choose me as their squire*, I thought and smiled. Fate was smiling at me today. I had won first place. Father would have to realize at last that I, Andrea, his fourth and youngest daughter, could be as good as the male heir he had always wanted—even without my uncle's prompting.

My feet barely touching the ground, I rushed to the castle.

Back in my room, I gave myself over to Ama Bernarda, my old nurse, to be dressed for dinner. For the first time ever, I did not argue when she slipped my fanciest dress over my underdress and combed my hair again and again in a useless attempt to make me look like a lady. I did not even complain when she scrubbed my nails with a sharp brush until my fingertips were red and sore.

Once I was ready, I looked in the mirror. A tall lanky girl with dark green eyes and short brown curls returned my stare. I couldn't recognize in her the mighty warrior I really was.

A sharp knock interrupted my musings. Margarida, I thought. When I opened the door, however, I didn't find my sister, but one of my father's footmen standing outside.

"Princess Andrea," he said. "His Majesty the King demands to see you."

I froze. Why should Father want to see me now? Had I already been chosen? Or . . .? Someone—Ama Bernarda, I realized—touched my elbow.

"Come on, Princess. Don't make Don Andrés wait."

"But . . ."

Ama smiled, her eyes so surprisingly blue in her worn-out face staring right at me. "Have no fear, my child. You have worked hard. Maybe we were all wrong and your father will grant you your wish to be a squire after all."

Encouraged by Ama's words, I rushed to Father's quarters, and after the footman's formal announcement, I hurried inside. From behind the immense mahogany table that dominated the room, Father looked up. "Pray have a seat, Princess," he said as I curtsied to him.

I did as ordered. My fingers tightly wrapped around the carved armrest of the chair, my feet on the deep red carpet, I leaned forward.

Father smiled—the unusual gesture making the old scar that ran down his right cheek stretch itself into a pale line. "Today has been a great day for you, Princess," he said. "One phase of your life has come to a close, and a new one is about to begin. So it is with joy that I dismiss you from my service as a page and welcome you as a lady into my family."

I jumped to my feet. "A lady? But, Father, I don't want to be a lady. I've won the golden arrow. I—"

"Silence!"

Father's voice was cold. Cold and hard as hail, and his eyes were ice. Under the soft silk of my skirts, my legs were shaking and refused to hold me. Gasping for air, I stumbled back.

Again Father smiled, a brief sharp grimace that did not reach his eyes. "You are right, Princess. You didn't do too badly this morning—for a girl—and I am proud of you. But you are almost fourteen now, and the queen and I have an agreement. Your time to play games with the pages is over."

"Games?"

Father raised his hand. "Yes, Princess, all you have done until now, I call games. Even if playing them has taught you the basic skills of a soldier, that is all they were. But from now on, your comrades will start the real training, and believe me, it will not be a place for a girl. You are a princess, Andrea, like it or not, and you have to learn to behave like a lady. One day you will understand and thank me for having sent you to your mother, Doña Jimena, today."

Pushing the heavy chair back, he got up and offered me his ring. The audience was over. As powerless as a bow under the skilled archer's hands, I rose and, bending over the polished table, kissed the blue stone on his middle finger: the symbol of Gothia, our kingdom.

Behind Father, from the tapestry that covered the wall, the brown damp eyes of the hunted stag were pleading with mine for help. Around him in a mêlée of bodies and legs, several hounds, fangs bared, were waiting for their master to finish the kill. I was the stag. And my time was over. I turned and the walls swirled in a blur of colors, while ahead of me the doors swung open without a noise.

When I came back to my senses, I found myself in the garden, standing by my old companion, the oak tree. Up on its branches, hidden by the dense foliage of summer, my secret hideout was waiting. I reached up, and grabbing its lowest limb firmly with my hands, I swung my body up. But my gown, entangled on the undergrowth, pulled me down.

Jerking the skirts over my knees, I kicked the trunk. "How can Father do this to me? Sending me to Mother? Isn't it obvious I'm not a lady? I don't look like a lady, I don't feel like a lady, and I definitely don't act like one."

I hit the tree again. Pain shot up my legs from my bruised toes, and brilliant points of light flashed in front of my eyes.

"Andrea!"

I ignored the call.

"Andrea," the voice repeated, closer now.

"Go away!"

I waited for the rustle of the skirt on the grass that would tell me Margarida was leaving. But my heavy breathing was the only answer.

"Ama Bernarda told me Father had summoned you," my sister said after a pause. "When you didn't come back, I guessed you would be here."

My nails biting deep into my clenched palms, I turned. "Leave me alone."

A flash of pain crossed my sister's eyes. "I gather Father said no," she said.

I wanted Margarida to hold me in her arms and hated myself for it. That would only prove my father was right, that I was only a girl. I shook my head. "I don't care what Father says," I cried. "I am a squire."

"Andrea, you are a lady."

"No, I'm not. I don't like to sew. And I hate curtsying."

Margarida smiled. "I don't like sewing either. But that is not all ladies do and you know it."

"The only thing I know is that I like to be outside in the meadows, and to shoot and fight, and that I only feel alive when I'm riding on Flecha."

"You can still ride Flecha."

"Sure, and when would that be? Once a month if I behave. That is not enough. You know I'll die if I have to stay inside."

"But Andrea, you cannot be a squire. If Father has forbidden it, no one in the castle will take you at his service."

I sulked. Margarida was right. No one in the castle would dare defy Father. No one in the castle. Suddenly the total implications of her words hit me, and I laughed. "Margarida, you are brilliant!" Rushing to her, I hugged her wildly.

My sister moved back and, holding me at arm's length, stared into my eyes. "What is it, Andrea? One of your crazy ideas?"

"My ideas are not crazy," I said. But as I was talking, I remembered the time some winters past when, annoyed at my sister Rosa's teasing, I ran away and almost froze to death in the snow. I shrugged. "This time I will plan my journey carefully."

"A journey? But where would you go?"

"It doesn't matter where as long as it's away from this awful castle. I will dress like a boy and offer my services as a squire to some distant lord."

"Andrea, please, don't go. You left once before, remember? And Father had to rescue you."

"Sure." I sighed in exasperation. "But thanks to my running away, Mother agreed I could train with the pages until my fourteenth birthday. Besides, it's summer now."

Margarida hesitated. I had to keep her busy so she could

not think to alert Mother. "I will need a page's clothes, a blanket, and some food."

"What you need is some sense, Andrea."

"You may be right, sister. But it wasn't my fault you took it all." Margarida laughed.

"So dear sister, would you be so kind as to get me some food from the kitchen?"

"You have made up your mind, haven't you?"

I nodded. "Please, Margarida, I need your help."

"All right, all right, I'll help you. But—"

"You will not regret it, I promise. Now go. And meet up with me at the stables."

I had almost reached the door to the keep when I remembered Ama Bernarda would be in my quarters. I hesitated. Ama would get suspicious if I were to change into my page's clothes. I could not take that risk. Turning back, I ran to the laundry house. I picked some plain tights and a soldier's tunic from the clean pile. I rolled them into a bundle under my arm and rushed across the cobblestones of the courtyard toward the stables.

From the darkness of her stall, Flecha greeted me with a loud nicker. Stretching her neck, she rubbed her head against my chest. I ran my hands through her golden mane. Flecha neighed.

"Shh. Nobody must hear us," I whispered into her soft warm ear.

Flecha's big limpid eyes looked at me for a moment, questioning. "We are going away," I told her. She snorted and remained still while I slid the bridle over her head.

While my hands worked on her saddle, the faces of the lords I had seen at my father's court flashed through my mind. I rejected them one by one until I found the perfect candidate.

"I've chosen Don Pelayo as my future lord," I told Margarida after she had joined me. "His castle is on the Boreal Island. Father will never imagine that I have crossed the ocean. He knows I hate boats."

"But the Boreal Island is so far away; Father will find you before you get there."

I thought for a minute. The shortest distance to the island from the mainland was from the village of Forcarei at the other side of the Northern Sierra. Although it was not far in a straight line, to actually reach Forcarei would take me several days because the road made a long detour east around the mountains. Unless . . .

"No," I said. "He won't."

Margarida frowned.

"I will not take the main road. I will go west until I hit the ocean, then continue north along the coast. I will be in Forcarei by morning."

Margarida gasped. "But you cannot do that, Andrea. You'd have to cross the Forbidden Lands. It is too dangerous. People disappear there without a trace, and strange creatures swim ashore at night."

"Come on, Margarida. You cannot seriously believe those stories."

"They are not stories. My dueña remembers. She saw the strangers they found by the shore in Grandfather's times. They looked like us, she says, but spoke a strange tongue, and they were naked like animals. Then one night they disappeared from the dungeon, through the castle walls, and were never seen again."

"So what? Even if that was true, which I very much doubt, why should I care? That was a long time ago."

"Please, Andrea. Be reasonable. Don't go."

Her face was tense with fear. I knew her resolve to help me was melting. I hugged her quickly. "Now sister, promise me you will not tell."

Margarida sighed. "Will you be careful?"

"I will. Don't worry. And before you know it, I'll be back. A real knight."

Margarida shook her head. I hugged her again. Then I turned to Flecha, and not wanting to waste any more time, I tucked the stolen uniform and the food in her saddlebag. The reins wrapped around my hand, I led her into the courtyard.

The castle gates were open. I jumped on Flecha's back and cantered toward the sentries. The guards came to attention as I approached and crossed their spears. But when I got close enough for them to see me, they moved back and saluted. I returned their salute and, pressing Flecha's flanks, sprang forward.

Soon I had left the drawbridge behind and, at full gallop, dashed ahead across the plains that surrounded the castle in the direction of the Northern Sierra. I wanted to pretend I was going north just in case someone was watching.

The evening was warm and clear, not a single cloud tainted the sky. On my right, beyond the thatched roofs of the village, over the eastern horizon, Athos the golden moon was rising. I could not have asked for a better night.

By the time I reached the forest, the sun was already on my left, sinking rapidly toward the raised lands that hid the ocean. The day would soon be over. I reined Flecha in and looked back toward the gray walls and towers of my father's castle. Nobody was following me. Yet.

I took a deep breath. The air smelled of grass and pine, of horse sweat and leather. It smelled of freedom. Over the repetitive call of the crickets, invisible birds were singing.

Flecha neighed. I pressed my legs, and her supple body turned at my command. Leaving the road I had followed so far, I headed west, toward the Forbidden Lands.

At first the woods seemed no different from the ones that flanked the highway. But little by little, trees became scarcer and were replaced by shrubs and bracken until finally, after a steady climb, I reached a plateau, a raised land that ended abruptly over sharp cliffs that plummeted to the sea. In front of me over the ocean, where the sun had been, the sky was burning red, orange, and purple, turning Athos the golden moon into a ball of fire.

Flecha neighed again, and the sound echoed in the distance like a warning. I shivered. "Let's go, Flecha. We must hurry. We have to reach Forcarei before Father's men."

I pressed Flecha's flanks, and at a fast canter, we continued north following a winding path along the coast. But before long, big boulders, still and menacing like giants turned to stone, blocked our way. Flecha reared.

I stroked her neck to calm her down and dismounted. Holding her reins, I stepped on the narrow ledge left between the rocks and the cliffs. Flecha reluctantly followed. We strode thus for a while, my eyes on the gravel to avoid taking a false step, until Flecha, letting out a loud snort, pulled at the reins and refused to go farther.

"Come on, Flecha. What is it now?" Tearing my eyes from the slippery ground, I looked up. What I saw was not encouraging.

Before me, the coastline had lost its battle against the ocean and receded inland to form a small bay. Except for a huge rock carved like an arch, which appeared to be still fighting the pull of the water, the cove was covered by the tide. Up the cliffs, where I was standing, the ledge we had been following didn't turn with the coast to surround the cove, but continued straight, took a deep descent, and disappeared. We couldn't go on. Still I hesitated. It didn't make sense. Paths are supposed to lead somewhere. They cannot just vanish.

My hands firmly on the reins, I looked to my right, trying to find a way to get around the cove, but the boulders, impressive and bare, formed an insurmountable wall.

"You are right, Flecha. We have to go back."

I was still talking when, over the roar of the waves breaking against the rocks, I heard a rumbling noise—like horses galloping. Down at the cove, the solitary arch I had noticed before seemed to fade away, and the water at its base withdrew as if caught in a whirlpool. Under my feet, the ground shook.

Flecha neighed in fear and reared, pulling at the bridle. Just as I turned to hold her still, I saw a dark form emerging from the broken rock in the cove. For a moment, I froze. Again Flecha pulled, and the leather ran through my fingers, burning them. I screamed in pain and let go of the reins so suddenly I fell backward. I heard Flecha's hooves against the ground, and I knew I had lost her. But I did not have time to worry about her. Under my weight, the gravel cracked and scratched my legs as I slid faster and faster down the broken trail that ended right where the cliffs began.

TWO

The Forbidden Lands

Brambles and bushes flashed by my side. I tried to grasp them. But they escaped through my fingers, leaving only their thorns in my scratched skin.

Blinded by pain, I screamed. Suddenly, over the cracking noise of loose gravel, I heard the sound of cloth tearing. Then I felt a strong pull on my legs, and I stopped moving.

I lay on my back, my whole body hurting, my head hanging over the edge of the cliffs. Down, down below, I could hear the roar of the waves breaking against the rocks and the cries of the seagulls fighting for food. I stayed still, barely breathing, waiting for my rescuer to help me up. No one came.

Slowly I raised my head. The sky was burning in a shimmering fire as Lua, the copper moon, rose from behind the boulders. For a moment I just stared, awed by its majestic beauty. But soon the pain of my beaten body reminded me of my dangerous predicament, and lifting my head as far as I could, I looked at my feet. Nobody was there. This didn't make any sense. Someone had grabbed my feet.

I squinted my eyes against the glow of the full moon and searched the ledge. No one was in sight. I shivered as the old stories of strange creatures that lived in the Forbidden Lands rushed to my mind. Were they true after all? It was then I heard the cracking sound of rocks falling; someone was climbing up the cliffs. I remembered the shadow I had seen emerging through the arch, and again I shivered.

I had to get out of there, and fast. Trying not to think of the ocean-beaten rocks below me, I lifted myself to a sitting position. But when I tried to crawl forward away from the cliffs, my skirts caught in a bush, holding me back. Suddenly I understood. It had not been a person but my long dress that had stopped my fall. How ironic, I thought, that my lady outfit had saved my life, when I was running away from all that it represented.

"Thank you, Mother," I said aloud and meant it. After all, she was the one who had insisted on my always wearing a gown for supper.

Once more I reached forward and pulled at my skirts. But the thorns pricked at my fingers, fighting for their prey. Over my heavy breathing, the sound of pebbles rolling was getting closer. Frantic, I pulled again and again, until my hands started bleeding. Still the thorns refused to let go.

I had no choice. I tore open the front laces of my bodice, and like a snake shedding its skin, I emerged from my gown. Wearing only my underdress, I ran to the boulders that flanked the ledge and squeezed myself into a crack. Barely breathing, I waited while the steps got louder and louder. Then suddenly they stopped.

After an indefinite time of anguished silence, I leaned forward and peeped through a gap in the rocks. A dark shape was bending over the bush that still held my dress. Although I couldn't see his face, something in his appearance was vaguely familiar. I was still trying to figure out what it was when the stranger straightened his back and, turning toward me, demanded in a heavily accented voice, "Andrea, would you please come out from wherever it is you are hiding?"

It was my uncle, Tío Ramiro.

I jumped to my feet, staring at him over the boulder. What was my uncle doing here? And more important, how was I to convince him not to tell Father he had seen me?

Tío Ramiro came over. "Hello, Andrea. It's always nice to see you, too." With a bow, he offered me his hand to help me climb over the rock.

I shook my head. "I don't have a dress, Tío."

Tío smiled. "Of course," he said. Sharply, he slid the strange jacket he was wearing over his head, handing it to me with a mock bow.

I held the garment in my hands. It was blue and tightly knitted in a soft material I had never seen before. Bright yellow letters on the front formed words I didn't understand. After a slight hesitation, I put it on and climbed the boulder.

Once more, Tío was kneeling by the bush. When I got closer, I realized he was cutting the thorns with a little knife. With a pull of his free hand, he lifted the dress. "I got it," he said and, getting up, faced me.

I stared in amazement. Several pebbles similar to my four-holed lucky charm formed a straight line down the front of his shirt.

"What's wrong, Andrea?" As Tío talked, he made the blade of the small knife disappear into its red handle with a sharp movement of his hand.

I gasped. "What is that?" I asked, pointing at his hand.

Tío hesitated. Then he shrugged. As quickly as it had vanished, the blade reappeared in his palm. "It's only a knife," he said. He handed it to me.

The blade was sharp only on one side; a thin crack ran along the other. The handle was . . . different. Memories of the wondrous gifts Tío Ramiro used to give me when I was a child rushed to my mind—toys made of soft materials that bent without breaking, books that talked when I touched them, musical boxes that didn't need to be rewound. I would play with them many happy days until one night they would vanish from my room. When in the morning I begged Ama to give them back to me, she would insist I had been dreaming.

"May I have it back?"

Once again, Tío made the blade disappear into the handle.

"Let's make a deal, Andrea," he said. "You will forget you ever saw my knife, and I will not tell your father I found you in the Forbidden Lands."

I considered his proposition for a moment. If Tío wanted me to forget the knife, I was sure it was worth knowing why. But if Father were to learn of my whereabouts, my plan would be doomed. "Deal," I said, and raising my hand, I hit my palm against Tío's. The pact was sealed.

Tío smiled. "And now, young lady," he said, turning to go, "I would appreciate it if you were to escort me to your father's castle. I'm afraid without your assistance I may fall down the cliffs or even worse, end up as food for the ferocious white wolves of the mountains."

Go back to the castle? Not in a million years. "I'm afraid, Tío, I can't go back with you now. I mean . . . I have to find Flecha."

"Really?" Tío Ramiro frowned. "Is that why you came here?"

"Well, yes. Flecha ran away. I have been looking for her all over. Why don't you go ahead? I will join you as soon as I find her."

"Don't you think, Andrea, that you have had enough adventures for one day? If I am not misreading the signs, you've barely missed falling down the cliffs. Don't waste your energies making up a story. You're coming back with me."

"No I'm not." I stamped my foot. "You cannot force me. And you promised not to tell Father you found me."

"I didn't promise not to tell your mother, did I?"

I sulked. "That is not fair. Besides, it's true. I do need to find Flecha."

"Fine. Go ahead then, while I get ready. But promise you'll wait for me at the end of the ledge."

"I'll think about it," I said and turned away.

"Andrea!"

I ignored his call, and as fast as the treacherous ground allowed, I rushed down the narrow rim I had walked with Flecha before. Soon I had reached the open plateau where we had joined the coast. My eyes swept eagerly over the barren landscape, looking for the golden shape of my mare. But Flecha was nowhere to be seen. Neither did she answer my repeated whistling and callings.

Systematically I searched the plain for hoofprints in wider and wider circles, but I couldn't find any—which was not strange, as the terrain was mostly rock. Hoarse and exhausted, I sat by one of the boulders flanking the ledge. What was I to do now? I couldn't escape on foot. Father's men would have no trouble finding me, especially now that Tío would tell them where to look. I might as well go back on my own and wait for a better chance.

So when I heard my uncle's steps coming down the path, I was still there, crouched under the boulder. I looked up at him as he approached, noticing he had changed into the long dark tunic he always wore in the castle. A leather bag I hadn't seen before was strapped to his back. He didn't seem surprised to see me.

"I have your dress here," he said.

Tío waited as I put my dress back on. But I still kept his jacket.

"You're going to need a new dress," he said when I was done, his eyes on the tears running down my skirts. "This one looks quite useless as it is." And then, as I nodded with embarrassment, he added, "Don't worry, Andrea. I think it was about time anyway. You've had this one for ages."

"You recognized my dress. That is how you knew it was me."

Tío smiled. "Of course. What did you think? I'm not a wizard."

Bending over, he offered me his hand. "Come on, now. We must get going. It would be better if we reach the castle before Don Andrés notices your absence."

He started walking on a narrow path heading south along the coast. I hesitated. Now that the moment had come to give up my dream, I just could not move. Maybe if I waited, Flecha would come back. Maybe Tío was bluffing and would not tell Mother he had seen me. After all, he had always approved of my training. If only he would have been at the Games and talked to Father. Why hadn't he? A flash of anger shot through my body. Jumping to my feet, I ran after Tío.

"Why didn't you come this morning?" I yelled at his back.

Tío turned and stared at me for a moment, his forehead creased in thought. "The Games," he said at last. "They were today, weren't they?"

"Of course! And you . . . you forgot."

Tío seemed genuinely upset. "I'm sorry, Andrea, but I couldn't come. Your father ordered me to patrol the Forbidden Lands."

He was lying. I knew he was lying. "But you promised. You promised to help me convince Father I could be a knight."

"And I did, Andrea. I did ask him on my last visit. Your father refused. Nothing I might have said today would have changed his mind."

I looked away. So it had all been decided in advance, and my winning at the Games had made no difference. Through my unshed tears, the pebbles glittered at my feet like jewels in the bright light of the two moons.

"Why don't you tell me what happened?" Tío asked, his voice warm and inviting. I tried to answer, but my words came out broken, as if a heavy hand were squeezing my throat.

"I guess things didn't go well for you at the Games," Tío he added.

My head shot up. "They did! I won the golden arrow."

"Congratulations, Andrea! I knew you could do it."

"Yeah, sure. But it was useless. Father has ordered me to join Mother tomorrow."

"Your father has ordered you to join your mother tomorrow? How cruel of him, indeed, my dear Andrea. Doesn't he know you need a vacation?"

"A vacation?"

"Yes, Andrea. A vacation. A couple of weeks on your own to get used to the idea."

I stared at him. What was he talking about?

Tío smiled. "I'll tell you what. Let's go back now, before your father gets angry with you for leaving. Tomorrow I'll ask him for permission to keep you as my helper. This will give you time to think about it."

Time to think of a better plan for leaving. I smiled back. "I guess I could do that."

Tío's eyes looked deeply into mine. He frowned. "But you must promise you will join your mother as soon as I leave."

I sulked.

"Come on, Andrea. Promise or there is no deal, and you'll have to join your mother tomorrow."

"All right, I promise."

Tío beamed at me and, with his arm behind my back, pushed me along.

"You know, Andrea, I don't know why you dread being with your mother so much. If you are not meant to be a lady, eventually she will have to desist."

"Do you really think Mother will give up?"

"Of course she will. Jen—I mean Doña Jimena is very strong-minded. She always has been. But not even she could make you into what you are not."

I wanted to believe him so badly, I pushed my fears to the back of my mind and lost myself in his stories. Stories of another time and place, of when Tío and Mother were children, of the smart and strong-minded girl Tío claimed had been my mother.

"Do you know your mother was determined to be a physician before she married your father?" he asked me sometime later.

"A physician? How disgusting!"

"Disgusting? Oh, well, I suppose you can call it that. Or maybe I got the story a little confused. But I am sure she had great aspirations once, before she grew up. We all do, don't we? Even princesses in torn dresses."

"What about you, Tío?" I asked him to hide my embarrassment. "What did you wish for when you were a child?"

Just then the path veered left, and as we turned, my father's castle came into view, glowing softly under the copper light of Lua. Over the keep, which was the tallest tower, the blue-and-white banner of Gothia, our kingdom, undulated in the evening breeze. The king was in the castle.

Tío didn't answer. He stood by my side, eyes wide open and staring ahead, a light of wonder in them. I waited, silent as well, breathing deeply the salty breeze flowing up from the ocean. Suddenly the sound of an owl hooting broke the evening silence. As if waking from a dream, Tío shook his head.

"I wished," he answered, resuming his walk, "to live in a castle where everybody would comply with my every whim."

"You can't be serious, Tío." I couldn't imagine anything more boring.

Tío laughed. "Andrea, today you are serious enough for the both of us."

And so I returned to my parents' castle, not as a knight covered in glory, galloping in front of an army as I had imagined, but escorted by my uncle, wearing his jacket over my torn dress and, alas, on foot.

I DO NOT KNOW WHAT TÍO RAMIRO TOLD MY PARENTS. BUT whatever it was, it worked. They never asked me about that evening, and Mother agreed to let me be on my own during the time Tío remained with us. On my part, I didn't tell anybody, not even Margarida, what had happened. My sister, discreet as usual, didn't ask.

Although I missed my comrades and the excitement of the training, I tried to make the best of my last days of freedom. And after Flecha reappeared, dirty and wild at the gate of the castle on the second day after my return, I rode often across the plain toward Mount Pindo, the sacred mountains of the Xarens, the old inhabitants of the kingdom. At other times, I would walk by myself deep into the woods, listening to the season of plenty burst upon the branches of the trees and watching the animals wander. They were collecting food to survive the winter. I felt I was also saving for harder times, although in my case it was not because of a physical hunger that I worried, but because of a longing inside me I could not name.

My uncle was busy with the kingdom's affairs. For as long as I could remember, he had been the arbiter of the complaints arising between the farmers and hunters and their lords. He was renowned for his unusual solutions, and everybody accepted his judgment.

When he managed to escape his duties, we would go for long walks. Then he would tell me fantastic stories of enchanted lands where girls were allowed to dress as they pleased and choose their own destinies. He had a great imagination and his stories sounded so real—sometimes more so than the trees in the orchard or the walls around my father's castle.

Four weeks passed like this, and finally the morning arrived when Tío told me he was leaving. I looked away to hide my disappointment.

"Come now, Andrea. Don't make it more difficult. You already knew I'd be leaving tonight."

"True," I replied. I had known all right. But knowing did not mean I had accepted it.

"You must keep up your part of the deal now. Promise you will join your mother tomorrow."

I nodded.

Tío grabbed my arms, forcing me to look into his eyes. "Also, Andrea, you must promise that you will never go down to the beach with the broken arch, the beach your people call *Cala dos Mortos*, 'The Cove of the Dead.'"

I pushed him away. "Why can't I go there?"

"Because it's forbidden. Believe me, Andrea, some things are better left alone."

I promised as he asked, thinking it was strange that my rational uncle would care about old superstitions. And his request had seemed irrational that morning in the bright sunlight. But later in the evening, while I watched him leave from my favorite place on the castle ramparts, and I could see the shadows crawling from behind every tree and every rock, I was not so sure anymore. It did seem possible then that something dark and evil might indeed be lurking down on the beach, by the arch not even the ocean had dared to destroy. And although the days were still warm, I wrapped my cape around me because suddenly I felt cold inside.

THREE

Among Ladies

The animal faces carved on the wooden door stared at me with malicious eyes, their mouths wide open in soundless laughter.

"Come on, they're not real," I said to myself, and taking a deep breath, I grabbed the knob. It felt as cold as water from a mountain stream against my sweaty palm. For a moment, I hesitated. It was a moment too long. The attack came from behind in the innocent form of a greeting.

"Good morning, dear sister!"

I dropped my hand and turned. An impeccably dressed young lady had materialized in the corridor, not a hair out of place, not a wrinkle in her gauzy pink gown. My sister Rosa, picture perfect as usual, was smiling at me. "I see you have forgotten your arrows," she said, her pale blue eyes sparkling with mischief. "But don't you worry, dear Andrea. You will find no foes among us gentle ladies."

Just what I need, I thought in dismay, *my conniving, torturing sister making fun of me*. As retreat was not an option, I clenched my fists and braced myself for the attack.

"Good morning, my precious older sister," I told her with my sweetest smile. "Such a pleasure to see you. But what are you doing all by yourself? How inconsiderate of your present admirer—sorry, I don't remember his name. You replace them so often, I just cannot keep up with them. As I was saying, how could he be so careless as to leave you unattended? Doesn't he fear a more attentive suitor could steal his prize?"

Rosa's cheeks turned red, and the smile froze on her face. Without a word, she collected her train and pushed her way past me into Mother's chamber. I sighed with relief. My sister Rosa, as mean and treacherous as a snake, had retreated.

"You shouldn't have said that, Andrea. You know she is not going to forget."

I looked back. My sister Margarida was coming down the corridor. "I went to your room, but you had already left," she said after I had greeted her. Then placing her arm around mine, she continued, "I thought you would like some company when entering the wolf's den."

"Thank you, Margarida." Her smile was so contagious, soon I was smiling back, silly Rosa and her ruses forgotten.

With renewed enthusiasm, I turned the knob and pushed the door open. I had always found the magnificent amplitude of the East Room intimidating. Now, in the early morning, with the sun's rays shining through the diamond-paneled windows on the far wall, the impression of unreality was so strong, I gasped.

"What is it?" Margarida whispered. "Mother will not eat you, I promise."

I blinked repeatedly so my eyes would adapt to the light and looked again. Mother was sitting on the dais along the farthest wall, talking with some ladies. I could make out the pinkish shape of my sister Rosa standing behind her chair. Happy indeed to have Margarida by my side, I stepped into the room.

Although Mother never looked at us, she must have noted our arrival because almost immediately she dismissed her company. Eager to show my good manners, I curtsied to the ladies as they passed by. The ladies stopped, glanced awkwardly at me, and curtsied back. They didn't seem pleased. Neither did Mother, I noticed, when I looked up at her. For a moment she stared sternly at me. Then she smiled and, lifting her hand, summoned me forward.

"Princess Andrea," she said as I raised myself from my curtsy. "You come to me today to begin your training for ladyship, and I welcome you with pleasure. And yet it is not for me to teach you what you already know."

I frowned.

"I can do no more than help to bring forward what is already in you. As I have done with your sisters."

As she talked, she turned to look at my sisters. Her hands tightened around the arms of her chair. "Where is Princess Sabela?" she asked, her voice as cold as winter snow.

Nobody answered.

"She has been late for several days now. I would like to know why."

From behind Mother's chair, my sister Rosa chuckled. Margarida moved closer to her, grabbing her arm. But Rosa shook herself free and, pushing Margarida aside, faced Mother. "Princess Sabela is probably talking to Captain García," she said and giggled. "They are engaged."

My mother's face turned even paler than her usual ivory color. She did not smile. In fact, not a muscle in her face moved. I knew from experience her silence was the prelude to a dangerous storm.

At the sound of a knob turning, I looked toward the door. As if conjured by Mother's wrath, my sister Sabela stood under the archway. For what seemed a long time, she remained still, her long auburn hair floating around her shoulders. Then lifting her dress over her silver slippers, she glided toward us, her eyes intent on Rosa's. Under Sabela's stare, Rosa's self-satisfied smile disappeared, a spark of fear flickered in her eyes, and she moved back.

"Princess Sabela." Mother's voice, cold and strained, broke the silence. "Have you disobeyed my direct orders regarding Captain García? Have you talked with him?"

Sabela bent slowly in what seemed to me a deliberate parody of a curtsy. "Yes, Mother, I have been with Captain García. Father has moved his guard duty so I cannot see him at any other time, and I had something important to tell him."

She let the last sentence float in the air like an open invitation Mother did not take.

"Princess Sabela, if you insist on seeing him, you will be confined to your quarters."

Sabela's eyes locked onto Mother's. "You command and I obey. But Her Majesty cannot keep me there forever."

Mother again avoided the confrontation. "Please take your seat now. We will discuss this matter later with your father, the King."

Her face raised in defiance, Sabela walked away, toward the farthest window. For a moment Mother did not move, her face a pale mask hiding her thoughts. Finally she turned toward me. "Princess," she said, her voice even, "you must always remember that being royalty is a big responsibility, one you must assume with dignity."

I nodded, not sure whether she was addressing me.

"Although being a lady is not only a matter of appearance," Mother continued, "we must not forget that sometimes appearance is all the world has to judge us by. Thus, it is your looks we must first consider. You are to learn how to walk properly and dress according to your rank. You will let your hair grow, and you will brush it until it outshines the sun itself."

Her eyes glided over me, lingering on my hands. I tried to hide them, but I did not find any pockets in my fancy gown. As I jerked them under my long loose sleeves, my right fingers found the flat pebble I had sewn there for luck—the way Tío Ramiro wore his on the front of his shirt—and I grabbed it so tightly that my hand began to ache.

Mother didn't need to mention my short broken nails, nor my rough-looking hands, to make her point. She simply raised her own perfect one and said, "And now, if you have nothing to add, we shall proceed with the day."

As I curtsied to her to take leave, she added almost in a whisper, "And please, Princess Andrea, never curtsy to my ladies again."

"Why?"

Mother ignored my question and, with a rustle of silk, rose majestically from her velvet chair and moved toward the window. Her train perfectly arranged around her slender waist, she sat on the window seat and started working on a tapestry.

"But why?" I repeated.

Rosa giggled. I jumped forward, fists ready.

"Andrea! No." Margarida's hands, surprisingly strong, grabbed my arms.

Slowly, deliberately, Rosa turned, and as she did, her hair fell over her back in a cascade of gold. If she had done it to impress me, she succeeded. I felt so dirty and ugly, it hurt. Not for the first time, a pang of jealousy twisted my heart. *Maybe,* I thought, *if I were fair and pretty like Rosa instead of tanned and skinny, I wouldn't mind being a lady.* Not that her dark complexion seemed to matter to Margarida. But Margarida was so content and loving, you would never think of her as plain. Actually, she had always had lots of suitors around her.

So maybe it was not my looks after all, but as Mother never tired of pointing out, my unruly temper that kept admirers away. Because the truth was that except for one of the kitchen boys when I was about seven, I had never had a single admirer. I still remembered with embarrassment all the stares imbued with deep feeling that I had wasted on Don Gonzalo, my trainer, a couple of years past, when I had been so hopelessly in love with him. Not only had he not returned any of my love notes, but soon afterward he had married boring Lady Alicia, at the time I had believed just to punish me. It had taken me a full year to get over my broken heart. And no one had captured my fancy since. Not that I cared. I did not need anyone. But still, it would have been nice to have a suitor. Rosa seemed to enjoy their company well enough, if her giggles were any measure of it.

Anyway, there was nothing I could do about it. Even if I let my hair grow and dyed it blond, how was I ever to change my very nature? As far as I was concerned, the matter was settled. I would never marry. Or worse still, Mother would marry me to some horrible lord just to get rid of me. So it was just as well my heart belonged only to me.

"Don't worry, Andrea," Margarida was saying as she pushed me toward the middle window. "You'll learn soon."

"Learn?"

"How to act like a lady, you silly."

"Oh, that." If ladyship meant being sneaky and vain like Rosa or ostracized like Sabela, it held no interest to me. As for being like Margarida, I could not even consider it. She was too different from me. She seemed to have an inborn desire to please others and do their bidding. But my will was too strong to accommodate anybody else's without a battle. Obeying did not come easily to me.

"Why can't I curtsy to the ladies?" I asked Margarida after we had taken our seats.

"Because they are below your rank. They thought you were making fun of them."

"But I have always curtsied to them."

Margarida pushed the needle through her embroidery. "You have indeed," she said. "But you are fourteen now, Andrea. You are not a child anymore."

"Right."

"Of course, you still have to curtsy to Lady Esmeralda and Lady Isabel," Margarida continued, her eyes on the cloth. "You know that Andrea, don't you?"

"No. Why?"

Margarida sighed and looked up from her work. "Because they have ancient titles and—"

I refused to listen anymore. It was all so complicated, I wanted to scream. As doing so in my mother's quarters was hardly acceptable, I closed my mouth and started to embroider some silly red flowers in a snow-white cloth I had somehow managed to arrange in its wooden frame. At least I knew that much from Ama Bernarda's patient instructions.

After a dozen roses, that dreadful first morning was over, and we were dismissed by my mother after more curtsying and a light kiss to her hand. I left the room excited at the prospect of seeing a good fight between Rosa and Sabela. But to my disappointment, they ignored each other and walked in opposite directions.

I grabbed Margarida's arm. "Isn't Sabela angry at Rosa for telling on her?" I whispered.

"Of course," Margarida said.

"Then why didn't they fight?"

Margarida moved back and stared at me. "Because we are ladies, Andrea. We do not punch each other like pages. Sabela will get back at Rosa eventually because she is smarter than Rosa, but she will do it in her own time, in a civilized way."

"I see," I said. But the truth was that life as a lady did not seem to me civilized at all, and made me yearn even more for my companions and their open friendship—and even more open disagreements.

I persevered. In the following months, I attended Mother in her numerous duties. And I obeyed her orders. But from time to time I would dress in my page's clothes and go on long rides on Flecha. Later, when the days grew colder, I would wear my uncle's jacket over my shirt—the knitted jacket Tío Ramiro had given to me up on the cliffs by the forbidden cove. He had never asked me to return it, so I had kept it buried at the bottom of my trunk.

University of California, read the golden letters in the front. Although the words made no sense, I memorized them anyway and repeated them to myself again and again as I rode on Flecha. Somehow they made me feel closer to my uncle, away in his distant manor where nobody had ever been invited. Not even my parents.

ONE AFTERNOON IN LATE SUMMER, MARGARIDA AND I HAPPENED to catch sight of my sister Sabela talking with her captain in the garden. They were so intent on each other, they didn't hear our approach. Tiptoeing behind some bushes, we hid from them. Not for a moment did I stop to consider that spying on them could be an intrusion of their privacy. After all, the garden was a public place, and their conversation our only window into the grown-up world. As far as I was concerned, listening was our right and duty.

When we arrived, the captain was pressing Sabela to marry him. My heart pounding wildly, I waited for her answer, certain she was going to accept him. Hadn't she defied Mother often enough on his behalf? Besides, I had to admit that the captain was indeed very handsome. But Sabela refused her lover's request. "I cannot marry you without my parents' approval," she said slowly, as if the words pained her.

"But you must. I cannot live without you. I know I am only a captain, but my arms are strong. With you by my side, the world will be ours."

"I know, my love. But I cannot defy my father's orders. If I do, he would ban you from his kingdom forever."

"Then escape with me. Tonight. My men will come with me." Sabela shook her head.

Her captain did not take the rejection well. His voice rose as he said, "You don't love me enough to give up the crown. You will just marry any lord in order to be queen."

"That is unfair!" I mumbled, and I started to get up to explain. Margarida tried to stop me, and I fought her back. By the time we settled our dispute and pushed the branches of the bush to listen again, Captain García was holding Sabela's hand while apologizing to her. Presently he took a step back, retrieved his sword from its scabbard, and with a knee on the ground, presented the tilt to Sabela. Then in an earnest whisper, he swore to love her forever. After my sister had returned his vows, he got up and took her in her arms. One minute he was kissing her. The next, he was gone.

Sabela kept her head up until the captain was out of sight. Then she collapsed on the grass. Although I could see her shoulders shaking, she made no sound.

I would have gone to Sabela and embarrassed us both if Margarida had not held me down once more. After a moment of confusion, I stopped fighting and quietly followed her back to the lane. Soon the hedges that ran along the path hid Sabela from us.

As we walked, the argument we had just witnessed kept playing in my mind. Hard as I tried, I couldn't understand my sister's rejection nor the bizarre behavior of the captain. Sure that I was missing some important point, I turned to Margarida. "Why didn't Sabela accept Captain García's proposal?"

Margarida stared at me, eyes wide open. "Do you realize what you are saying, Andrea?" There was a note of irritation in her voice. "Sabela is the primogenitor of the House of Montemaior. She will inherit the crown. She cannot marry a captain."

"Why not? She is in love with him. Besides, Captain García is a respected officer in Father's army."

"Have you forgotten that whoever marries Sabela will be the next king? Sabela must marry into one of the Houses of Old. It is the law."

I pondered her words for a moment. Then I remembered my sister's silent crying after her lover's departure, and somehow I knew Sabela would never break her promise to him.

"What if she refuses? Would Father force her to marry against her will?"

Margarida did not answer immediately. "I don't know," she finally said. "But I do hope she will oblige. For her own sake and for the kingdom's as well."

"Why?"

A stream of giggles answered my question. I looked up and saw Rosa, a blinding vision in white, emerging from a bend in the path. As usual, one of her admirers was in her wake.

"That's why," Margarida said, pointing at them.

As I looked at the approaching figures, trying to make sense of Margarida's puzzling answer, the young man whispered something into Rosa's ears. Again Rosa laughed.

Before I could question Margarida further, the couple was upon us. I moved to the side to let them pass, while offering them my greetings. But Rosa, balancing a lacy parasol in her gloved hands with the mastery of a soldier brandishing a sword, hid her face from us and ignored my salute.

I would have gone after her, angry at her slight. But Margarida stopped me. "See what I mean?" she whispered. I shook my head. "If Sabela doesn't agree to marry into the Houses of Old, Rosa will be the next queen."

I gasped. Rosa our queen? That was indeed a scary prospect.

FOUR

The Ball

Summer passed and the harvest came. Soon the snow covered the walls and the courtyard and the fields beyond. The warm weather was gone, it seemed, forever. Captain García was gone, too.

On the morning following the conversation between my sister Sabela and her captain, Ama Bernarda had said while she helped me get dressed, "Captain García has left your father's guard."

A little later Lucia, the kitchen maid, had whispered eagerly in my ear after setting the breakfast on the table, "Captain García's gone, Princess. And many good men with him."

Even Margarida, usually so self-controlled, had rushed into my room with her version of the event.

Only in my mother's quarters did the captain's name go unmentioned. Still, the astonishing news was written everywhere: in the tight lips of the ladies, in the insidious solicitude of Rosa toward Sabela, and of course in Sabela's impossibly sad stare. But in my mother's presence, not a word was said about the brave captain who had deserted my father's army for love.

Although I was forbidden to talk with my old comrades, that night I made an exception and joined them in the barracks. There I learned that Captain García and his followers had headed east toward the wastelands. They planned to cross the rugged mountains and try their fortune in the eastern lands.

For days, everybody talked about the captain and his courage in defying my father. Time passed and no news came. The rumors died. And the name of Captain García was heard no more. But Sabela didn't forget. Although she never mentioned his name, I saw her atop the castle ramparts on many an evening staring into the distant mountains where morning awaited.

OVER THE WINTER MONTHS, MY TRAINING AS A LADY CONTINUED. Soon my hair was long enough to dress, and I had to spend long hours brushing it. Eventually my hands became soft and white, and my nails stopped breaking. On the outside, I was starting to look like a lady.

Inside, though, something was missing, some sixth sense ladies seem to possess. Hard as I tried to fit in, I still felt awkward. To add to my misery, my sister Rosa was always there, ready to point out to my mother whatever it was I had not done, or not done well enough. The maddening thing was that whenever she told on me, she always managed to appear as innocent as a baby.

Tío Ramiro did not visit that winter. I did not really expect him to, as the roads had all disappeared under the snow, making travel impossible. But still, I missed him. Without Tío to talk to, only Margarida stood between me and despair.

"Wait until the spring," my sister kept telling me after listening to my complaints. "Mother will introduce you to the court at the Spring Ball. You may change your mind then." And so, obediently I waited for the spring and the mysterious ball that would make a lady of me.

Finally, when the snow started to melt in the fields and the trees to bloom with new flowers, Mother made the announcement. "As it is customary every spring," she said, "a ball will be held in the palace. This year all the heirs of the Houses of Old will be invited. Over the following days, a contest will take place. The winner, should he win Princess Sabela's favor, will be proclaimed heir to our kingdom."

With a rustle of silk, Sabela rose from her chair and moved toward Mother. Ignoring the curtsy protocol demanded, she stared at Mother. "I will not marry any of the Lords of the Houses of Old, Your Majesty," she said, her voice even.

"In that case, Princess, you will not marry anyone. Your birthright will go to Princess Rosa."

Sabela's answer came without hesitation as if she had rehearsed it many times. "So it will," she said, and after a formal curtsy, she swirled around and left the room.

Rosa, her eyes beaming with delight, rose from her chair. But Mother raised her hand and motioned her to sit back.

After a long strained silence, Mother spoke. "Princess Andrea."

I jumped forward and, in my excitement, tripped over the long train of my dress and almost fell. Behind me, Rosa giggled. I grabbed my skirts tight in my fists and jerked them from the wool rug, wishing they were Rosa's arms. I walked up to Mother.

When I looked up from my curtsy, Mother was staring at me, but her pale blue eyes gave away nothing. "Princess Andrea," she said in an even voice, "you are welcome to attend the ball. But remember that until that day you are under my supervision. Never forget: Your duty as a lady comes first." I nodded and moved back.

After several weeks of exciting preparations, spoiled only by Rosa's constant harping, the morning of the ball arrived. As I waited for the couturier to make the last adjustments on my new dress, I could not stop daydreaming. In a few hours, Mother would accept me as a lady in front of the whole court, and somehow I would understand my place in the world.

"As you can clearly see, Princess," the couturier was saying, "the effect of the lace over the elbow is striking."

I nodded my agreement absentmindedly. In fact, I was sure she had told me the previous week how the absence of lace in the sleeves added to the simple charm of the dress or something along those lines. I didn't argue. The dress seemed fine either way.

I closed my eyes, too bored to listen. When I opened them again, my sister Rosa was smiling at me in the mirror. She was wearing a layered dress, each layer a different shade of pink, her favorite color. Suddenly my pale yellow gown seemed subdued. To feel better, I remembered how very becoming the hue was to my dark complexion, as the dressmaker had assured me. Apparently my sister did not find it so. "Asparagus has never looked better, slim sister," she said sweetly.

I turned, my cheeks burning. "Look who is talking, Miss Plump Strawberry Queen." The anger at my sister suppressed for so many years blinded me. I pushed her to the floor. Rosa screamed and covered her face with her hands. I jerked at her arms to reach her mouth and stop her cries. But Rosa shook her head and screamed again.

"Princess Andrea!"

I looked up, and my heart stopped. Mother was standing by the doorway, her eyes, two slits of ice.

I stood up and moved back while Mother came over. After helping Rosa up, she turned to face me. "No ball for you, young lady," she said in a hoarse whisper. "You are dismissed to your quarters."

With a final look of disapproval, she swirled around and left the room, her ladies-in-waiting silent witnesses to her indignation and my shame in her wake.

I remained still for a moment, stunned by the enormity of her punishment. Blind with anger, I picked up the skirts of my dress and rushed to my room.

Pieces of my frock were flying around me when Ama Bernarda appeared in the doorway that opens into her bedroom. "What is it, Princess?"

"Rosa got me in trouble again, and Mother has forbidden me to go to the ball. I will never be a lady now."

"But you are a lady," Ama said, holding me in her arms. "A perfect little lady, you have always been for me."

I eyed her suspiciously. A perfect lady? That was new. Hadn't she insisted, only a year past, what a perfect squire I would be? Memories of the Games came to my mind. I remembered Don Gonzalo's cries of encouragement and the acrid smell of sweat. I remembered the trembling of the string in my hands and the exhilarating feeling of victory when the king had given me the golden arrow. Then I remembered my father's ultimate decree, and my spirits sank again.

Ama hugged me. "Don't cry, dear child," she said. "It is all your father's fault, if I may say so, that you are so confused. Storming out of the room like that the day you were born, without even looking at you. Just because you were a girl. And such a beautiful girl you were, too. Staring after him with your big blue eyes wide open, as if trying to understand what his anger was about."

I lost myself in the familiar, probably untruthful story with a guilty pleasure. When I calmed down, Ama helped me to the bed. She left, returning with a bowl of soup she insisted I drink. I knew she would not leave me alone until I did, and I obeyed her. It was only later, as I drifted off to sleep, that I realized Ama's trick. She had added some of her sleeping herbs to the brew.

A bright light flashing in my eyes woke me up. I sat up in bed. I knew something important was supposed to happen that day, and I also knew something was not right. For one, the sun was in the wrong place. My room faced west, so the sun was not supposed to come in until late afternoon. But the shining rays cutting through an opening in my bed curtains were only too real. I blinked and my memories came back. The morning was over, the ball had probably started already, and I was forbidden to attend.

I moaned and, burying my head into the pillows, let my fingers run freely through my hair, undoing with a wicked pleasure my elaborate hairdo—my mother's idea of a lady's look. No more lady this, lady that for me! Tío had told me once that if I was not meant to be a lady, no one could force me. Well, I had tried and failed. It was over.

At least Ama was gone. I knew she would be in the kitchen by now, the best place, she claimed, to hear the gossip from the ball firsthand. I got out of bed, and sitting in front of the oblong face of the mirror, I dressed my hair into a single braid. Once I had finished, I held it with the golden arrow—the arrow I had won the day of the Games, which the smith had turned into a barrette.

"Mother can keep me out of the ballroom," I said to the angry girl in the mirror. "But she can't force me to stay in my quarters. I'll go to the garden and watch the ball from my secret place."

It was not what I had planned. I had expected my childhood days of spying to end today, but destiny—with a little help from my family—had decided otherwise. I was sure, though, that seeing through the window the incomprehensible display of manners of the grown-up world would be the perfect cure for my silly desire to be there.

I rushed to my trunk. Under the piles of carefully folded dresses, almost invisible against the dark wooden planks, I found my old hunting outfit. Happy to have kept it from Ama Bernarda's frequent cleaning sprees, I put it on. It was so worn out it fit me like a second skin, my movements its own.

No fancy frills, I thought with relief. My time as a lady is over. Andrea the Princess was gone forever. Good riddance! I was not going to miss her.

I was about to close the chest when I saw my uncle's dark blue jacket. I grabbed it and threw it over my shoulders.

My leather boots made no sound on the wooden floors as I stole out of my room and through the empty corridors into the garden. Careful to keep off the public paths so I wouldn't be seen, I ran noiselessly on the soft grass until I reached my old companion, the oak tree. I stopped then, out of breath, and my back against its rugged bark, I let my eyes wander toward the castle. Up on the second floor, behind the windows of the Great Hall, I could see shadows moving. The ball had started. I stretched my arms to the lower branches and pulled myself up.

The moss tickled my face and arms as I climbed, bringing to my mind memories of a time long ago, when Margarida and I used to come here to play. I could still remember the evening we had discovered that from the top of this oak, we could spy inside the ballroom, and the magical summer we had spent building a clumsy platform from planks and ropes we had gathered in the castle. By the time I reached our secret hideout, I was smiling; the anger at my sister Rosa, the frustration about my mother's unfair decision, and my disappointment for not being allowed at the ball seemed far away now. They were like feelings belonging to somebody else, a close friend maybe, but definitely not me.

I squatted on the platform and, closing my eyes, breathed deeply, losing myself in the warm sweet smell of new flowers. Along with the music of the fiddles and lutes coming muffled through the closed windows, another song was playing in my mind, a long-forgotten song the wind used to sing for me when I was a child. It was a tune without words, a tune of happiness I had once understood, but whose meaning I had lost as I struggled to grow up.

For an indefinite time, the music played, soothing my discontent until suddenly, with a heavy thump, the branch shook under me. I shot up, eyes wide open, my hand already on the golden arrow buried in my hair. A dark shape, large as a mountain lion, was crouching at the end of the platform. Just as I watched, the shadow sprang to its feet and turned. And I found myself staring into the deep blue eyes of the most handsome boy I had ever seen.

FIVE

The Prince

I flung myself forward and, grabbing the intruder's arm, twisted it behind his back. "Who are you?" I said, my arrow already on his neck.

The young man stared at me in bold defiance. "I am Don Alfonso de Alvar," he said, his voice as calm and even as if we had just been formally introduced. "I have no weapons upon me, so until you withdraw yours, I refuse to elaborate further."

I dropped my hands and, moving back two steps, examined him carefully. He was smartly dressed in a black uniform with the rising sun, the emblem of his House embroidered on the front. I found the fact that he had kept his perfect looks, even though he had just climbed a tree, extremely irritating. I knew that, dressed as I was in my hunting clothes, he had assumed I was a page, and for the first time in my life, I was upset by the mistake.

"I am Princess Andrea de Montemaior," I told him with all the majesty I could muster. "Everything around us belongs to my family."

I didn't care for my family just then, but I wanted to impress this pretentious prince. And impressed he was. His eyes widened and his body tensed as I spoke. Even before I had finished my sentence, he had started to apologize.

"I am deeply sorry, my fair lady, for not having recognized you. But the shadows had hidden from my eyes the beauty of your face. Ashamed of my impudence, I bend before you now, not daring to ask for your forgiveness."

And true to his words, he bowed to me.

"I don't have time for pleasantries, Sir. Would you please tell me directly what are you doing here in my—garden?"

Don Alfonso smiled. "Indeed, my lady, indeed."

Setting his feet wide apart on the tree trunk, he started brightly, "The reason for my being here in this, your palace, my dear lady, is none other than to act as tutor and companion to King Julián, my beloved brother, whose name, I am sure, is not unknown to you."

Don Julián de Alvar was indeed a familiar name in our kingdom, although not a welcome one. Five years past, he had defeated our kingdom and taken from us some borderlands that had been in dispute for generations. I had heard my father and his lords comment on Don Julián's courage in battle and his cunning in the peace negotiations. As far as I knew, our kingdoms were not on social terms. Apparently I was mistaken.

"You must also know, my fair lady," he continued, "that since the purpose of this magnificent ball is to obtain the favor and eventually the hand of Princess Rosa, Don Julián, as heir to our House, was requested to attend. But the invitation was not extended to me, a younger prince with no kingdom to inherit.

"Your ladyship can imagine how my heart broke at the injustice a mere trifle of birth order imposed upon me. I had already resigned myself to the unfair laws of this world when fortune smiled at me in the most unexpected way."

Good grief, I thought, *suppressing a yawn. If I don't do something quick, this charming prince is going to tell me his entire uneventful life and that of his dear brother, too.*

"My lord," I said in my most commanding voice, "would you please answer my question directly?"

Don Alfonso frowned. "That is exactly what I am doing, Princess," he said, his voice rising in surprise. "As you will soon understand if you were only to indulge me a little longer."

Without waiting for my answer, he continued in this elaborate style that so reminded me of Father. "Don Julián is, nobody would argue, a brave warrior and a distinguished statesman. But in matters of gallant love, he is—let's simply say—inexperienced. Not by any fault of his own, of course, but only because he has not been exposed to the company of your fair sex. His duties as king and his studies have taken all his time.

"On the other hand, I, your humble servant, with my perfect blend of natural charm and worldly knowledge, am a master in all the intricacies of courtship."

From time to time as the prince spoke, his eyes wandered toward the balcony that stood between us and the castle. Through the ballroom windows, I could see figures dancing. But the balcony doors remained closed and the balcony empty.

What he was looking for, I could not tell. Neither did he give me the opportunity to ask. "It was only natural that my brother would seek my advice," he was saying. "How could I resist his eager request? After a heated discussion, an agreement was made that satisfied us both. I would teach Don Julián the language of love in return for access to the ballroom. And that, my dear lady, is the reason for my being here."

"I am not your dear lady," I said and was about to ask him to leave when Don Alfonso, his eyes on the castle, resumed his talking. "Wouldn't you agree, Princess, in the easy parallel that can be drawn between the door destiny has closed for me and the one my brother so stubbornly seeks? And most of all, in how they are both connected? Because had my brother found his door, he would be gone by now, and I would be the one attending the ball."

"What door?"

"The door to the world beyond, of course." There was surprise in his voice and something else, like distrust, which made me even angrier.

Jumping forward, I grabbed his arm. "What are you talking about?"

Gently but firmly, Don Alfonso pushed me away. "Are you really a princess of the House de Montemaior?"

I tightened my hand around my arrow and bent my legs ready to attack. How did he dare to doubt my words? Don Alfonso did not move. His puzzled eyes intent on mine, he seemed lost in thought. Suddenly he smiled. "But of course! You don't know about other worlds. Why should you? You are a girl. It is only natural that your father did not want to bother a delicate lady as yourself with the knowledge of the door. Sorry to have mentioned it."

After bowing gracefully to me, he turned his attention to the balcony. He seemed to consider the matter closed. I did not. Being a princess was hard enough without having to endure some stupid prince bragging about secrets I would never share because they were reserved for men.

I lifted my arm and pressed the arrow against his neck. "Tell me about the door. Now!" I whispered through clenched teeth. "Or else."

Don Alfonso stared at me. "All right, all right. I will explain," he said, while with a quick movement of his arm, he snatched the arrow from my hand. Swiftly he jumped back, bowed deeply to me, and placed it at my feet. Then, a mocking smile dancing on his handsome face, he addressed me formally.

"Do you know the story of the beginning of the Houses of Old, Princess? How far away, in a world beyond our own—"

I cut him short. "Of course I do."

I, and every child in the kingdom, had heard the story of King Roderic, of how after being defeated by the Arabian invaders, he fled north with his men. To help them escape pursuit, the Celtic tribes of the high mountains led them through a door that connected their world to ours. The king planned to return, but soon after their arrival, the door was destroyed forcing them to remain in, Xaren-Ra our world, forever. According to legend King Roderic and his knights were the founders of the Houses of Old.

I had heard the story. I had also outgrown this and other fairy tales long ago, about the same time I had outgrown the crib. Evidently somebody had not.

"Yes," he continued, "everybody knows the legend of the origin of the Houses of Old, but only the royal families know that the Xarens, the aborigines of this world, knew of other doors."

"What does it matter now? The Xarens are dead."

"You are wrong, Princess. Our ancestors destroyed their culture, but after so many centuries of intermarriage, they are in all of us."

"But their knowledge is lost."

"Not totally. Some of their scrolls have survived to our days. Don Julián has studied them over the years and has deciphered their writings. From what he has already translated, he is positive other doors exist. And he is determined to find them."

"Why should your brother care about other doors?"

"Because the Arabs who overcame King Roderic were said to possess the knowledge of how to convert a desert into a garden. And nothing would please my brother more than to bring water to our desert lands. Actually, when Don Julián was invited to the ball, he was more interested in the opportunity to discuss his theories with your uncle, Don Ramiro, than he was in the prospect of dancing with the most beautiful ladies this world beholds."

"Talking with my uncle? Why?"

"Because your uncle is the most learned man in both our kingdoms, and . . ."

I stopped listening. Conjured by his words, an image was forming in my mind. The image was of a shadow emerging through an arch carved in a broken rock down at the Cove of the Dead—an arch that my memory had awkwardly distorted into resembling a door.

"Shh!" Don Alfonso whispered. "He's coming."

I bolted back to reality. "Who's coming?"

Don Alfonso raised a hand to his lips. Then he signaled toward the castle.

The doors to the balcony were now wide open, and a lady in a pink dress was coming through the doorway. It was Rosa. A tall man dressed in black walked behind her.

"Who is he?"

"My brother," Don Alfonso whispered in my ear.

"Your brother?" I repeated, not sure of what I was seeing, because Rosa, my overwhelming and bossy sister, was not flirting as usual but seemed strangely subdued. She was talking softly to her new admirer, and he was answering back in the same tone. The vision was too impossible to be a dream.

Puzzled by Rosa's peculiar behavior, I moved closer to the balcony to get a better view. But in my haste I forgot to check my step, and with a crack, the old plank complained under my feet and started swaying. It was too late. For a moment I struggled for balance while leaves and sky swung around me. Then, just as I thought I would fall, two arms grabbed my waist and dragged me back to the branch.

Rosa's voice came from above. "Who's there?"

I heard the rustling of silk against stone. Looking up, I saw Rosa leaning over the balustrade. She was so close, I could have touched the hem of her skirts by extending my arm. I waited, shaking with frustration at the idea of being found spying on the ball—and by Rosa of all people. But instead of her teasing laugh, I heard a grave, reassuring voice. "Do not worry, Princess. It was only an owl calling."

At these magical words, Rosa turned and faced the man. Her voice came soft and hesitant, almost pleading. "But Sire. I am most certain that someone is in the tree."

"Princess. I assure you no one is there."

"But . . ."

The king took her hands. "Come with me, my love," he implored her in a compelling voice. "Come sit by my side. For how am I to live if you don't allow me to quench my thirst in the ocean of your eyes?"

After a slight hesitation, Rosa accepted the arm the king was offering. Slowly they moved away.

What a nice young man, I thought with relief. Obviously pomposity ran in the family, but at least Don Julián had put it to good use by distracting my sister.

"My lessons have been successful," Don Alfonso whispered.

"What lessons?" Suddenly I realized I was still leaning against him. I moved quickly away. "Thank you very much, Sir, for helping me before," I told him with a deep curtsy.

"You are welcome, my lady," Don Alfonso replied, his eyes still on the balcony.

I followed his stare. Half-hidden under the brambles hanging from the trellis, Rosa was sitting on a bench. Don Julián, a knee on the ground, was talking to her in earnest. The king had a beautiful voice, and knowing Rosa, I had no doubt his words would be as welcome to her ears as the first drops of rain in a dry field.

"Open your eyes to the beauty of the evening," Don Julián was saying. "Feel the caress of the breeze over your shoulders. Let the fragrance of the flowers fill your senses. And fear nothing, my love, because my life is yours, and yours is sacred."

Presently he paused and reached for one of the roses that hung over the balcony. With a swift movement, he tore it from the brambles and presented it to my sister. His voice, like a wave swelling into a crest before kissing the sand, flowed into the warm air of the evening.

"Accept this rose, Princess, as a token of my love. Keep it always by your side and I will be with you forever, because it is my own bleeding heart you are holding in your hands."

He waited for a moment as Rosa accepted his offering. Then he bent and kissed her on the lips. Rosa didn't resist.

"The lady is his," Don Alfonso whispered to himself.

For what seemed to me a long time, Rosa and her lover remained together, looking into each other's eyes, whispering impossible promises of eternal love. Finally, when my legs were so numb I thought they had turned to stone, Don Julián rose. "It is getting cold, my love," he said gently, as if talking to a child. "Let's go inside. I would never pardon myself if you were to become ill."

His hands around her waist, he motioned her toward the castle.

"What a great performance," Don Alfonso said with a smile after Rosa and her lover had returned to the Hall.

"From what I have seen, Sir," I replied, annoyed at his self-complacency, "your brother doesn't need your help."

"Of course he does, my dear lady. Of course he does. What you have seen here was just lesson number one: 'Wrap the lady with words of praise and, before she has time to react, make her yours.'"

Don Alfonso seemed unaware that revealing his tactics of conquest to me was awkward at best. After all, I was a princess, too, if only in name, and Rosa was my sister. Although a part of me rejoiced that somebody had made a fool of Rosa, another part felt insulted by Don Julián's technical approach to winning her love.

Don Alfonso gasped. "What an adorable lady!" he said, his voice trailing off as if he were at a sudden loss for words.

I looked up, surprised at this dramatic change, but saw only my sister Margarida standing by one of the windows. The mysterious lady who had so impressed the prince was gone.

"And now, my fair lady," Don Alfonso said, back to his normal chatty self, "we must part. The Goddess of Love has called, and I, her humble servant, must obey."

After bending before me in an exaggerated bow, he jumped swiftly onto the balcony and disappeared behind the doors his brother had left open for him.

Through the windows, I could see the dancing couples swirling like rainbows in perfect synchrony across the ballroom floor. The whole palace seemed to be lost in a happy dream from which I was the only one excluded. Not that I cared. Actually, if this glimpse into the adult world was in any way accurate, I, Andrea de Montemaior, was in no hurry to grow up.

I squatted against the tree, relieved to be alone. But I could not rest. Disturbing images kept playing in my mind: the image of a king looking for the knowledge of an ancient race; the image of my sister Rosa falling under the spell of her cunning lover's words; and, above all, the image of Tío Ramiro as I had seen him the evening of my frustrated escapade, coming through a broken rock down at the Cove of the Dead.

Could Don Alfonso be right? Could the arch really open into another world? Feeling suddenly cold, I reached for the jacket I had wrapped around my shoulders.

As I touched my uncle's jacket, I remembered the unusual words written on the front. Then I remembered the blade that had vanished in Tío's hands, which he had so insistently urged me to forget. I remembered all the mysterious gifts he used to bring me when I was a child. I remembered his strange accent and the secrecy surrounding the location of his manor. And as the idea that Tío Ramiro was from another world sunk into me as certitude, I climbed to my feet. I had to go back to the cove. I had to see for myself whether the arch was really a door.

I was already halfway down the tree when I remembered I had sworn to my uncle I would never go there. But my indecision didn't last long. To break a promise that Tío had extorted from me under false pretenses seemed a small price to pay for the possibility of finding a new world. Besides, I had no choice.

I couldn't go back to the castle and pretend to be a lady. What was there for me but to wait for some prince to woo me with lies into marriage? Not a cheerful thought. My world seemed too narrow, too hopelessly confining. Perhaps Tío Ramiro's offered a better alternative for me.

SIX

The Door

The ocean had already cut the sun in half when I reached the ledge overlooking the Cove of the Dead. The thorn bush that had saved my life was still there at the end of the broken trail, and down at the cove, the arch, like the remnant of a dwelling carved in solid rock by ancient giants, loomed majestically over the sand.

Trying not to think of my previous mishap, I bent over the cliffs, looking for a path. I knew it had to be there—after all, I had heard Tío Ramiro climbing while I was trying to disentangle my dress from the thorns—but I searched in vain.

I was about to give up when I saw crude steps carved in the rock cleverly hidden behind a bush. My back to the ocean to avoid looking down and being pulled into the void, I started my descent.

When I finally reached the sand, my heart was beating so furiously against my chest I had to lean against the cliffs and rest for a moment. Then, followed by the piercing cries of the seagulls, I dashed toward the arch along the stretch of land covered by dead algae and broken shells the tide had just started to reclaim.

It was cold under the arch, cold and damp, and the air was filled with strange groans and whispers. It took me a moment—a long frightening moment—to understand that the noises did not come from living beings, but from the water dripping between hidden cracks in the rock.

Trying to laugh away my fears, I crossed the cave formed by the arch and stepped outside into the unknown. But the same cove and the same cliffs still surrounded me. High above, Athos the golden moon stared at me unblinkingly from the same sky. I was still in my own world!

I kicked the arch in frustration. Pain shot through my leg, but the rocks remained. Not ready to give up, I dashed back inside and examined the cave, looking for an opening that could be a passage into the other world. But I couldn't find any, and although I pushed all the bumps I found on the rocks, no hidden door opened.

Defeated, I collapsed on a small ledge that ran along the back of the cave. My mind empty of thought, I watched the waves break against the arch and, after turning into swirls of white foam, flood the cave. Soon the water reached my knees. I knew I must leave if I didn't want to get trapped inside, but a strange lassitude overcame my limbs and prevented me from moving.

Suddenly a tremor shook the arch. For a moment the rocks, the water, and even the air seemed to melt away as if caught in a blaze. Then, as quickly as it had come, the quivering left, and the cave resumed its former shape. But not quite. Something was wrong. I strained my eyes and looked around until it hit me. It was darker now, and the water—the water was gone! I jumped to my feet in alarm and ran to the opening.

It was also dark outside the cave, darker than it had been only moments ago. And when I looked up, my heart jumped inside my chest—the sky was just an empty extension of blue-tainted purple over the ocean, and Athos the golden moon was gone. And the cove was gone, too. Instead, a white sandy beach stretched itself along the ocean for as far as I could see. Further inland, over the dunes that had replaced the cliffs, a full moon was rising. It was a foreign moon, small and pale.

Don Alfonso was right, I thought in awe. *I really am in another world!*

Something hard hit me on the back, and as I fell to the sand, I heard footsteps closing in on me. Before I could react, a strong hand grabbed mine and was helping me up. A deep baritone voice was speaking in words I couldn't understand. Instinctively I reached for my arrow. Then froze. A tall boy with very short hair was staring at me. His completely shaved face wore the most disarming smile.

"Who are you?" I said.

The boy spoke again in his incomprehensible language. I shrugged and was about to repeat my question when I heard voices calling, "John!" Looking up, I saw two figures coming toward us. The boy sprinted past me and, after picking up a ball from the sand, ran back to his friends. As he passed me again, he shouted something I took for a good-bye.

Once he had joined them, they all walked away laughing and talking in their foreign tongue, tossing the ball back and forth. They were similarly dressed in long pants and loose tunics and wore the most unusual white shoes. By their voices, I realized that one of them was a girl.

I waited, still frozen, until I felt confident they would not see me. Then I followed them along the beach, hiding behind dead trees resembling the antlers of gigantic deer that lay scattered on the sand. Soon they turned right, and after crossing the dunes, they reached a house that stood alone on top of a hill. The house reminded me of the dwellings the peasants have in my kingdom. Only this one seemed to have two floors, because it had two stacked rows of perfectly square windows.

As the young people entered the house, an incredibly bright light appeared in one of the windows. I could see the boys as clearly as if it were day, moving about in a room. The girl joined them, and then they all settled down in front of a wall where images kept changing at an extraordinary speed.

I watched them, fascinated. After a while my fingers felt numb, and my knees hurt from crouching behind the low bushes, the only hideout I had found on the bare sandy hill. My pants were still wet up to the knees where the waves had reached me, and in spite of my uncle's jacket, I was cold.

Inside, the young people were drinking. I could see the steam dancing on top of their cups and their flushed faces laughing. I yearned to be with them. But I resisted. After all, this was not my world, and as far as I knew, they could be enemies. Yet they seemed so friendly. And they had no weapons. What harm could they do to me? Besides, I needed a place to spend the night, and—my stomach rumbled—I was hungry. Throwing caution away, I got up and walked to the house.

I was about to knock when the door opened, and the dark shape of a man appeared in the doorway. Instinctively I moved back, squinting to see his face. But the light coming from inside kept it in the shadows. After a brief hesitation, the man stepped outside and closed the door carefully. "Andrea, is that you?" he asked in a heavily accented voice.

"Tío Ramiro?" My lady manners forgotten, I ran into his arms.

Tío held me back. "Andrea, what are you doing here? Has your mother sent you?"

I shook my head.

"I see." Tío frowned. "So it was your idea. After I warned you not to come here!"

"No, you didn't," I said, angry at his unfriendly welcome. "You never told me where you lived. So how could you have forbidden me to come?"

He sighed. "Well, I guess this was inevitable. At least I found you before you got yourself in trouble."

"Found me? How did you know I was here?"

"I didn't. Kelsey told me they had met a girl by the arch. And today being the full moon, I thought I'd check."

I was about to ask more about this Kelsey, but Tío was already walking away from the house. "Come on, Andrea," he called over his shoulder. "Let's go for a walk."

"For a walk? But I want to meet your friends."

Tío turned. "No, Andrea. Not now. We must talk first." His arm firmly set over my shoulders, he guided me toward the beach. "Andrea, how did you find the way here?" Tío asked as we crossed the dunes.

I struggled to put into words the strange events that had brought me there. "Don Alfonso told me about doors that opened into another world. And I remembered your coming through the arch. So I went to the Cove of the Dead, but there was no door, at first I mean, and then—"

"Don Alfonso de Alvar? Where did you meet him?" Tío asked. But before I could answer he continued, "Never mind. The fact is you are here. So I suppose it's time for me to explain."

He remained silent for a moment as if collecting his thoughts. "Andrea," he finally started, "You are not in your world anymore. We are on a planet called Earth—but how could you understand this? Your education was not exactly heavy in science."

I moved back, freeing myself from his arm. "Excuse me, Tío. But I didn't come here to be insulted. I understand. Look at the sky. There is only one moon, and it is smaller and paler than any of ours. And the stars are all wrong. And the cliffs are gone. I know, Tío. I know this is not my world."

"It seems I have underestimated you. I will not do it again."

We had reached the arch as we talked. Tío stepped through the opening and disappeared. I hesitated. Was he trying to send me back to my world?

"Please, come in," Tío's voice urged me from inside. "It's safe. The door will not open again, not tonight anyway."

I took a deep breath and stepped inside. The cave was again an ordinary cave, a perfect copy of the one I had entered in my world, only darker. Leaning against the rocks, my uncle was waiting. I crossed over the dry sand and sat by his side.

"My involvement with your world," Tío continued, his voice distorted as it echoed against the walls, "happened by chance almost thirty years ago. Your mother and I were kids then, younger than you are now. We had just moved here to California into the house you just saw."

"California?" The word was familiar, and yet I couldn't remember where I had heard it before.

"Yes, Andrea, California. That is what this area is called."

Suddenly I remembered. The words written on Tio's tunic. "University of California," I said aloud.

Tío smiled. "University of California," he repeated, correcting my pronunciation. "I see you have kept my jacket and had the good sense to wear it when coming over to conceal your clothes."

"What's wrong with my clothes?"

"Nothing. But handmade leather boots and tights are not in fashion right now here."

I shrugged. Why did everybody always criticize my appearance? "Come on, Tío! Tell me how you got to my world," I asked him, eager to change the subject.

Tío resumed his story. "That summer, my first one by the ocean, was magical." Tío laughed. "Even before we found the door, I mean. Your mother and I had a wonderful time building castles in the sand and playing hide-and-seek among the dunes. Then one day, Jennifer—"

"Who is Jennifer?"

"Your mother. Jennifer was her name in this world. She changed to Jimena to blend with your people, as I changed mine to Ramiro."

"You mean Ramiro is not your real name?"

"No, Andrea. My name is Raymond, Raymond Miller. And please stop interrupting.

"One day your mother hid from me under the arch. When after a long search I finally found her, I was a little scared. Jennifer, who was always happy to pick on me, insisted the cave was haunted and teased me into coming back after sunset to prove I was not frightened. Of course I accepted the challenge, and that night we returned to the arch.

"From the beginning, the cave seemed to hold an inexplicable attraction to your mother—or maybe it was just the fun of seeing me scared. In any case, from that day on, we escaped every night after supper and played inside the cave until dark. Then one evening, unknown to us, the door opened into your world. The next thing we knew, we were swimming for our lives. And no, Andrea, I don't know how it happens. I only know that it opens once a month when the full moon of my world rises over the eastern horizon here, or Lua the copper moon rises in yours.

"When the waves finally threw us against the cliffs, we were too shaken to think. Acting on instinct, we started up the cliffs. It was a difficult climb as there was no path, and the rocks were slippery with the mist from the ocean. The steps you probably followed down to the cove were added later.

"By the time we reached the ledge, we were exhausted. Crawling under one of the boulders that formed a little cave, we fell asleep. The following morning, the soldiers of your kingdom found us. You can imagine our confusion when we saw them pointing their spears at us and shouting orders we couldn't understand."

"I know, Tío. I was shocked, too, when I couldn't understand what your friends were saying. Does anybody in this world speak like me?"

"Yes, Andrea." Tío's voice was stern. "Some people in my world speak a different version of your language. It is called Spanish. But yours seems to have evolved in a unique way with the influence of the Xarens' tongue. But that is another story. Would you mind if I finish mine first?"

"Of course, Tío. Tell me what happened. Did my father keep you prisoner?"

"Your father, Andrea, was not the king. He was just a boy himself, a couple of years older than we were. Your grandfather was king. He was a brave man, although his customs were a little barbaric for my taste. To him, we were no more than demons from the underworld. He would have burned us alive if your father hadn't taken us back to the cave and let us go."

"But Tío, how did Father know when the door would open?"

"Because the knowledge of the Xarens, the native inhabitants of your world, had been transmitted for generations down through the members of your family. The Xarens knew about the doors between our two worlds and how the full moon opens them."

"Just what Don Alfonso told me," I mumbled. "He's not crazy after all."

"Let's go back," Tío said, his eyes on a circular object tied around his wrist. "Kelsey and her friends will probably be in bed by now."

"What is that, Tío? A portable sundial? But it's night, how can you read it?"

"It's a watch, Andrea. A time reader, you could say. Let's leave it at that for now."

I knew my uncle well enough to know it would be useless to insist. So I swallowed my questions and followed him onto the beach. As we left the arch, I noticed that the tide had turned, and the water was starting to reach the rocks.

For a while, nobody spoke. Against the sound of the waves on the sand and the shrieking call of the seagulls, my uncle's words played in my mind. Suddenly I realized something in his story was wrong.

"But Tío, if you both returned to California, why is Mother still in my world?"

My uncle did not hesitate. "That happened later. Many years later. Your mother was already in college studying to be a physician. She would have been a good one, I'm sure. She was so strong-willed, I don't think any patient of hers could have refused to get better. But your father had other plans. He came over one night, alone. By then your grandfather had died in one of his glorious battles, and your father was king. So Don Andrés came and took your mother to be his queen."

"Really, Tío? But Mother couldn't have been so easy to convince."

"Well, it is true it was not so simple. But your mother was not the problem. She was willing to go as soon as she saw him. I think she had fallen in love with him when she first met him. The real problem was how to explain to our family why she would never return. And how to keep her disappearance from the papers."

"The Papers?" He had said the word in a curious way, as if it carried a capital P.

"Yes, the papers and the TV and . . ." He laughed. "Don't worry, you'll understand soon enough."

Suddenly Tío stopped. Following his stare, I saw a dark figure standing still over the dunes. "Kelsey!" my uncle whispered, visibly upset. Then, after ordering me to wait, he walked in long strides toward the girl.

The girl addressed him first in an angry voice. Bewildered, I watched them argue. I had assumed until then that the young people were Tío's pupils, but the girl was not showing any respect for Tío Ramiro. In fact, if the tone of their voices was any indication of their respective ranks, she seemed to be the one in charge.

After a couple of minutes of furious shouting, the girl turned her back on my uncle and stalked away. After a slight hesitation, Tío shrugged his shoulders and came back to where I was waiting. "Come, Andrea. Let's go," he said sharply, already walking away. "And whatever you do, don't say anything about your world."

I nodded. What difference could it make what I said to them? Had Tío forgotten I could not understand their language anyway?

I ran after him. "Tío, who is the girl? Why is she upset?"

Tío turned and stared deep into my eyes. "She's Kelsey. My daughter."

I gasped. "Your daughter! You have a daughter and never told me?"

"Why should I have told you about Kelsey?" Tio's voice was annoyingly calm. "You were not supposed to meet her. Ever. Your world and mine can never mix. I'm sorry Andrea, but you have to go back."

"Go back? I don't want to go back!"

"Let's go to the house. Tomorrow we will discuss the matter further. But don't get your hopes up, Princess. Whether you want it or not, you will return to your world."

I will not, I said to myself. But I knew better than to start an argument with Tío when he was angry. Pretending to agree, I rushed after him.

In front of us, over the dunes, the pale moon of the new world was watching. As I stared in wonder at its mysterious silvery light, my uncle's words came back to me: *The door only opens when the full moon rises over the eastern horizon.* I smiled. Tío had no choice. I was staying. At least for a while.

SEVEN

The New World

The shrieking call of a seagull woke me up. Across the room, framed in the window, I could see a long stretch of sand rolling gently to the shore and the blue mantle of the ocean lost in the mist. Where was I? The seagull cried again, and as its second call died in the distance, memories of the previous evening flashed through my mind.

Wide awake now, I pushed away the blanket and jumped from the narrow bed Tío Ramiro had referred to as "sofa." My hand on the doorknob, I hesitated. More than anything, I wanted to go downstairs to meet my cousin and her friends—Tío had whisked me upstairs as soon as we entered the house, and I hadn't seen them yet—but I had promised my uncle I would stay in the room until he came for me. Not daring to disobey his orders on this, my very first day in his world, I dropped my hand and moved back.

The room Tío had called "his study" was small, the size of a cell in my parents' castle, but so amazingly crowded, I barely had space to move about. I was certain I had never seen so many things together in my entire life. Some I recognized—a table and chairs, books, and paintings. Others challenged my imagination, like the square shiny box staring at me with my own bewildered face reflecting from its black surface. Close to it, by the candle that burned without fire, a tray with food had mysteriously appeared. A rumbling noise in my stomach made me realize I was starving. That was not surprising, for I had not eaten anything since the soup Ama Bernarda had given me the previous day in my own world, after my fight with Rosa.

I had already finished the fruit and bread and was drinking the surprisingly sweet orange liquid when, with a knock at the door, Tío Ramiro came in. "Good morning."

I ran to him. "Where is everybody, Tío? I can't wait to meet them."

"I'm afraid the meeting will have to wait, Andrea," Tío said coldly. "As a matter of fact, it'll have to wait forever. Kelsey and her friends are gone."

"Gone? But . . . why? Where?"

"Kelsey was so upset I hadn't told her about you that she left last night. As for where, she went back to Davis, the town where she actually lives."

I frowned, confused. "Doesn't she live here with you?"

"I live in Davis, too. We only come here on the week-ends—I mean, sometimes."

"What about your wife? Is she here?"

"My wife? I don't have a wife. Kelsey's mother and I don't live together. Haven't in ages."

It was obvious my uncle did not want to elaborate further, so I changed the subject. "I'm sorry, Tío. I didn't mean to cause you trouble with your daughter."

Tío nodded. "It's all right. She'll get over it soon enough. As for you, young lady, you are staying here with me until the next full moon. And then, like it or not, you go back to your world."

"But—"

"No buts, Princess, or you will not so much as step out of this house for the entire month. So now," he continued as he handed me some clothes, "put these on. They're Kelsey's. I think they'll fit you." Without giving me time to answer, he turned and left.

I stared at the door, and for a moment I even considered opening it, outrunning Tío, and leaving the house. But where could I go? Besides, Tío was right about one thing: I had to get rid of my old clothes if I was to blend in. Curious about the strange garments, I put them on. They fit me. At least I thought they did, as I was not sure how they were supposed to look—my only glance at the New World's fashion having been in the dark.

Once I was ready, we left the house and Tío helped me into his so-called "car." With a deafening explosion, the car came to life and started roaring as if an angry beast was inside fighting to get free. I screamed and grabbed onto the exit handle.

"It's all right, Andrea," Tío said. But the noise did not stop, and even worse, the car started moving.

I screamed again. And again Tío Ramiro told me to relax; according to him, there was no cause for alarm. Then, as the car rolled forward into the black wide path, a wave of nausea grabbed me, and for a moment, I was too busy keeping my breakfast down to think of anything else.

Tío, oblivious to my discomfort, was talking. "I want you to understand that your coming here was a mistake. As far as my world is concerned, yours does not exist. And that is how things must remain. It is not safe otherwise."

Sitting in the car didn't seem to me safe, either. Through the window, trees zoomed by, while in front of us, the road twisted itself like a gigantic snake ready to swallow us. Still, somehow my uncle managed to stay on the winding path by moving a black wheel he was holding in his hands.

Tío looked at me, and the car swayed slightly to the right. "Are you listening, Andrea?"

I swallowed. "Yes. No. I mean . . ." I couldn't just give up. Besides, why was he the only one allowed to move between both worlds? The only one to—But he wasn't. Tío was not the only one. Not according to the legend, not according to Don Alfonso.

"Tío, your world must know about mine. After all, the founders of our Houses came from here."

My uncle shook his head. "No, Andrea. Although I personally believe your legend is true, only the first part, the story of King Roderic's defeat at the hands of the Arabs, is known in my world. According to the history of this world, it happened in a country we called Spain almost thirteen centuries ago. But there is no record anywhere of your ancestors leaving for another world."

I sulked. "But they did. You know they did. So why can't I stay?"

"Because . . . because it's dangerous. Do you remember the story of the Xarens? They lived in your world when your ancestors arrived from Spain. The Xarens were more civilized in a cultural sense than King Roderic's men, but they were peaceful people. In the clash of cultures, theirs was destroyed. That is why your world must remain unknown to mine. Do you understand?"

"Yes, Tío. Of course I do. Your civilization wouldn't stand a chance if my people would learn you are here, waiting to be conquered."

My uncle laughed. "That's one way of looking at it." Then, again his grumpy self, he continued, "I'm glad you understand.

Do you see now why you cannot talk with Kelsey? Why you must return to your world as soon as possible?"

"No, I don't. I am not an army. And I have no intention of bringing one to conquer anybody. All I want is to stay here for a moon time. Please, Tío. Let me stay with Kelsey. I promise I will never mention my world to her."

It was not easy, but I wanted it so badly I begged and whined and compromised, and by the time the car stopped in its allotted place in front of the gigantic cubic rock Tío called "the mall," he had agreed to my request.

I left the car then and followed Tío through an amazing glass door into an enchanted place right out of a dream. All around us the walls were glass, and through them I saw rooms full of clothes and shoes and all sort of things, most of which I didn't recognize.

My surprise was beyond words when, after we had entered one of the rooms, I saw the same dress I had chosen in the window in different sizes. So instead of waiting for someone to take my measurements and make the dress, I tried several on. When I found the one that fit me, a lady put it in a colorful bag, and that very same moment, I walked out of the store with it. Of course, I thought it a waste of time to sew all those dresses for me to pick just one, but Tío said it didn't work like that here, and that he would explain later.

My uncle bought me several outfits and comfortable white shoes with laces to replace my leather boots. Then, when I couldn't think of anything I could possibly need for the next five years, we sat at a little table in a big hall and I ate some cold sweet cream that melted in my mouth.

Just before leaving, we walked into a library. Tío called it a bookstore. It was a friendly place, not at all dark and gloomy like the one at my father's castle, but bright from lights hanging from the ceiling. My uncle took me to the back of the room and picked lots of books for me. Books, he said, would teach me how to speak this language.

On the way home, as I sat in the car surrounded by my wonderful presents, Tío Ramiro pushed one of the little books into a black hole, and it started talking. I listened carefully to the magical words, and when we reached Tío's house, I was able to repeat them to him.

Tío seemed surprised. "Do you remember every single thing you've heard?"

"Of course I do, Tío. Why should I forget?"

"Never mind. Why don't you watch these now," he said, giving me some very thin books.

"Watch them?"

Tío smiled. "I keep forgetting. Come, I'll show you how to use the DVD player and the TV."

I went through all the English DVDs that evening and fell asleep reading the English books. The following day in the car, I listened to more English CDs, and by the time we arrived at Davis, the university town where my cousin lived, I could understand English well enough to carry on a conversation. I had also learned the strange symbols that represent numbers in Tío's world. Apparently our numbers—Roman numerals Tío had called them—were no longer fashionable and hadn't been for centuries.

"I am impressed with you, Andrea. Really impressed," my uncle told me as we walked through the garden he called the "campus."

"Your mother kept telling me all these years that your people had an amazing memory. But I never believed she meant it so literally," Tío said. "Unless . . . are you sure she didn't teach you English when you were a child, and it's coming back to you now?"

I laughed. "*Querido Tío*, dear Uncle, as you must be the first to know, Mother has tried to teach me many things over the years without much success. But English, I assure you, was not one of them."

Tío smiled. "All right. I believe you." He stopped, and pointing to a big building looming four stories tall in front of us, he added, "Here we are. This is where Kelsey lives."

Kelsey's house was big—much bigger than my uncle's. When I asked him whether my cousin lived there all by herself, Tío laughed. "No, of course not. Kelsey lives in one of the rooms. You'll see. Now remember your story. You grew up in Spain where your mother is a doctor. You've come to live in the States for a month to practice your English. And do not forget, please, that you're seventeen years old."

"Yes, I know. I am seventeen because the months in your world are shorter—five or six days shorter than in ours. That means our year has fourteen of your months."

Tío nodded. "You'll do fine," he said and, holding the glass door open, motioned me forward. We walked down a long hall flanked by many doors and up two flights of stairs onto another floor that was an exact replica of the one below. There he turned right and knocked on the second door to the left.

After a short wait, the door opened, and the girl I had seen at the beach appeared in the doorway. She was still angry—I could tell by the way her pale blue eyes were flashing, eyes the exact same color as my sister Rosa's.

"Kelsey, this is your cousin Andrea," my uncle said.

I extended my hand, as Tío had instructed me to do. Kelsey did not take it, but stared at me with contempt. I returned her

stare without blinking. I had not come this far to be intimidat-
ed by a girl my own age. Finally Kelsey looked away. "Hi," she
said and, turning her back on us, moved inside.

I looked at my uncle. What kind of welcome was this? But
Tío only shrugged his shoulders and signaled me to follow.

"Kelsey," my uncle said once the door had closed behind us,
"as I told you on the phone, Andrea will be staying at the dorms
for the next month. I'll bring her bags to her room while you
get acquainted. Then I have to go. I would appreciate it if you
would show her around the campus today."

From the bed where she was sitting, the girl stared at us,
her lips set in a thin line, and gave no answer. Tío Ramiro did
not seem to have expected one, because with a nod in my
direction, he started back to the door. Before I could say anything, he was gone.

As soon as Tío left, Kelsey stretched her long legs over the
side of the bed and came over.

"Well, Andrea. It seems that we're stuck with each other,
so I guess it would be better if we try to make it work." I nodded. "I don't know why Dad never mentioned you or your
family before," she continued, " and I couldn't care less. I do
think it was really rude of him not to tell me you were in the
house when we arrived last Friday. But since I guess it was not
your idea, I'm willing to give you a chance."

"Thank you."

"No problem. Now about the baby-sitting part. I have plans
for today, and I'm not going to change them for you. You can
come with me or be a good girl and visit the campus on your
own."

It was not a difficult decision. After Tío Ramiro came back
with the key to my own room and we were sure he was gone,

we left the dorms and walked across campus to the building with the word "gymnasium" written over the door. I followed Kelsey inside, keeping my questions to myself so I wouldn't show my ignorance.

Soon after we had taken our seats high on the stairs that surrounded the central area, the game started. I watched as ten boys threw a ball to each other and, from time to time, into a hanging basket. I was starting to recognize the pattern of the game, when one of the players was replaced. I looked at the new player, and my heart started beating one hundred times faster. The boy was tall and lean with short brown hair, and his eyes were brown. I knew they were light brown, although I was too far to see them now. I knew that because he was the boy who had smiled at me the previous evening at the beach. The boy they had called John.

I remembered the blow of the ball to my back and the boy's warm hand on mine, and the court became a blur. From then on, the game was not about following a ball anymore, but about following John. Although I clapped and screamed from time to time so Kelsey would not realize I had no clue of what was going on, I saw only John.

When the game was over, we waited outside the gym, talking with other girls until the players came through the back door of the building. I couldn't tear my eyes from John. He was tall with the sinewy build of a warrior. I had already learned by then that most men in his world did not grow beards, but I still found his short hair and shaved face utterly fascinating.

With long strides, John came toward us, talking with another boy. His eyes were pale brown, as I remembered them, the color of the honey I used to steal from honeycombs back in my world to please my mother.

"Andrea! Hello!" Kelsey was shaking my arm. "Meet Richard and John."

Instinctively I started a curtsy, but just as I bent, the other boy, Richard, took my hand and shook it firmly. "Hi," he said. Without waiting for my answer, he moved toward Kelsey and kissed her. I was still staring at them, shocked by their public display of affection, when a deep voice spoke by my side.

"Hi, Andrea. Nice to meet you."

I looked back at him and my mind froze. John was smiling at me with the same friendly smile I remembered from the first time I had seen him at the beach.

"Nice to meet you, too," I mumbled, trying to keep my knees from shaking.

"Come on, you two. We are going to Al's," Kelsey called. Holding Richard's hand, she walked away.

"So what's your story?" John asked as we followed them.

"My story?"

"I mean, where are you from?"

"I . . . I'm from Spain."

"Oh really?" John seemed pleased. "My grandparents came from Spain, too."

"What do you study?" I asked hastily. I did not want him to start asking me questions about my supposed country. Questions, I was certain, I would not know how to answer.

"Archaeology," he said. "And you?"

"English," I told him, dutifully following Tio's instructions. "I want to be an English teacher when I go back to Spain."

John nodded, praised my English, and gave me a funny overview of what to expect in the following weeks and how to survive college life. Soon we reached the open patio where Kelsey and Richard were already waiting.

Soon the rest of the team joined us, and we all sat around a big table. Interrupting each other's sentences, they discussed the game they had just won and the strategy for the next one while we shared some food called "nachos" and cold bubbly drinks.

By the time I said goodbye to Kelsey at the door of my room, we were already friends, and I was absolutely crazy about John. Of course, I knew only too well that John was not from my world and that my days in his world were numbered, but that could not stop me from dreaming.

Through the open window, the pale white moon of the new world was staring at me. Resting my elbows on the windowsill, I leaned forward, and as I watched it glowing majestically in the evening sky, a peaceful feeling overcame me. A feeling of belonging, as if I had finally found my place, the place I had been hunting for since before I was born.

The full moon was already waning, following the inexorable cycle of death and rebirth that would mark the end of my stay. Still, painfully beautiful, it smiled at me with its half-hidden face. Lost in its magic, I smiled back.

EIGHT

The Spanish Missions

Enrolling at the university was pretty easy. My mother, Tío Ramiro told me, had asked him to register my sisters and me as citizens of this world when we were born. In spite of my hard feelings toward Mother, I was deeply impressed by her foresight.

More difficult to explain to my uncle was why I had been late to meet him. The fact that I didn't have an alarm clock—one of the devices people use in Tio's world to measure time instead of our marked candles—was no excuse, as he had specifically told Kelsey to lend me one the previous day. She had forgotten. Things got worse when he asked me how I had liked the library, and I stammered something like, "It was very nice," but I could not tell him where it was or which books I had taken home.

My uncle sighed. "Andrea, I'm not going to ask you what you did yesterday. You are not a child anymore, and I cannot supervise your every move. But I do hope you didn't do or say anything that would jeopardize the secrecy of your world."

"Of course not, Tío," I said, trying to look appropriately outraged at the suggestion.

Tío shrugged. He didn't seem convinced, but at least he didn't pry further.

"As we discussed yesterday," Tío told me as we left the registration office, "the best thing to do now is to pretend you have come from Spain to stay for a month and improve your English. So I have signed you up for several classes in the English department."

"Classes have already started," he continued as I nodded. "But you've only missed a week, so I don't think you'll have any problem catching up."

"I'll work hard, Tío, I promise."

Tío grabbed my arm to steer me away from a bicycle coming straight at me, and after warning me again to watch for the bicycles darting around us like arrows in the practice field, he handed me a book.

"Here is your schedule," he said, and after opening the book, he pointed at the top of the page. "We're at the beginning of the fall term—"

I had noticed the leaves on the trees were turning, but as Tío mentioned it, this struck me as odd: it had been early spring in my world, only two days ago.

"How come it is fall?"

Tío frowned. "Why not?"

"But in my world . . ."

"Oh, I see. That is because your world takes fourteen of our months to circle your sun. So the seasons in both worlds usually don't match."

"I'm glad I came now and not in a couple of months. Imagine, I could have ended up in the middle of a snow storm."

"You don't have to worry about that. There is no snow in California."

"No snow! This world is indeed magic. I think I will like it here."

Tío Ramiro laughed. "I'm sure you will, Andrea. But remember, you must go back to your world in a month."

I sulked. *How could I forget if you remind me constantly?* I wanted to say. But I knew Tío was still mad at me for having come to his world, and as I did not want to upset him further, I said nothing. Eyes wide open, I followed him along perfectly straight paths flanked by trees and across square patches of green to a big rectangular building that seemed to be made entirely of glass. Through its walls, sitting on sofas randomly arranged, I could see young people talking.

Tío opened the door and motioned me inside. "This is the Recreation Hall where students come to relax," he said, his words barely audible over the loud chattering.

I paused for a moment, longing to join them, but Tío urged me forward to a long table where a young man smiled at us from under a banner that read "Information." At Tío's request, the boy handed me a map. It was a miniature representation of the campus, with little drawings of buildings on it. They were so cool, I could not stop looking at them.

Tío snatched the paper from my hands. "We are here," he said, marking the place with a cross. "This building is your dorm, and this is the English department." Folding the map, he squeezed it into the outside pocket of my backpack. "Come on. You can study it later. Let's go to the Coffee House now and get something to eat."

Holding my arm, he led me through an open door into a big noisy room that smelled of spices and broiled meat. It reminded me of the kitchens in Father's castle, only here students walked around the tall tables not cooking, but picking dishes and putting them on small trays. "Self-service," Tío called it. I called it paradise.

Just like in the paradise of Ama Bernarda's stories, some food was forbidden, at least until I had learned how to use a fork in the proper manner. For now, to be on the safe side, I chose only a bowl of soup and a sandwich, while promising myself I would practice hard that night so I could try anything I wanted to the following day.

After we had paid for our lunches, we walked into an open patio where around little tables symmetrically arranged under huge striped parasols, students talked, ate, and laughed with a contagious exuberance.

Once we were seated, Tío gave me one of the small boxes he had on his trays and showed me how to drink from it with a bright yellow straw. "It's chocolate milk," he said, laughing when I asked what kind of cow made such a wonderful milk. He also offered me crunchy chips from a fluffy metallic bag. He said they were potatoes, but they were nothing like the potatoes of my world. They were flat and crispy and made me hungry for more. But Tío, claiming I would get sick if I did not stop eating, forbade me to go back inside to get another bag.

"Besides," he said, getting up, "I want to show you the library. And since I have to teach a class at two, we have to hurry."

"May I come with you?" I asked after he had explained he was a professor in the anthropology department.

"Sure," he said, but didn't sound sure at all. "Just don't ask any questions."

I found Tio's talk on "The Psychology of the Medieval Warrior" fascinating. His students kept interrupting him, and he answered their questions promptly. But when I raised my hand as everybody else was doing, he ignored me. Upset, I left as soon as the class was over without waiting for him and wandered around the campus by myself, intoxicated by the freedom I was allowed in this world with no Ama to chaperone me everywhere and no Mother to force me to act against my nature.

The following day, I attended my first real classes. I was nervous at first, but soon I realized I had no problem keeping up with the teachers, and I relaxed. In between classes I talked with some of my classmates, and by the end of the morning, I had already made friends.

John kept a promise he had made at Al's and took me downtown for lunch. Happy to practice my newly acquired ability with the fork, I ordered a salad. But John insisted I try his "pizza." He offered the triangular pie to me that he was holding in his hand, and so I dropped my fork and took the pie in mine. I imagined John sitting at my father's table in the Great Hall, grabbing the food from the common trays with his bare fingers as he had done with the pizza, and smiled at the thought: He would fit right in.

I liked the pizza so much, John just let me eat his piece and bought himself another one.

Once we were finished, we strolled along the streets on our way back to the campus. Unlike the random pattern that the alleys of the villages in my world follow, these streets were neatly arranged in a perfectly straight grid. Although I found each and every one of the shops that occupied the first floor of the houses fascinating, the most amazing thing of all was to be close to John. And to stop staring at him required amazing effort.

Several days passed this way, swift and pleasant like a summer breeze. And every day I felt more comfortable in my new life. I loved the freedom this world allowed me. I loved its people and its food and the rhythm of the new language. And above all, I loved the thrill of knowing I would see John playing basketball the following Sunday.

But Tío had other plans.

"Good news, Andrea," he told me on Thursday as I left my English class. "I've been able to rearrange my schedule and free up this weekend for you."

I didn't say anything, but my eyes must have conveyed my total lack of enthusiasm at spending time with him, because he added. "That means we're going on a road trip. We'll be visiting some of the Spanish missions." He said this brightly, as if I should be thrilled.

I wasn't. I would have preferred to stay in Davis. But I couldn't tell Tío about my wish to see John—Tío would have guessed my interest in John and probably forbidden me from seeing him altogether to avoid further trouble. So I had no believable excuse for staying, and in the end, I agreed to accompany Tío Ramiro on his trip.

Kelsey laughed when I asked her if she wanted to come. "Go with you to see the missions? No thanks. I saw them all when I was a child, once too often, actually, and have no interest in seeing them again. They all look the same to me. Very nice, very pretty, very boring."

"Why is your father taking me there, then?"

Kelsey shrugged. "Who knows? He may actually believe everybody shares his passion for them. You see, Dad has been studying the missions for so long he may have lost perspective. He even runs a field course in one of them over the summer." And then after a pause, she added with a knowing smile, "John helps him."

"John?"

"Yes. He's one of dad's graduate students. Hasn't John told you that? Oh, I see you have other, more important things to talk about. Or maybe you don't even need to talk."

Just then, she reminded me more of Rosa than I cared to contemplate. Trying not to blush, I asked her what time the basketball game was on Sunday. Maybe if it was not too early, I could still make it back in time to watch it.

Kelsey laughed. "Don't worry, Andrea. Their team doesn't play in Davis this Sunday. But I'll tell John you asked."

I blushed anyway.

KELSEY WAS RIGHT ABOUT THE MISSIONS. THEY WERE NICE. SHE WAS also totally wrong: nice did not begin to convey the magnificent beauty of the Mission Santa Inés, the first place we visited.

Set in a wide open valley against a background of distant hills, the mission seemed to grow out of the earth as we approached it, seeming both eternal and dispensable, like a white speck dropped on the canvas by mistake one day and later embraced and made the center of the painter's picture.

We left the car in the parking lot—empty, since the mission was closed that day—and walked up to the front of the church.

Two cypresses—vertical lines of green against the whitewashed walls—framed its wooden door; high above, the roof—a triangle of red tiles—stood out against the blue sky. To our right rose the bell tower, a metallic cross on top and three arched openings set in two rows where the bells hung. Beyond the tower was a long wall with a single arch that served as the entrance to the graveyard. To our left stood the cloister, a succession of arches growing smaller in the distance under a red-tiled roof.

"Who built this mission?" I asked Tío, my voice barely above a whisper so as not to disturb the majestic simplicity of the place.

"The Spaniards," Tío said. "The descendants of the same people that crossed from Spain into your world." And finding the door to the church locked, he rang the bell.

I waited for the clear sound of the bell to die in the distance and then spoke again, "I thought Spain was far from here."

"So it is, Andrea."

"But then how——"

Just then the door opened, and a man dressed in jeans and a plaid shirt stood in the doorway. The man smiled at Tío; they shook hands and exchanged greetings. After Tío introduced him to me as the director of the mission, he motioned us to come inside.

The church consisted of a single rectangular room. Pictures topped by crosses hung along its whitewashed walls, and in two places, roughly in the middle, frescos painted in green and pink and blue depicted flowers surrounding a religious scene.

Two rows of wooden benches faced the main altar from where the image of Santa Inés watched over us. The brass candelabra, hanging from the wooden beams in the shape of a wheel and full of candles, would have felt at home in my father's castle.

We left the church and entered the cloister, a gallery of arches built around a square courtyard. A fountain sat in its center. The murmur of the water singing in the stillness of the morning filled the air, while the neatly kept hedges reminded me of the queen's garden back in my world.

As we walked under the arches, our steps unexpectedly loud on the tiled floor, I noticed that the windows that opened to the cloister were blocked with iron bars. And yet the place didn't feel like a prison to me, more like a sanctuary, a refuge out of time.

Tío and his friend excused themselves as they had things to discuss and left me alone. And as I sat by myself on one of the benches against the wall, I had the sudden feeling of being watched, the feeling that all the people who had ever lived in the mission were still here in some other dimension, and that if I moved my eyes ever so slightly, I would be able to see them, and if I listened hard enough, I would be able to hear their steps. The steps of the Spaniards who had built this place, the descendants of the people who were also my ancestors. And then the bells tolled, and the spell was broken.

Tío returned and we went inside, into a room plainly furnished with a long wooden table and benches, where we shared lunch with his friend.

Later in the afternoon, we drove away toward the rolling hills, and the mission receded again into the distance, a speck of white lost in the valley.

WE REACHED THE MISSION OF SANTA MARÍA EARLY IN THE evening. At least that's what the sign by the side of the road indicated. But this time, instead of buildings to welcome us, only a bare landscape of shrubs and broken earth mounds was visible when the car stopped.

"Here we are," Tío said, holding open the car door for me.

I stared at him. "We are where? I mean, where is the mission?"

Tío pointed up the hill and nodded. "There. Those walls were once the mission of Santa María."

I could not believe we had driven all the way here to see . . . nothing. Surely Tío was joking.

But he was not. He just stood there holding my door open. And when he spoke again, his voice was pressing. "Come on, Andrea. We have to set up the tents and start a fire before sunset. It gets cold quickly here. And I want you to see the ruins beforehand."

We were going to sleep here? Was Tío out of his mind? Not knowing what else to do, I got out of the car and followed him up the hill.

"Why didn't you tell me this mission was in ruins?" I asked him as I ran to keep up with him.

Tío shrugged. "I thought I did."

He was not being entirely forthright. Somehow I knew he did not want me to know the mission was in ruins until I had seen it. But why?

NINE

The Conquest

All that was left of the mission were some broken walls and a solitary arch holding up the sky. There were no stones around the ruins, either. Had later peoples stolen them to build their houses?

"No, Andrea," Tío told me when I asked him. "There were no stones. The mission was built with adobe bricks. Bricks made out of earth and dried in the sun."

"But what about the rain . . ."

"It doesn't rain much here, Andrea. As you can see, there is not much water, either."

"Why did they build a mission then, if there is no water?" My kingdom being a land of green mountains and running streams, I had trouble imagining a world without water.

"The Spaniards knew how to build aqueducts to bring water down from the mountains," Tío explained. "This was once a rich valley. They grew crops of olives and corn, peppers and almonds."

As Tío talked, I heard Don Alfonso's voice in my mind. *The Arabs who overcame King Roderic were said to possess the knowledge of converting a desert into a garden. And nothing would please my brother more than to give water to our desert lands.*

I shrugged the memory away. "Is Spain dry, Tío?" I asked, as that would explain their expertise in transporting water from place to place.

Tío nodded. "The southern part is. And remind me when we get back to Davis to find you some books about Spain. You're supposed to be from there."

"But not from the south, okay? I don't know anything about deserts."

Tío smiled. "All right, then. We'll say you are from Asturias. I did the research for my dissertation there, searching for remains from the time when your ancestors left Spain."

"Did you find any?"

Tío was so lost in his own thoughts, I had to repeat my question.

"Find what?"

"Remains from the time of my ancestors."

"Yes, I did. But no proof of your ancestors crossing to another world. Of course."

He did not say more and I did not press him. But I knew there was something else he was not telling me. I wondered what he had found there that still gave him such a faraway look after all these years.

"What happened?" I asked Tío later as we sat around the fire. "Why was the mission destroyed?" We had erected the tents already, farther down the hill from where the mission once stood, under the protection of an ugly modern compound my uncle explained held restrooms and showers for summer field courses held there.

Tío sighed. "It is a long story. Do you really want to hear it?"

I nodded, and Tío smiled at me in a sad kind of way. Eyes deep in the fire, he started talking.

"After your ancestors left Spain, the Spaniards wrested their country back from under Arab control. It was a long process that lasted over seven hundred years. And when they were done, well, I guess they were used to the conquest, so they crossed the ocean and came to America to continue.

"First they conquered the Aztec empire south of here, in the country that is now called Mexico. Then they traveled north and west and eventually came to California. The first Spaniards to arrive here were the padres, religious people who didn't want to conquer, but to convert the natives to their own religion.

"The Native Americans, at least in this particular area, were peaceful. They didn't fight the foreign people. Some even volunteered to help the Spaniards build the missions and, when they were finished, came to live in them as well.

"But the Native Americans were not happy. They were not used to living in closed spaces. They hated the bells tolling throughout the day, telling them when to rise, when to pray, when to eat, and reminding them of their lost freedom.

"Then things got worse. The Spaniards were defeated by the new elite that had evolved in Mexico, and the new government stopped paying the soldiers garrisoned in the missions. The Native Americans had to feed the soldiers who were supposed to protect them from a danger they couldn't fathom. So eventually, they rebelled against the soldiers and burned the missions down."

"But not Santa Inés?"

"They burned Santa Inés, too. They burned the barracks that housed the soldiers. But when the church caught fire, they put down their weapons and helped the padres save it. Then they disappeared into the wild. They never lived in the mission again."

I stood still, gazing into the flames.

"Why did the Spaniards come in the first place, Tío?"

Tío bent over the fire and grabbed a branch, stirring sparks into the night air. "Some came for gold," he said, "some for glory. But I think the padres, the men who founded the missions, were not interested in gold or glory. They were "holy fools." They really believed they were saving their souls by converting the Native Americans to their religion."

A coyote cried in the distance, and I looked up. But I couldn't see it. The night was dark; the moon was not to rise until midnight.

I bent closer to Tío. "You think the Spaniards shouldn't have come, don't you, Tío?"

Tío looked at me and smiled. "On the contrary. If there had been no missions, I wouldn't have a job, would I?"

We remained in silence for a while, watching the flames dance in the wind. And then, when the fire died, we went inside our tents. And for the first time ever, I slept in the open, only a thin canvas separating me from the stars.

THE NEXT DAY, TÍO WANTED TO VISIT ANOTHER MISSION. FEARING another disappointing bunch of ruins, I demurred. But La Purísima, Tío reassured me, was fully restored, by which he meant it had been rebuilt after its destruction.

"I promise you'll like it," Tío said.

And he was right. La Purísima had been constructed by a stream against a red-sand hillside covered with trees and, like Santa Inés, was unbelievably beautiful in its simplicity.

But Tío had not told me everything. He had failed to mention the fact that the mission was inhabited. And not only by tourists like us, wearing jeans or shorts and bright shirts, but by men in the brown robes of the padres and women wearing white loose shirts and long skirts with handkerchiefs over their heads. I could also see men dressed in peasant clothes, working in the fields or attending to the cattle and sheep grazing in the enclosed pastures behind the whitewashed buildings of the mission.

"They are not for real," Tío said as he led me to the main door that opened to the cloister where a small crowd had gathered.

"What do you mean they are not for real?"

"I mean they are people pretending to live as if they were at the end of the 1800s, when this mission was first established."

"Why?"

"You'll see," he said. He signed me for a tour. But he excused himself to go speak with the director of the mission.

And so I found myself following a cheerful middle-aged woman, who was split in two by a red scarf around her waist, through different rooms where people in similar attire per-formed different tasks, such as grinding corn on flat stones for tortillas, making candles and soap, or spinning wool and weav-ing the yarn into colorful blankets. And all these chores, our guide explained, closely mimicked life as it had been when the Spanish padres had lived there.

Everyone in my group seemed to enjoy the visit, but for reasons I could not understand, I found it unbearably sad, and when the guide led us out of the church, I fell behind. I strolled along the fiery red wall that started to the right of the church until I found a wooden double door that opened into the old mission graveyard.

I walked about the tombs, reading the windswept gravestones, and again and again I found the same year inscribed on them.

"Did they die when the Indians attacked the mission?" I asked Tío when he finally found me.

Tío shook his head. "No. Yesterday I didn't tell you the whole story. These people didn't die by the sword. They were killed by one of the diseases the Spaniards brought with them. The Spaniards had become resistant to various illnesses over the years. But the natives, having never been exposed to them, died by the thousands. Millions, if you consider the whole continent."

Unable to grasp the enormity of what Tío was saying, I turned my eyes to the stone sitting at my feet: *1818–1820*, I read. The girl or boy lying here had been only two years old. And for a moment, the red walls I had found soothing before seemed painted in blood. I felt sick.

So this is what would become of my world, I thought, *if Tío's ever learns about it. A graveyard for the dead, a museum for the living.*

I looked up. "This is why you brought me here, isn't it? So that I'd agree to go back to my world." It wasn't a question.

But Tío shook his head. "No, Andrea. I brought you here so you would understand why. So you would understand how dangerous it is for your world to be discovered, and so you would never again tread lightly between your world and mine."

I nodded. "I won't, Tío. I'll go back to my world when the moon grows full again and stay there."

And despite all the beauty of the place, I felt like crying.

BY THE TIME WE HEADED BACK TO DAVIS, MY RESOLUTION TO return to my world had started to dwindle. Yes, I knew our worlds should never meet, but at the thought of passing another uneventful winter, not to mention the rest of my life, in the company of my mother's ladies, I felt half-dead already. Surely there had to be a flaw in Tio's careful reconstruction of the destruction of one way of life by another. To start with, how was he so sure what had happened in the missions these two hundred years past? Tío was old, but not that old. He could not have been there in person.

My uncle laughed at my suggestion. "Of course I wasn't, Andrea. And no, we can't ever be one hundred percent sure we got the facts right. But there are ways of getting close to the truth. That's what archaeology is about: the study of cultures and people long gone."

"But how? I mean, could you teach me how to learn about the past?"

"And why would you like to learn that?"

"So that I could study the Xarens back in my world."

Tío smiled. "To study the Xarens? Now that is actually an old dream of mine."

"Is that a yes, Tío? Will you teach me now, and then, when I'm back in my world, will you ask my parents to let me study the old cities of the Xarens?"

Tío shook his head. "Sorry, Andrea. But I don't think your parents would approve. As you know, in your world, ladies do not roam the countryside in search of ruins."

I scowled. "I'm not a lady."

Tío laughed. "So you say."

I sulked. But not for long. I knew Tío was interested in studying the Xarens, and as he could not stay in my world for long due to his responsibilities in his own world, it would be in his best interests to allow me to help. He just needed a little convincing. And I knew just how to tempt him.

"You know, Tío, that the king of Suavia has a collection of Xarens' texts?"

Tío turned to face me, his eyes eagerly bright. "Really?" he said, the car swerving briefly out of its lane and crunching into the shoulder. "How do you know that?"

"Don Alfonso told me. I could ask him to let me see them."

Tío laughed. "I see. And is it the Xarens or Don Alfonso you want to study?"

I blushed. I blushed even though there was nothing to blush about, as I found the thought of a romance with Don Alfonso nothing short of appalling. I was about to tell Tío this when it occurred to me that if Tío thought my interest in the Xarens was just a way of getting a boyfriend, a prince of my world no less, he might be more inclined to indulge my learning. And besides, if Tío thought I fancied the haughty prince of Suavia, he would never realize I liked John and thus would not think of preventing me from seeing him.

So I said nothing, and trying hard not to smile, I lay back in my comfortable leather seat and watched the hills pass by my window. I was pleased with myself. My future already looked brighter in my world.

And I still had three weeks left in California to work things out. I was not going to let the certainty of my return to my boring world spoil my fun.

TEN

The Storm

After Tío dropped me off at the dorms, I went straight to Kelsey's room. I could not wait to tell her I had changed my mind about studying to be an English teacher—the official explanation for my being in California—and had decided to take up classes in archaeology. But Kelsey had news of her own: she was not going to be Juliet in the play, but Mercutio. And that, I gathered by the anger in her voice, was not good news.

I had helped Kelsey a couple of times the previous week prepare for her audition. Once I got over the unbelievable fact that she was a student in the Drama Department—which basically meant she was studying to be on stage, something no lady would ever do in my world—I had actually enjoyed it. At her request, I had read Romeo's lines to her Juliet. So I knew Romeo and Juliet were the main characters. I did not remember anyone named Mercutio.

Kelsey went livid when I told her that. "See what I mean? No one remembers Mercutio. And why should they? He is so dispensable he dies at the beginning of the play."

"He? Mercutio is a boy? But how . . ."

"There are not enough boys for the play," Kelsey said matter-of-factly.

That was not what I meant. It was strange enough for me to accept that acting was something so widely accepted in this world it was even taught at the university. But for a woman to impersonate a boy in front of an audience . . .

What would Mother think of this? I wondered, Mother who had totally forbidden me to dress like a boy and be a squire once I turned fourteen. But then I remembered my mother had lived in California as a girl and thus must have been familiar with this world's customs. Mother living in California was in itself a shocking thought. But not ready to dwell on this right then, I pushed it aside and turned my attention back to Kelsey. My cousin was still rumbling about the injustice of the world at large and her drama teacher in particular, who obviously had a personal interest in Lindsay as she, Kelsey, was a much better actress. Lindsay, I imagined, had gotten the part of Juliet. I did not ask.

Instead I asked her again about Mercutio. Kelsey grabbed one of the books lying on her bed and tossed it to me. "There, see for yourself. Page eleven. List of characters."

I took the book and read the description under Mercutio, Romeo's friend. And what I read about him was not as bad as Kelsey's mood had made me fear. In fact, it was pretty flattering.

"Listen, Kelsey. It says here Shakespeare killed Mercutio because he was becoming a more interesting character than Romeo or even Juliet."

"Yeah right. Except you're missing the key word: *killed*. As in Shakespeare *killed* Mercutio. He killed him in the first scene of Act III. The play has five acts. So you do the math."

"Well, yes. You are only in three of the acts. But you have some of the best lines in the play," I reminded her, flipping quickly through the book. "And you die in a sword fight."

"So?"

"Come on, Kelsey, don't be so pessimistic. I can teach you how to fence. I bet no one else will know how to fight with a sword. You'll totally stand out."

Kelsey looked at me in surprise. "You know how to fence?"

"Well, yes—I mean, I took classes when I was young."

Kelsey's eyes opened wide with excitement. "Why didn't you say so before? We'll expand the fighting scenes! We'll make them the center of the play! That would give the play a new angle. One I'm sure has never been done before. And Lindsay, being Juliet, will not be in any of them." She beamed at me. "Andrea, you're a genius."

The next day, Kelsey took me with her to the rehearsal and explained to Dan, the stage director, her new ideas about the play. Then at his request, we performed the steps we had practiced the previous evening for Mercutio's fight and death. Dan was dutifully impressed and agreed to let Kelsey choreograph the fighting scenes. As for me, I was asked to teach Kelsey and the other actors the proper moves in a sword fight.

And so, after being forbidden by my parents to ever be a squire, I found an unexpected use for my long and hard training as a page, one that made me incredibly popular among the actors at first, and later among their friends as well, who would come to watch the practice and then stay after the rehearsal and ask me to teach them, too. One of the friends who came to ask was Richard, Kelsey's boyfriend. And then on the second week, he brought John.

I was ecstatic. Thanks to Kelsey and her play, I had a legitimate reason to see and teach John three times a week. Sometimes he would walk me home after class. Other times we went for drinks with the rest of the cast late into the evening or to parties on the weekends. And I would have been completely happy but for the moon that grew fuller and fuller every night, until the last day of my stay finally arrived. That night, the moon would be full again.

I got up early that morning and, sitting on my bed, waited for my uncle to come and pick me up. And when he came, I quietly said goodbye to my cozy little room and followed him outside.

Tío Ramiro didn't take me to his car as I expected, but turning away from the parking lot, walked deep into the campus. "Let's go for a walk," he said. "We have to talk."

What about? I wondered. I didn't remember having done anything wrong, except for my forbidden crush on John, that is. But even if Tío knew my secret, what difference would it make now that I was leaving? Only after we had reached the pond in front of the English department and taken seats on one of the benches that flanked the water did he break his silence.

"How are you doing, Andrea?" he said. His voice, flat and even, gave me no clue of what he was thinking.

I shrugged and said, "Fine," because I didn't have words in any language to describe how much I loved being there. And yet the moon's journey had come full circle. At the beach, the arch was waiting.

As an echo to my thoughts, I heard Tío saying, "Tonight is the full moon."

"I know, Tío. I'm ready."

"I know you are. But . . . I guess what I'm trying to say is, do you want to go?"

I looked up. "No. I don't want to go."

Tío smiled. "I didn't think so. And that's why I was think-ing . . .You see, Andrea, I must admit that over these last weeks you've shown a genuine interest in learning. I think you deserve a chance to continue your studies. If you want me to, I'll go to your parents and ask their permission to let you stay here for a while longer."

I stared at him in total shock. "You'll go in my stead? But . . . but what about your classes?"

I had been attending Tio's lectures for the last few weeks and knew they were supposed to continue until the end of the term, which was still two months away. Tío could not just quit, could he?

"How thoughtful of you," Tío said, still smiling. "Don't worry. I've asked John to cover for me. He's been my graduate student for almost a year. He'll do fine."

I gasped and tried to speak, but my mouth was so dry no words came out. Instead, I jumped up and hugged my perfect-ly dressed uncle. "Thank you, Tío. You are my best uncle."

Tío pushed me away. "Of course I am. I am the only uncle you have. Now seriously, Andrea, is there anything you want me to tell your parents?"

At his words, memories rushed to my mind: the smell of the grass covered in dew in the early morning before the hunt, Flecha's nostrils flaring in anticipation; the thrill of victory upon disarming my opponent; and the amusement in Margarida's eyes after one of my many social blunders. I missed my sister and my stubborn mare. I missed Ama Bernarda and her constant complaints. And maybe, just maybe, I also missed my parents. "Tell them . . . just tell them that I miss them."

Tío nodded. "So I will," he said and walked away.

Barely avoiding being run over by the ever-present bicycles, I made it back to the dorms and then up the stairs to Kelsey's room.

"Guess what, Kelsey? I'm staying. I'm staying for the whole term."

I had it all figured out. Even if my parents did not agree to my staying longer, they would have to wait until the next full moon to send their orders for Tío Ramiro. After that, I'd still have another four weeks before the door would open again.

Kelsey looked at me, her pale blue eyes showing no surprise. "I know," she said. Bending over, she placed the dress she had been folding in a duffel bag. "Dad just told me."

"Your dad? But I was just with him. He couldn't possibly . . ."

Kelsey rolled her eyes. "Really, Andrea! What planet are you from? Dad called me. Called me, you get it? As in 'on the phone.' You know that magic thing you talk into?"

"Of course!" I said and smiled to hide my confusion. But all of a sudden I didn't feel like smiling. For a moment, I had felt so sure this was my world, my real world, and now I was an outsider again. Would I ever fit in here? "I know what a phone is," I said, the words bitter in my mouth.

Kelsey laughed. "Sometimes I wonder," she said.

Before I knew it, I was laughing, too.

"Well, anyway," Kelsey continued after we had calmed down, "Dad said you were staying and that he was leaving, and he asked me to take care of you. And that is exactly what I'm doing." At her last words, she waved at all the clothes piled on her bed.

"You're giving me your clothes?"

My cousin dropped the shirt she was holding and shrugged. "Andrea, please! Stop trying to be funny and listen.

We're going on a trip. You've been in California for a month and all you've seen is this boring, depressing college town. What idea of this country are you going to take home?"

"I have been to the missions, too."

Kelsey rolled her eyes. "My point exactly. Come on! Go to your room and start packing. I am going to show you what California is really about."

"But I like it here . . ."

"Oh, brother. You like it here. I can't imagine what your country is like if you like it here, and really, I wouldn't care to find out either. As for you, if you think this is so great, wait until you see San Francisco and Berkeley and Monterey!"

Kelsey was packing her shoes now. Whether I wanted to go or not didn't seem to matter to her. Still I insisted. "I cannot go, Kelsey. What about my classes? And the play? And what about Richard?"

"The play. Well, I guess not being Juliet is an advantage after all. I think they can manage without me for a couple of days. As for Richard, he and I are history."

Now it was my turn to roll my eyes. "You fought again?"

"You make it sound like we fight all the time, which is so totally untrue. Oh well, who cares? This time it's for real. And I need a break. So I'm taking a week off. And you should, too. Come on, Andrea, we'll have fun."

"But . . ."

"Oh, I see. It's because of John you want to stay. Right, cousin?"

"It is not."

"Then why are you turning red?"

"I'm not. I mean, I was just running to come speak with you. That's why."

"Is that so? Well then, prove it. Say you're coming."

I did. And that very afternoon, I found myself in Kelsey's red convertible, speeding along the brown rolling hills of northern California. By early evening, we had reached San Francisco and any reservation I could have had about the trip disappeared. San Francisco was a dream come true—if I could ever have dreamed of such a marvelous place.

For the next two days, we explored the city. We crossed the bay and watched the sunset from the Golden Gate Bridge. I could not hold back my awe as we watched the blaze of color, nor my panic when Kelsey drove down the steep hills of the city as if she had forgotten that cars had brakes.

Then we continued up the coast, stopping wherever we wanted and wherever the steep cliffs allowed. We ate the most incredible food in colorful restaurants, which soon seemed as familiar to me as the Great Hall of my parents' castle. At night we watched TV, mainly shows about doctors and hospitals. I didn't have to ask to know that my cousin, for all her talk, was not done with Richard, who I knew was studying to be a physician. But I also knew better than to tease her, as I didn't want her to tease me back about John.

By Friday, Kelsey and Richard had made up. I was deeply relieved, tired of watching the road speed by me too fast as they argued over the phone.

By mutual agreement, we started back. We arrived in Davis on Sunday just in time to watch the basketball game. It was the perfect ending to the perfect vacation.

DURING THE FOLLOWING WEEKS, JOHN TAUGHT ME HOW TO READ history in stones and broken pottery, and I taught him how to fence. And every other week, I went with Kelsey to the gym and watched John's team play basketball. And day by day, the moon grew until it was full again, and Tío returned.

"You can stay," he told me as we sat in the small café where we had agreed to meet through Kelsey.

I almost fainted with relief. "You convinced them? You convinced my parents to let me study here? I mean, thank you! Thank you so much."

Tío shrugged my thanks away. "Actually, you should thank your sister Rosa."

I stared blankly at him. "Rosa?"

"Yes, Rosa. After you left, your sister got engaged to Don Julián de Alvar, the king of Suavia. And your father is so enraged at her choice, I don't think he was really listening when I asked him to let you stay. So he said yes. I hope he gets over his anger soon. Your father's kingdom and Suavia have been enemies long enough. I hope this marriage will end their bloody feud. And I hope your father has enough sense to see it this way."

Like Father, I was only half listening. All I could think was that I was staying.

When prompted, Tío told me about Margarida and Ama Bernarda who had sent their love, and about Flecha, my golden mare. And thinking of them made me feel homesick and even a little angry with my parents for having dismissed me so easily, as if they were only too happy to get rid of me. But I didn't dwell on my hurt feelings for long. Regardless of their reasons, for once their wishes agreed with mine. And I was more than willing to leave it at that.

BETWEEN ATTENDING LECTURES IN THE MORNINGS AND PARTIES ON the weekends, between basketball games and fencing classes, the term came to an end, and suddenly the day of the performance was upon us.

As I was not needed backstage, I sat with Richard and John among the audience, and for the first time ever, I saw the play in real time. I was enthralled. It was one thing to see the actors dressed in jeans and sweaters delivering lines out of context while Dan interrupted them constantly with sharp remarks. It was another to see the story develop before my eyes, played by actors dressed in bright fancy costumes that made them look like gods. Even the swords I knew to be fake, as I had used them myself often enough, seemed fashioned from brushed steel as they flashed on the stage.

Kelsey, her blonde hair held back in a low ponytail, her long legs dressed in boots up to her knees, was magnificent. And seeing her thrust and parry, first with words and then with sword, I believed she was fighting for her life. And when she died, stabbed through the heart, I hurt with her.

But despite the beautifully staged fights and the realistic-looking blood on Mercutio's and Tybalt's fake wounds, the play still belonged to the two lovers, even if Juliet, as played by Lindsay with eager helplessness, reminded me of my sister Rosa, especially during the balcony scene.

And while Romeo wooed Juliet with words of love, just like Don Julián had wooed my sister in my father's castle, I found myself wondering whether Rosa had already married her king. But then I remembered Tío saying it would take at least a year to get my father and Don Julián to come to a final agreement that would settle their dispute once and for all, if indeed they were able to reach a truce.

Unlike my sister and her lover, Romeo and Juliet were married the next day. Three days later, they were dead. And although

I knew they were only actors reading lines someone else had written, I almost believed their doomed love and cried for them.

Tío joined us backstage after the play. He had brought flowers for Kelsey, as is the custom in his world. And after Kelsey disappeared into the crowd, he turned to me.

"I'm proud of you, too," he said to me. "You passed all your classes. Including mine. This is for you."

He handed me a small box with a red bow, just like the ones he used to give me when I was a child. Inside the box, I found a watch. A magical watch with a golden moon. The moon, Tío explained, would move in a circle following the phases of the real one.

Tío put it on my wrist. "Wear it always," he said. "So you don't forget that being here is a gift."

Dan had planned a party at his house for the cast after the play, and as usual, I joined them.

Many people came to me throughout the evening. They all praised the realism of the fighting scenes and congratulated me for my contribution. But John ignored me. I had long suspected his coming to the rehearsals had more to do with seeing Lindsay than with a real interest in improving his fencing skills. But I had dismissed his infatuation as a passing fancy related to Lindsay's romantic role in the play. After all, as I had also noticed, John was not the only one sighing after her, and Lindsay already had a boyfriend.

Still, that night it seemed to me that Lindsay was gladly enjoying John's attention. Tired of pretending I did not care, I left the party early and went back to my dorm.

The next morning, Kelsey came into my room and invited me to spend a couple of days at her father's house by the ocean. I did not want to go at first, as I knew Tío would not be there—he had told me he would be attending a conference in Los Angeles. But Kelsey, as usual, knew how to convince me.

"Come on, Andrea. It's the only day Richard has free. And," she added with a sly smile, "I've already invited John."

Quickly averting my eyes, I busied myself picking up the clothes I had dropped on the floor the previous night. "So?"

Kelsey laughed. "So you'll come, right cousin?" And before I could react, she added, "I'll be back at two." The door closed behind her.

I dropped my clothes again, and sitting back against my bed, I tried in vain to slow down my beating heart. I had decided the previous night to forget about John. But now my resolution felt shaky. Surely John's infatuation with Lindsay would be over as soon as he realized she was not really Juliet. Maybe a couple of days with me by the ocean was all he needed to see me in another light, a more flattering one.

Of course I knew that my feelings for John were forbidden—John was not from my world—but knowing didn't make me any wiser, and when Kelsey came to pick me up, I was ready.

It was a glorious day. We played volleyball on the beach and hide-and-seek behind the dunes. Then, tired of chasing the waves, we built a fire on the sand and cooked hot dogs and marshmallows, which we ate sitting on a dead tree washed ashore by the tides—maybe the same trunk I had used to hide from them so long ago, the evening I had appeared in their world.

We were singing at the top of our voices, silly songs I found extremely funny, when out of nowhere, the sky opened up and began to pour as if a gigantic faucet had opened above us.

In my haste to get up, I tripped and fell. By the time John helped me to my feet, Kelsey and Richard were out of sight. As the rain wrapped itself around us like a curtain, my uncle's house, lost in the dunes, seemed impossibly far away. Suddenly lightning broke the sky and illuminated the arch, dark and distorted, on its eternal watch over the beach.

"Wait!" I called to John. "We can stay under the arch until the rain stops." But the roar of thunder covered my words. Reaching forward, I grabbed his arm, signaling toward the broken rock. John nodded and ran toward it.

I rushed after him, while the storm, raging now in all its fury, threw angry gusts of rain at us. We had barely reached the cave when another clap of thunder shook the arch. Startled, I lost my balance and fell. Just as I hit the sand, I noticed the change, a subtle change as if millions of ants were running over my skin—as if the consistency of the air was slightly off. Then I felt cold water running over my body and a salty taste in my mouth. The tide was in.

I jumped to my feet, refusing to believe my senses. But when I glanced through the entrance of the arch, I couldn't deny it any longer. It was not only that the rain had stopped and the clouds were gone. The light was different, too. It was the unmistakable yellow light of Athos the golden moon. With a painful sense of loss I had to admit to myself, I had unwillingly returned to my world.

Before I had time to dwell on my disappointment, an immense wave rolled over me and sent me breathless against the rocks. As the water receded to collect its force and strike again, I saw John farther to my right, lying like a heap of soaked clothing on the sand.

"John! John! Are you all right?" I called at the top of my voice. But the thundering noise of the waves breaking against the rocks drowned my words.

I plunged forward, wading against the receding water, while in front of me, the shapeless form moved. Again I screamed to him, and forcing my legs to move still faster, I plodded ahead. Slowly John rose to his knees. By the time I reached him, he was already up.

"What happened?" he asked, staring at his drenched clothes in disbelief.

"Let's go, John. The tide is rising. The water will soon close the doorway. We have to hurry."

John did not move. "What are you talking about? The tide was low two minutes ago. How could it . . ." As his eyes wandered around the walls of the arch, his voice trailed off. A look of utter shock on his clean-shaven face, he stared back at me. "Unless . . . unless I've been unconscious for a while?"

I hesitated for a moment, then nodded. This was not the time to explain. "That's right, you were. Now come quick. We have to get out."

I grabbed his arm and pulled at him. But John stalled. "Wait," he said, pointing over my shoulder. I knew—even before I turned and saw the wave, an immense wave closing upon us with the roar of a wounded bear—I knew it was too late, that the strength of the water would pull us under and I would drown, because although I had lived by the ocean all my life, the truth was, I could not swim.

I took a deep breath and, with my legs firmly set on the ground, braced myself for the impact. The crest broke against my chest with the force of a hundred horses, and losing my balance, I stumbled back. Just as I fell, I felt John's arms around my body holding me up. Coughing and gulping water, I clung to him while the wave wasted itself against the rocks.

John put me down as the surf withdrew and, pulling at my arm, headed outside. It was the impulse of the following wave that finally pushed us onto the cliffs surrounding the cove, the Cove of the Dead. Gasping for air, I collapsed on the rocks.

For a while John was quiet, which suited me fine; I needed time to think about how to explain to him what had happened. I had sworn to my uncle not to tell anyone about my world. But what else could I say? Just my luck the door had opened at the wrong time.

Despondent, I dropped my head into my hands, and as I did, my eyes rested on the watch my uncle had given me the previous evening. Perfectly still on the blue dial, the golden circle of a full moon was staring at me in silent warning.

John's voice cut through my brooding. "Let's go back to the house."

I looked up. "We can't, John," I said without thinking. "The house is not there anymore."

John rolled his eyes. "Yeah, right. The house is gone, and we're on the moon."

"Yes. No. I mean . . . what I mean is that we're no longer in California."

"Come on, Andrea. You're not funny," John said, getting up. But as he turned, his body froze. Eyes wide open, he stared at the imposing walls surrounding the cove. *What could he think*, I wondered, *of the huge yellow moon of my world hanging over the cliffs?*

"What's going on?" John cried. "The sky, the beach. Why is everything different?"

"I told you. We are not in California anymore."

"Give me a break, Andrea. Where are we, then? In a planetarium?"

Grateful, I grabbed the rope he was throwing to me. "Exactly."

"Right. And how on earth did we get here?"

"I'm sorry, John, but I promised not to tell."

"Really?" He paused, waiting for me to explain. When I did not say anything, he continued, "Okay, fine. If you wanted to fool me, you win. I totally admit it. So now let's go back."

"But we can't. I mean, not yet."

"And what do you propose that we do, then?"

"We can go to my parents' place."

"Your parents? I thought they were in Spain."

"I . . . they . . . vacation. They're here on vacation. They have a summerhouse. I don't get along with them that well, so I don't visit them often."

"All right, Andrea. Have it your way. I'm wet and tired. I'll play along since it seems that's the only way I'm gonna get some dry clothes. But you'd better have a good explanation later."

An explanation I had. That he would accept it, I very much doubted. I grunted under my breath in a noncommittal way, and turning from him, started walking along the cove toward the steps carved into the wall.

"Is it a big-screen projection, like a hologram?" John asked as we climbed the cliffs. Again I didn't know what to say, so I pretended to be busy finding my footing. By the time we reached the top of the cliffs, he had stopped talking. In silence, we started down the winding path that led to my parents' castle.

What John was thinking, I couldn't imagine. Neither could I think of what to tell him. Except for the truth, that is. But even if I dared to tell him the truth, would he believe me? *Probably not*, I thought, as I remembered his awkward attempts to find a logical explanation for all this. Although maybe it was better for him to believe we were in some fantastic high-tech park. At least for the moment.

And yet when the path turned inland and my father's castle came into view, burning softly in the copper light of Lua, I realized the time for explanations had come, and my legs started shaking so badly that I couldn't walk any further. Luckily John didn't notice. He had stopped, too, and with a look of wonder in his light-brown eyes, he was staring at the castle. "Jeez, Andrea," he said, letting out a loud whistle. "It's so cool! I can't believe I've never heard of this place."

I almost fainted with relief. He still believed he was in his world. Happily I jumped into the game. "My father likes his privacy," I told him. "The area is closed to outsiders."

"What a total waste. People would go nuts over a place like this!" he said.

He was probably right, I thought, as I remembered the

mission I had visited with my uncle so long ago in my first week in California. I pushed back the memory and ran after John, who was already walking toward the castle.

"Wait, John. We must stay away from the gatehouse, I mean the door."

"Why?"

"Because . . . it's . . . closed. We have to climb over the walls."

John frowned. "Climb the walls? Are you out of your mind?"

I grabbed his arm. "You must do as I say, John. The door is electrified. If I turn the alarm off, I'll get in trouble." What I really meant was that we couldn't show up at the gatehouse dressed as we were in jeans and sweaters and sneakers. They hang people in my world for lesser crimes than wearing such bizarre clothes.

John considered my explanation for a moment. "Okay," he said, "let's play thieves." And without further argument he followed me.

My nights on the ramparts paid off. I knew exactly where the blind spot for the guard was, the place where the ivy had made its home. Without being noticed, we reached the courtyard, and keeping to the shadows, we hurried to the northern tower of the keep. There our luck ran out; the door was locked.

"Now what?" John said.

I stared at the walls. The vertical gaps that provided light and air to the spiral staircase were too narrow for us to crawl through. Besides, the big granite stones, although crudely carved, would provide no purchase for our fingers. We could walk around the keep and climb a tree to one of the windows of the lower floors. But the windows would be locked as well. Frustrated, I rammed the door with my shoulder. The heavy wooden planks didn't move. We needed the key. It was the only way to open the latch. Suddenly I remembered the golden arrow that, as always, held my hair. I grabbed it from my braid and tackled the narrow point into the keyhole. After only two tries I had it unlocked. Again I pushed at the door, and this time it swung open with a loud creak. Motioning John to follow, I rushed inside and up the stairs.

Behind me, John was quiet. When I glanced over my shoulder, I saw he was staring around with apprehension. As if I were seeing them for the first time, I noticed how dark and gloomy the walls were, how strong and pungent was the smell of smoke and burned fat that came from the torches hanging on brackets above our heads. And for a moment, the place I had always called home struck me as foreign. The feeling was so disturbing, I felt dizzy.

Finally we reached my quarters. I was closing the door carefully so it wouldn't slam, when John grabbed my arm. "Andrea!" he said, his voice a pressing whisper, "someone's in the room."

I looked back into my room. Compared to my white cozy dorm in Davis, the room now seemed strangely big and bare. And yet it was as it had always been: A tapestry covered the stone wall behind my canopy bed, the cedar trunk lay at its foot, and—a shadow was crawling on the floor. It was the shadow of a woman, standing by the doorway opening into my dueña's room.

Letting out a cry of joy, I ran to her. "Ama Bernarda! *¡Soy yo!* It's me, Andrea."

Ama didn't move. "*Mi princesa*, is it really you?"

"Of course it's me."

Slowly Ama reached for my face with her wrinkled hands, while tears ran down her weathered face.

"Andrea," John's voice reached me through Ama's tight embrace. "What's going on? I don't understand a word you're saying."

I looked up. "I'm sorry, John. But Ama doesn't speak English."

"Give me a break!"

"It's true, John. Ama is from Spain."

"Oh, I see." John smiled his dashing smile and, his right hand extended in front of him, came toward Ama. "Nice to meet you."

Ama moved back. Her arms straight out in front of her as if to ward him off, she looked at John with unconcealed fear.

I stepped between them and faced my dueña. "Ama Bernarda, this is Jo—Don Juan. He is one of Tío Ramiro's knights. He will be staying with us for a moon period."

Ama hesitated. I guessed our sudden appearance and bizarre clothes didn't make my case any stronger. But finally Ama Bernarda calmed down and agreed to take John to a guest room.

As soon as they left, I climbed under the blue canopy of my bed and closed my eyes. When I opened them again, the soft light of morning was pouring through the cracks of the wooden shutters. Bending over me, Ama Bernarda was shaking my shoulders. "Princess, you must wake up. Don Andrés has asked to see you at once."

"My father?" Still half asleep, I rubbed my eyes. "But how does he know I'm here?"

"Your father is the king, Princess. He knows everything. And if I may say so, His Majesty is bound to be curious about Don Juan."

Don Juan! John! Panic flooded my mind. The previous night I had been so worried about bringing John to the castle,

I had forgotten all about my father. I knew Father would not be pleased about John's unexpected arrival. And even though John's coming to my world had been an accident, would Father believe me, or would he be so upset with me that he wouldn't let me go back to California?

I jumped out of bed, and after throwing some water over my face from the jug sitting on the table, I walked back to Ama Bernarda to get dressed. Ama was shocked by my outfit—I was still wearing the jeans and sweater of the New World—and let me know so in a torrent of words.

"You are totally right, Ama," I told her. And while she frowned, probably wondering whether I meant it or was just humoring her, I said, "Ama Bernarda, do you know whether Father was in a good mood when he asked to see me?"

Ama shook her head. "I wouldn't think so, Princess. Since your sister's engagement was announced, Don Andrés has been in quite a mood."

"Why is he so angry, Ama? I mean, if Father didn't want Rosa to marry Don Julián, why did he invite him to the ball in the first place?"

"Because he had to, Princess. By law, all the heirs of the Houses of Old must be invited. Of course nobody had ever considered the possibility that Princess Rosa would accept Don Julián. Princess Rosa knew Don Julián and your father are enemies. Maybe that's why she did it. Your sister Rosa has a strange sense of humor."

Sense of humor? What a curious way of explaining Rosa's choice. Of course, I knew better. I knew Father's hate for Don Julián had nothing to do with my sister's decision. Hadn't I seen Rosa falling under Don Julián's spell while he wooed her on the balcony, her total abandon as he kissed her? And the memory brought to my mind the image of Juliet. Juliet—who by falling in love and marrying Romeo, the son of her father's enemy, had ended up dead. I shivered. Rosa was my least favorite sister, but I didn't want her dead.

For a little longer, Ama Bernarda fussed over me, talking incessantly about Rosa's engagement, until finally I was ready. Transformed once more into a princess by the magic of a dress, I rushed toward my father's quarters.

Not one but two soldiers kept guard at the doors. Crossing their spears, they saluted me. Then they moved aside, and while one of them held the door open, the other announced my name. *So much for a cozy family reunion*, I thought, my spirits sinking even lower.

From their thrones over the dais at the end of the room, my parents were staring at me. Their cold glares confirmed my fears: They knew about John, and he was not welcome. I stepped forward, my heart beating in my chest like a galloping horse, and knelt before them.

"Welcome back, Princess Andrea," Mother said. With a wave of her hand, she motioned me to sit. "Your arrival, Princess," she continued after I had done so, "has been a pleasant surprise to us. On the last full moon, we sent our word with Don Ramiro, allowing you to stay in his world for as long as you desired. We assume, then, that you have returned to stay. And we rejoice."

"Thank you, Mother. I—"

"But you have brought with you an outsider. And that we cannot accept lightly. I do hope, Princess, that you had a good reason for doing so."

"Mother, Father. I am most grateful for your permission to stay in Tio's world. Permission, I hope, that still holds. Because the truth is, I didn't want to leave California. I mean, I did miss you very much and wanted to see you, but my return has been a mistake. Yesterday John and I entered the cave below the arch to escape from a storm. As we waited for the rain to stop, the door opened and we found ourselves in the Cove of the Dead."

Father rose from his throne. Looming over me in all his imposing majesty, he bellowed, "Do you mean to say that your friend has not been properly instructed by Don Ramiro?"

"Yes, Father. I mean, no, Father . . . Tío Ramiro doesn't know."

"Princess Andrea," Father's voice, harsh like thunder, echoed against the walls, "you give me no choice. The outsider must die."

"No!" I jumped forward. "John doesn't know about the door, Father. He believes he is still in his world. I will not tell him the truth, and in the next full moon, I will take him back."

"That would not be safe," Father said. "He would talk about us. And eventually someone would find the way here."

"But you cannot kill him. He has done nothing wrong."

The white scar on Father's cheek was throbbing as his eyes flashed in anger. But before he could answer, Mother spoke. "Your Majesty," she said. "I agree that Andrea's friend cannot go back. If he does, he will indeed pose a danger to our world. But I think we could give him a chance, a chance to stay voluntarily."

Father shook his head. "No," he said. "He already knows too much."

This could not be happening! Father had always been unreasonable and old-fashioned, but this . . . this was barbaric. Barbaric! That was the word Tío Ramiro had used to describe how my grandfather had thrown him and Mother into the dungeon upon their arrival. Tío and Mother had escaped from certain death only because Father had helped them. So Father had not been so narrow-minded then. Hadn't he gone back to California, years later, looking for Mother?

"But Father, you upset the order of the worlds when you brought Mother here. And everything still turned out all right."

"Enough, Princess Andrea," Mother said. "Bringing up the past will not change the present. Besides, when I came, I did it with full knowledge of the decision and of my own will. And I never returned."

"Not the first time. The first time, when you came with Tío, you came by chance, too. And you returned to your world." I turned to Father. "And you helped them escape. You disobeyed your father's orders and let them go."

"That was different. They were only children."

Although his voice was still angry, something had changed. He was listening now.

"It was not different. They could have talked about our world. But they didn't. So you see, Father, you were right to let them go. You were right then, as I am now when I ask you to let John go."

Father didn't answer. His eyes staring blankly at me, he seemed to be lost in his memories. Finally he shook his head. "I suppose you are right, Princess Andrea. I did let them go." Turning to Mother, he smiled. "And I have never regretted it." Then his eyes grew cold again. "As for the outsider, Princess, we will welcome him as our guest for the time being. The rest is up to him. You will explain to him the truth about our world. If by the next full moon he agrees to stay and become one of us, he will live. If not, he will die."

I gasped.

Father raised his hand in dismissal. "Go now and bring the outsider to us."

Afraid my voice would break if I tried to speak, I nodded. After curtsying to him and then to Mother, I left the room.

TWELVE

Courtship

"They won't let me out," John snapped before I could say hello. "What do they think they're doing?" He was referring to the two soldiers standing outside his door. "And that's not even the worst of it. I mean, if they want to be in a play and dress like idiots, good for them. But look at me," he added, his arms outstretched in mocking display, "Someone took my clothes and left me this . . . this ridiculous outfit! Who do they think I am? Romeo?"

Romeo, indeed. Dressed in a white open shirt and tight blue pants that disappeared at the knees into brown leather boots, John did not look ridiculous at all. He looked stunning. So much so that my words stumbled on my tongue, and I couldn't answer. John looked up and, as if seeing me for the first time, started laughing.

"And what about you?" he said. "What are you supposed to be? A princess?"

I had had enough. "Yes. I am a princess. And this is my castle. And my father, the king, has ordered me to take you to meet him."

"What?"

"It is true, John. Well, at least the part about Father wanting to see you. So why don't you come? You can complain to him all you want."

John stared at me for a moment, his eyes flashing. Then, as suddenly as a summer storm, the anger left his face and he smiled. "Now you're talking," he said, rushing to the door.

Holding the door open, he turned to me. "After you, my lady," he said, bending to me in a poor imitation of a bow.

I walked outside and, escorted by the soldiers, started down the corridor. John sauntered by my side, talking nonstop about the amazing realism of the guards' weapons and costumes that "put to shame the ones Dan had created for the play." He marveled at the authentic look of the stone walls and tapestries. Not even the acrid smell of the fat-burning torches failed to cool his upbeat mood.

I listened to him, nodding here and there at his enthusiastic comments, relieved that no answer was expected of me. In my mind, I was terrified. Nothing good could come of my parents meeting John. And what John's reaction might be to Father's demands, I didn't dare to imagine.

Too soon we reached Father's quarters. The sentries at the door came to attention and crossed their spears with an ominous clank of metal. Then they stepped aside and opened the door for us. Without hesitation John rushed inside, while I ran after him as fast as my long skirts allowed. Wishing against hope that he would keep quiet, I curtsied to my parents.

When I looked up, Father had left the throne where he had been sitting and was now standing in front of John. Taking John's hand into his, he shook it firmly, as if he had done this all his life.

I blinked and looked again. Mother was now smiling at John, leading him to one of the windows.

In broken English, Father asked John about his studies and his plans after college, while I looked on in disbelief. Was this the same person who had threatened to kill John a minute ago? Baffled by the sudden change, I kept silent, and while they discussed John's hypothetical future in California, I searched my mind for a way to convince John to stay so that he could have a future at all.

My thoughts kept returning to the same basic question: Why should John ever agree to live in our backward world without computers, electricity, or even running water? I couldn't imagine how anybody in his right mind would. Anybody except Mother, of course. But Mother had stayed because—as unbelievable as it seemed to me—she was in love with Father. And John, to my deepest regret, didn't love me. But what if . . . what if he were to fall in love with me? Wouldn't he want to stay then?

I had to give it a try. After all, I thought, if Don Julián had talked my sister Rosa into marrying him, why couldn't I persuade John to marry me? John was likely to be impressed by my being a real princess, as he had never seen one before. Besides, he already liked me in a friendly kind of way. All I needed was a romantic setting to spark the flame, and he would be at my feet in no time. And so when we took leave of my parents, my mind was made up: thanks to Father's narrow-mindness, my forbidden wish to date John had now become the only way to save his life.

John, I was happy to see, was in the best of moods. "Andrea," he told me after the guards had closed the doors behind us, "your father is a remarkable person. I totally admire his creativity. It was kind of disappointing when he refused to explain how he made that cool sky projection last night. Oh! And by the way, Andrea, *you* didn't help me much either."

"I'm sorry. But I . . ."

John did not wait for me to find a suitable excuse. "It's all right," he said. "I'm sure he'll tell me some other time. Right now, he's invited me to stay for as long as I want and enjoy his kingdom, as he calls it. I've accepted. We're in winter break after all. And besides, this recreation of a medieval castle is so authentic, I wouldn't mind having a closer look. So if you're not busy, why don't you show me around?"

I nodded.

"Great. So why don't we start by getting some breakfast? I'm starving."

John found the kitchen fascinating. His eyes widened as he looked at the rabbits, partridges, quails, and waterfowl hanging from the ceiling, and he asked all kinds of questions. Without pausing to hear my answers, he walked up and down the tables, watching as the kitchen apprentices kneaded the bread, cut the vegetables, and mixed the meat with spices, talking to them in his outspoken and friendly way. Luckily nobody could understand a word he was saying, and my translation of his enthusiastic comments was dutifully censored. I was certain the servants, uneasy already by being addressed directly by someone they took for a lord, would not appreciate being called quaint and old-fashioned.

Finally I managed to steer him to the hearth where the porridge was cooking. Rejecting any help, he so eagerly applied himself to pouring it into bowls that he badly burned his fingers. He insisted that such a delicacy was worth the pain.

We were crossing the courtyard on our way to the stables when John stopped. Further down by the ramparts, some squires were training. His eyes bright with excitement, John stared. "Can I join them?" he asked, already moving toward them.

I bounced after him and jerked at his arm. "No, John. You can't." My voice, higher than I had intended, betrayed my fear.

John turned to me. "Why not? Isn't this a great opportunity to expand on what you've already taught me?"

"Yes, yes, of course. But I . . . you . . . you need to make an appointment."

John shook his head. "What a drag! They're obviously having a ball. And look at their weapons. They look totally accurate. Right from a history book. Not like those fake ones they used in the play."

If I were not careful, I thought as I dragged a reluctant John away from the ramparts, Father would not have to worry about killing him. He would get himself killed on his own. And again the urgency of my rescue mission weighed on me like a ton of rocks. But as soon as we reached the stables and I saw Flecha's head over the half door of her stall, I forgot all my worries.

Flecha was happy to see me—*more so than my parents had been*, I thought with a pang of anger—and in her enthusiasm, she rubbed her muzzle against my chest, hitting me so hard I fell to the ground. With a bruised ego and dust and hay all over my gown, I struggled to my feet while John laughed.

When I asked him if he could ride, John told me he had ridden before in a place he called "summer camp." But knowing his exaggerated optimism about his abilities, I asked the stable boy to find us the tamest horse in the stables.

The boy dutifully complied and came back with a brown pony I was sure even Rosa could have mounted. John didn't want to ride it at first, saying it was way too small for him. He was right, of course, as he was several inches taller than the average man in my world. But I refused to let him ride any other horse, and eventually he agreed. We rode out of the castle. Steering clear of the village to avoid further complications, we headed east along the river until we reached the outskirts of Mount Pindo.

As always, watching the solitary mountain looming majestically over me, I was overcome by awe. It was no wonder that the Xarens, the old inhabitants of my world, had made it the dwelling of their gods. With its summit lost in the clouds and its slope deep into the waters, the mountain seemed to hold heaven and earth together and apart in an impossible balance of wills.

After we had tethered the horses by a small grove and climbed up the steep slope to my favorite place, I sat by John's side—our backs against the jagged rocks, our legs hanging over the ledge—and waited for the magic of the mountain to work. Down below, we could see the river stretch itself lazily between the shores as if in no hurry to end its journey, while straight ahead, through the wisps of mist swaying over the waters, the other bank played hide-and-seek.

I had brought John there with the idea of telling him the truth about my world. But overwhelmed by the beauty of the place, I couldn't bring myself to break the silence. And so when we returned to the castle later in the afternoon, John was still living in his own distorted reality, and I—I was still terrified. My plan was not working. I was no closer to John's heart than I had been the previous day in California. What was wrong with him? Mount Pindo was as magical a place as you could find in my world. And I, well, I was a princess. What more did he want?

"Dinner," John said, startling me. "When are we going to have dinner?"

"As soon as we get back. And don't you worry. I'm sure Father has ordered a banquet in your honor."

"A banquet? You mean like one of those Renaissance fair reenactments? I can't wait."

I couldn't wait either—for the banquet to be over. The idea of John sharing a table with Father's knights and their ladies was more than I could bear. But I had no choice. Father had demanded his attendance. In my world, nobody disobeyed the king.

THE GREAT HALL WAS ALREADY FULL WHEN WE ARRIVED. JOHN rushed in without waiting for me. His long legs moving with the ease of a basketball player fending off a block, he made his way toward the center of the room. Above us, in the golden light of the evening sun, the massive iron chandeliers hanging from the wooden beams spread their arms like giant spiders in search of prey. Around the long trestle tables, ladies and gentlemen dressed in colorful garments moved about in small groups, sharing news and laughing at each other's wit.

John was impressed. "Wow, Andrea! This is so cool! I don't understand why you don't like to come here."

I forced my lips into a smile. "I'm glad you like it, John. But—" *I would rather be sitting at one of the tables in the Coffee House in Davis*, I was about to say, when I saw my sister Margarida coming toward me. Leaving my sentence unfinished, I ran to her.

"Ama Bernarda told me you had returned," my sister said, her voice full of reproach. "I've been looking for you all day."

"I'm sorry, Margarida. I really am. But I had to show Don Juan around."

"Of course you did, little sister. I understand your wish to be with him. But you could have at least stopped to say hello."

"You're right. I should have." Although her tone was stern, her eyes were twinkling, and I knew she wasn't really angry. "Come, I'll introduce you to him now."

Weaving my arm into my sister's, I turned toward the place where I had left John, and the easy smile Margarida had awakened in me faded. John was gone. For a long terrifying moment, I searched for him among the different groups. Being taller than most of the people in my world, he would have been easy to spot had he been in the room. He wasn't.

I thought of John wandering alone through the castle and shivered. As fast as I could, I pushed my way toward the entrance. I had almost reached the door when I saw him. Standing by the doorway, he was helping a lady into the hall. And as the lady leaning slightly on his arm glided inside, my heart jumped to my throat and then sank so low it missed a beat: The lady was Rosa.

As usual, my sister was wearing one of those elaborate and cumbersome outfits that rendered her helpless. They were absolutely ridiculous outfits if you asked me, but men, I had often noticed, found them irresistible. Apparently John was no exception. "Brain dead," I said to myself, quoting my cousin Kelsey's favorite remark after many of her fights with Richard. It didn't help.

"He is handsome, your prince," Margarida was saying. "And he has good manners."

Just then, a yelp of trumpets from the gallery announced the king's arrival. At once the Great Hall grew quiet, and the courtiers, as if touched by magic, froze in the place where the sound had found them, their faces turned to the door.

Holding my breath until my lungs hurt, I watched as Father, in an incredible breach of protocol, left Mother's side and advanced toward John. After saying some words to him I couldn't hear, he walked back to Mother and proceeded to the center of the high table. John, still holding Rosa's arm, followed him and took the seat to the king's right.

To sit beside Father was an honor I was sure John didn't appreciate—an honor I had never shared, and neither had Rosa before then. It took me a moment to understand that she did now, not because she was with John, but because she was engaged to a king.

"Andrea, why don't you sit by Don Juan?" Margarida asked me as we took our places at the end of the table. "Aren't you two . . ."

"Not exactly. Don Juan is only a friend."

"But . . . I thought you brought Don Juan to introduce him to Father." She paused for a moment and looked deep into my eyes. Then she smiled. "You wish he were more than friends, don't you?"

I did not answer. I knew my burning face had already given me away.

John, after a brief talk with Father, turned again toward Rosa. My sister smiled and batted her eyelashes at him. I started to get up. Gently but firmly, Margarida held me down. "Please don't let Rosa's behavior bother you. You know her. She flirts as easily and thoughtlessly as she breathes. It doesn't mean anything. Besides, to my regret, she's engaged to be married."

"Your regret? Why should you care that Rosa is engaged?"

"It's . . . complicated. Listen, Andrea. There's something I have to tell you. I'm tired of keeping it to myself." My eyes on John, I was only half listening. "You see, I have also met my prince. I met him at the Spring Ball, the very night you went away. I was standing by the window alone, remembering how as children we used to spy on the ball from the oak tree, when I heard someone talking. I turned, and there he was: the most handsome man I have ever seen. He smiled at me and asked for a dance. We danced all night—"

"And when dawn was breaking, he disappeared in the east," I finished for her, trying to keep calm while Rosa giggled with John.

"Andrea! It isn't funny."

"I'm sorry. I was . . . Please tell me what happened."

"Over the following days, while the eligible Lords competed for Rosa's hand, we met in secret. And when he asked for my hand, I gave him my word that I would marry him. But then, before he could ask Father's consent, Don Julián won the contest, and Rosa surprised us all by accepting him. And well, now we can't get married."

"Why not?"

Margarida moved closer. "Because he is Don Alfonso de Alvar, Andrea. He is Don Julián's brother . . ."

I gasped. Don Alfonso, my boring companion in the tree, my sister's lover?

". . . and Father is so furious that Rosa is marrying Don Julián, he will never agree to my marrying his brother."

At the center of the table, his face almost touching hers, John was helping Rosa to some food. Her coy smile made me sick. John would never fall in love with me if Rosa chose to play with him. And knowing my sister, her interest in John would last for about a week, then she would turn her attention to somebody else. John, angry with her, would want to leave the castle. And Father would kill him for sure.

"And yet, I cannot give him up," Margarida was saying. "I've tried, but I can't."

My eyes on John, I nodded. "I know, sister. I know exactly what you mean." And to my despair, I did.

THIRTEEN

The Engagement

Over the following days, I introduced John to my world. Every morning we would leave at sunrise and ride for hours over the plains surrounding the castle. In the afternoon, Don Gonzalo, my former instructor, would teach John how to fight with a sword and shoot arrows at targets drawn on bales of hay, while I watched from one of the balconies on the first floor. I'd have loved to be down in the bailey with them, but I didn't dare challenge my mother's orders to behave like a lady. I needed her on my side when the time came to confront Father again and plead for John's life.

In the meantime, John was enjoying himself. That was evident, and it filled my heart with hope. As the days passed, he had stopped asking questions about the obvious differences between our worlds. Out of fear of spoiling his good mood, I had postponed the explanation.

Yet any progress I could have made during the day to gain John's attention, I lost as soon as Rosa came into the Great Hall every mealtime. Although the signs were there, I stubbornly refused to acknowledge any attraction between them and never mentioned Rosa to John, nor told him of her engagement.

And then one morning, as I waited for John outside the stables, I saw framed against the first rays of the rising sun the unexpected silhouette of a maiden. My surprise soon turned to concern when I realized that the lady was Rosa.

Even if I hadn't known that my sister hates riding, her silk embroidered gown, her white slippers, and her sophisticated hairdo would have given her away: she was not really there for a ride. In a flash of anger, I remembered her flirtatious behavior at the table and the effect her batting eyelashes and pretend blushes had on John. Until then, I had tolerated her silly advances, thinking of them as coming naturally from a hopeless flirt. But deliberately seeking him out was beyond my sisterly understanding.

Ignoring my killer stares, Rosa smiled. "Good morning, Andrea," she said lightly.

"Good morning? Not for me, dear sister. Not until you go back inside."

"Really? And why should I do that?"

"Because the sun is already rising, and if you don't leave immediately, it may harm your fair skin. And we wouldn't like that to happen, would we?"

"You are totally right, sister. How nice of you to warn me."

But Rosa did not leave. Instead she turned back to her dueña, who had stopped two steps behind her, and ordered her to go fetch a parasol.

As soon as her dueña disappeared into the keep, I grabbed Rosa by the arms and pulled her to me. "Come on, Rosa, we both know why you are here, and enough is enough. You are going back to the castle this very moment, and if you don't stop playing your stupid games with Don Juan, I—"

"Playing with Don Juan? Why would I do that? Why waste my time on such an impossible endeavor? Isn't it only too plain that the poor boy is madly in love with you?"

Just as Rosa spoke, the sun, a burning ball of fire, rose from behind the castle walls, blinding me and blurring in my mind the thin line between right and wrong. Before I realized what I was doing, I heard myself screaming, "Maybe you're right, Rosa. Maybe Don Juan is not in love with me. But at least he doesn't lie about it! He doesn't whisper sweet nothings somebody else has taught him, pretending he just made them up for me. At least the day he might tell me he loves me, I would know he loves me and not my crown. But of course, that is why you cling to Don Juan, isn't it? To feel alive once more before you become the property of a king, a king who only sees in you an easy way to conquer his enemy's kingdom!"

Rosa stumbled back. "You! You! How dare you?" Hiding her eyes behind a lacy handkerchief she had conveniently produced from her sleeve, she started sobbing.

I was about to congratulate her on her acting skills when a shadow fell upon us.

"Andrea!" John's voice, harsh with anger, lashed at me. "What have you done to the princess?"

I gasped. The princess? What a nerve! As if she were the only princess in the universe. As if I were not a princess as well!

"I haven't done anything at all to your princess!"

But John was not listening. Already by Rosa's side, he was talking to her in eager whispers. At his words, Rosa stopped crying and, eyes coyly averted, smiled at him. As if bewitched, John offered her his arm and, without a glance in my direction, led her away.

Through the closed windows of the castle, I could hear the muffled voices of the servants greeting each other and the new day. In the courtyard, the sun's rays had already dispersed the shadows and warmed the stones. But my heart was cold. How could I have ever imagined John would fall in love with me? How could I have forgotten that as a princess, I was a total failure? Now it was too late. John had become another of Rosa's puppets, at least until he understood that Rosa was already engaged. Then he would refuse to stay, and Father would have him killed.

FROM THAT DAY ON, JOHN DID NOT HANG OUT WITH ME ANY-MORE. Tired of seeing him with Rosa, I would leave the castle at dawn and ride on Flecha to Mount Pindo. High above the river, by the rocky outcrop where I had failed to inform John that he could never return to his world, I would sit for hours, waiting for the sun to complete its journey.

It was there where, many days later, John found me. With a cheerful "Hello, Andrea!" repeated several times as it bounced against the boulders, he shook me out of my brooding.

"Hi, John," I said, my voice laughing because at the sound of his, I believed myself back in Davis: he and I alone by the pond and the bicycles zooming behind us, along the straight paths of the campus.

But as soon as I turned, the spell was broken. Instead of sneakers, John was wearing leather boots folded over his calves, his pants tight against his legs before they disappeared under a short embroidered tunic. Blue and white. The colors of Father's kingdom.

John bent forward, "So, what have you been up to? I haven't seen much of you lately." Awkwardly folding his long legs, he sat by my side.

"Really? I haven't noticed."

"Well, anyway. Now that I've found you, I would like to ask you a couple of questions—about Rosa."

At the mention of my sister's name, my anger returned, and with it an uncontrollable desire to hurt him. "Come on, John. Forget about Rosa. There are more important things to talk about. Like, where are we? Look, John. Look at the moon, the golden moon rising as always one hour before sunset. Look at the trees, almost but not quite the same as the ones you grew up with, and at the sky where no plane ever crosses. I'm sorry John, but the game is over. We're not in California."

"I know."

"You know?"

"Yes, I know. I've known for a while. I'm not that thick. I can't explain where I am, and at this point I don't care, but I do know this is not California. Or Earth for that matter."

He knew. He knew and did not care. Did he also know about Father's decision to kill him if he tried to go back to California?

Over the ragged cry of a crow, I heard John's voice. "Andrea, your sister is striking."

"Strikingly stupid."

"What did you say?"

"I said that Rosa is engaged, so forget whatever it is you're thinking."

"But she loves me."

"What?"

"I understand it may be difficult for you to believe, but Rosa loves me."

"Excuse me, John, but how are you so sure? As far as I know, my sister doesn't speak English, and you don't speak Spanish."

"Your sister is teaching me. *Te quiero, mi amor.*"

I looked away, my face burning. "What did you say?"

"It means 'I love you, my love.'"

"Thanks for the translation."

"I'm serious, Andrea. Your sister is the most incredible girl I've ever met."

"She's incredible all right."

"I mean it, Andrea. I've already decided to stay another week. Then I'll ask her to return with me to California."

"You've decided to stay another week?" *As if you had a choice*, I finished in my mind.

"I know, I know. I know what you're thinking: Winter break is over. But big deal if I blow a couple of classes. I'll make up for them later."

I shrugged. "Have you talked with my father lately?"

John's face brightened. "What a great suggestion! I'll talk with him immediately. You're totally right. My Spanish is not good enough to ask her out. So I'll do it the old-fashioned way. I'll ask your father's permission."

"You can't do that, John. Aren't you listening? Rosa is engaged."

But John was already on his feet. "Thanks so much. It was great catching up with you." And rushing back to the path, he disappeared down the steep slope of the mountain.

THAT NIGHT, AS AMA BERNARDA WAS GETTING ME READY FOR BED, Mother came into my room. In answer to an unspoken signal, Ama stopped yanking at my tangled hair and, bent into a deep curtsy, moved back.

Eyes carefully averted, I curtsied, too. My legs, I noticed then, were shaking. Mother was not supposed to come to me, but to summon me to her presence. In fact, for as long as I could remember, only once before had she come into my chamber. And even that once I was not sure it had not been a dream. My only memory was of her face looking down at me as I lay in bed delirious during my one serious illness as a child. What was so important that she had decided to come tonight? Had something happened to John?

My head shot up. "Mother, has Father passed sentence on John?" Mother did not answer. Whether because the ominous thump of the door closing had covered my words or because she chose not to, I did not know. Instead, she stared at me with her pale blue eyes, so cold and distant that I shivered. Still in silence, she glided toward the bed and, arranging her skirts gracefully over the cover, took a seat.

"Princess Andrea," she said as she motioned me to sit by her side, "your sister, Princess Rosa, has informed us of your conversation regarding Don Julián. Don Andrés and I have been discussing the matter thoroughly. Don Andrés insists that Don Julián lied to your sister and to us, with the only intention of becoming heir to our kingdom. I am not convinced. That is why I am here. I want you to tell me the truth about Don Julián's real intention when he proposed to your sister."

"His intentions? How am I to know of Don Julián's intentions, Mother? I have never spoken to him."

"Do not play games with me, Princess," she said, her deep blue eyes probing mine. "I need to know."

Although I tried, I could not evade her questions, and soon I was telling her how the night of my failed first ball, I had climbed to my hideout in the oak tree. Ashamed at what now seemed to me childish behavior, I recounted to her my conversation with Don Alfonso and his claim that he had made a deal with his brother to teach him how to talk to a lady to gain access to the ballroom. I was careful to emphasize my opinion that Don Alfonso was just making everything up in order to impress me. But Mother didn't believe that part.

"Then it is true. Don Julián had a secret agenda all along."

"No, Mother. Don Julián just needed some help because he is shy."

"Princess Andrea, you are too young and inexperienced to understand. I will be the one to draw the conclusions."

Mother got up, and I, bound to obedience by years of training, followed suit, saying nothing.

Already at the door, Mother stopped and, facing me again, smiled. "Actually, Princess, you may have just saved your friend's life. Don Juan has asked Don Andrés's permission to court Princess Rosa. Don Andrés has agreed to his proposition, annulling Rosa's previous engagement to Don Julián. His reasons you have just validated. Now, I suppose, Don Juan will decide to stay. So in the end, Princess, everything has turned out to be for the best."

"Not everything," I said. But Mother had already left.

Feeling empty and cold, as if winter had suddenly settled in my heart, I threw myself onto my bed. Why had I lied to Rosa? From what dark place inside my hate had those crazy words come? Now, thanks to my stupid blunder, I had lost John forever. Sobbing desperately, I buried my head in the pillows.

For days I remained in my bed feeling sorry for myself and, rejecting Ama's insistent calls to reason, refused to see any-one—until one morning, Tío Ramiro came into my room unannounced. "Come on, Andrea," he said. "Stop this nonsen-sical brooding at once and get dressed. You must help me stop the war."

"Stop the war? I didn't know we were at war."

"You don't know your kingdom is at war? On what planet do you live, Andrea?"

"Xaren-Ra. Of course I know that, Tío. How stupid do you think I am?"

Tío was not listening. "Haven't you heard that Don Julián has declared war against your father? And the truth is, the way things work in your world, I don't blame him. Breaking an engagement is a big insult. To clear his honor by destroying your kingdom seems, indeed, the only honorable solution."

Tío Ramiro's logical mind was missing the point this time. What did he know of broken hearts? Don Julián, in pain for having lost his lover, was trying to win her back. I would have done the same myself if only I had an army behind me. But a princess does not have the same resources as a king.

"Listen, Andrea, I thought you understood when I took you to see the missions the danger your world would face if discovered by mine. Obviously, I was mistaken. But at the time, I believed you when you said your coming to California had been an accident. That is why I helped you to stay there. But to bring John into yours, that I cannot excuse."

"But Tío, coming back was also an accident. We entered the cave to get away from the storm. How was I to know that under the clouded sky the full moon was rising?"

"Don't try to fool me, Andrea. It will not work. Have you forgotten I was the one to give you the watch? And anyway, that's irrelevant now. The point is you both left. And do you have any idea how difficult it was to convince your cousin that you had just gone to visit your parents? Yes, I am sure you appreciate my help very much, but why don't you prove it by helping me out of this terrible mess you have started?

"Of course, this time you are not the only one to blame," Tío continued, without waiting for my answer. "Look at your father. I knew he was an old-fashioned fool, wasting his time waiting for a male heir instead of attending to the education of the daughters he already had. But now, for sure, he has lost his mind. What did he think he was doing, breaking the engagement between Rosa and Don Julián and accepting John into this world? As far as I know, with Sabela—the smartest one in the family—confined to her rooms and out of the line of succession, and Rosa being such an airhead, the kingdom will someday be in the hands of John. And John doesn't belong here. He was not raised in this world and will not survive in it. He must go back. Do you understand?"

"Yes, Tío. I—"

"Good. Then what are you waiting for? Get up this minute and go talk to John. You have to convince him he must forget this nonsense about marrying Rosa and return to California."

"But, Tío, Father will not let him go. He doesn't want anyone in your world to know about ours."

"I see. Well, leave that to me. I will deal with Don Andrés presently."

"And while you talk with him, would you please ask him if I may go back, too?"

Tío rolled his eyes. "What a great idea." And shooting an angry stare at me that contradicted his words, he walked away.

My mind in turmoil, I paced the room. Tío Ramiro had certainly been most unsympathetic to my predicament. But still he was the only person who could help me go back to California. Hurt feelings or not, I had no choice but to follow his orders.

And so, for the first time in what seemed to me ages, I left my room. It was not until I found myself in the corridor that I realized I hadn't the foggiest idea of what to say to John to convince him to return to his world. I did have the suspicion, though, that asking him nicely wouldn't accomplish anything. But lacking a better plan, I yanked my skirts up and started toward the stairs in search of John.

FOURTEEN

War

What I found instead was trouble. Dressed in a pink gown with a tight bodice that disappeared below her waist in a cascade of frills, Rosa was standing at the end of the corridor. I moved back in haste, trying to blend in the shadows. But it was too late. A smile dancing on her perfectly made-up face, Rosa came toward me. War or no war, she had kept her priorities straight, and as usual, she was stunning.

"I am so glad to see you, dear sister," she said, almost singing, "looking so well and healthy. Please, tell me you are not mad at me. I couldn't bear the idea of anybody being upset when I am so very happy."

She said this as if nothing had happened since the last time we had seen each other. As if she had not stolen my boyfriend in the meantime. Well, my boyfriend-to-be more exactly. And what a nerve she had to ask me whether I was upset. I was not upset. I was way past upset. I was furious. I wanted to grab her naked shoulders and shake her until she asked my forgiveness. But that would only prove I still cared about John, and I was not going to give her that pleasure. My sister, who knew as much about decency as a hungry wolf knew about

149

mercy, would be thrilled to use that knowledge to hurt me
further.

I smiled. "Of course I'm not mad at you, dear. Not at all.
Don't you know I only live to make you happy?"

Rosa eyed me suspiciously. "Really?"

"But you see, Rosa, if there is a war, Don Juan could die.
And that would be most unpleasant for you. So why don't you
try to do something to help him?"

"Oh, but I am! I'm embroidering a beautiful scarf for Don
Juan to wear in battle as a token of my love."

"Your Don Juan is going to need more than a scarf to stay
alive."

"Why do you always have to be so nasty?"

"Come on, Rosa, wake up! This has nothing to do with me.
Don Juan will be in mortal danger if he goes into battle. And
you may be the only one who can stop this war."

"Stop the war? Why should I do that? You know what I
think, Andrea? I think you are jealous because they are fighting
over me. That is why you say such horrible things. Nothing will
happen to Don Juan. He is the greatest warrior of all."

"Not the last time I checked."

"How would you know, anyway? All these days you have
been hidden in your room like a scared rabbit, Don Juan has
been training and—"

"Where?"

Rosa stared blankly at me.

"Where does Don Juan train?"

"Outside in the fields by the river. Why?"

"Never mind, dear. Just get back to your scarf."

I left her there, a startled look in her pale blue eyes, and
dove down the stairs two steps at a time. I couldn't get away

from her fast enough. She certainly had an empty shell for a head, this sister of mine. *What in the world does John see in her?* I wondered. Apart from the obvious, of course. But was he really so stupid that he couldn't see beyond her looks?

Picking up the skirts of my gown over my knees, I ran faster and faster, down the spiral stairway to the bottom of the tower, and jerking the door open, I stepped outside. Then, a strangled cry on my throat, I stumbled back.

Neither Tio's angry words nor Rosa's smug self-complacency had prepared me for this. Like mushrooms after the rain, a multitude of workshops had sprouted during the days I had kept to my room and now covered the totality of the bailey. Apart from the usual shops of the shoemakers and dressmakers, carpenters and candlers, there were others in which the atilliators were making crossbows, and the mail artisans were skillfully inserting rings into rows—shops that clearly spoke of war.

From the blacksmith shop at the end of the stables came the deafening clank of iron on iron. I didn't need to go there to know that not only horseshoes, but arrowheads, swords, and mail rings were the product of the ceaseless hammering.

And as I stared into the courtyard, blinking in the bright light of midmorning, the reality of the upcoming war sank in. I shivered. Tio was right: John had to go back to California before he got himself killed. Again I dashed forward, fighting my way through men and tents, reaching the inner courtyard. The town gate, the closest exit to the river, was at the other end.

But getting there was not so simple. A continuous stream of carts with grain and vegetables, fruits and poultry was pouring into the castle, blocking my advance. My back to the wall to avoid being crushed under their wheels, I climbed into the first empty wagon I saw heading toward the village and waited, hidden under the canvas, until we had crossed the drawbridge. Then, bending my knees, I jumped far and high onto the tall grass that flanked the road.

Nursing a bruised elbow, I ran down toward the river, guided by the clink of metal on metal and the sharp cries of the warriors. But when the training fields finally came into view, my doubts returned. Swords and shields flashing in the sun, men were fighting for as far as I could see. How was I supposed to locate John among them?

I was about to give up and wait for John to return to the castle, when a solitary couple farther down by the bank caught my attention. One of the men was Don Gonzalo, my former instructor—I recognized him by the crossed spears of his coat of arms embroidered on the front of his tunic. His opponent was tall and slim, and although he was simply dressed in the blue-and-white colors of my kingdom, a deep void in my stomach told me it was John.

Edging my way among the fighters, I moved closer. John had improved since the last time I had seen him. But still, I realized with a pang of fear, he was no match for Don Gonzalo. As the fight was going, I was sure it wouldn't last much longer. John was hardly stopping the blows. And yet the fight went on. Don Gonzalo was making impossible mistakes and eventually lost his sword. John raised his arm, and in a flash of metal, his blade rested on his opponent's chest.

I stepped forward as they bowed to each other and called his name. John looked up and smiled at me, the same disarming smile with which he had welcomed me into his world. "*Buenos días, Princesa,*" he said. And a sharp pain inside my chest left me no doubt—his magic was still working on me.

"I love these fights," John said after Don Gonzalo had left. "They're so totally unreal."

Unreal? Does he still believe our world is a pyrotechnical gimmick? I wondered while John, oblivious to my worries, returned his sword to its scabbard. The precision and dexterity of his movements told me better than any words could, he was not going to be easy to convince.

"John, there's something we have to discuss."

Again John stared at me, and as I stared back into his eyes, bright with victory and brown like honey, I forgot my speech.

John shrugged. "I'm listening."

"Right. What I want to say is that this world is not a quaint recreation of your imagination. It is real, as real as California. And you don't belong in it. Your coming here was a mistake. My mistake. And that is why it is up to me to take you back."

John laughed. "Of course. I'll go back, Andrea, don't you worry. Just as soon as the war is over."

"No, John. Not after the war is over. You have to leave now, before it starts. Don't you see the war is happening because of you, because you took Rosa from Don Julián? If you leave and Rosa apologizes to Don Julián, there will be no war. But if you refuse to go, many will die. And it would be your fault. And mine."

"I can't leave now! I can't leave Princess Rosa. I'm a gentleman, and—"

"A gentleman? Come on, John, cut it out. You're not even from this world."

John's face turned red and his hand moved toward his scabbard. I jumped forward and, grabbing his arm, jerked it away from the sword.

"That's enough, Princess Andrea!" The voice, hoarse like a lion roar, came from behind. The voice of the king. Releasing John's arm, I turned.

Father had left the shadow of the willows under which he had probably been watching the fight and was coming up the riverbank, his long hair flying loose over his shoulders.

"Don Juan knows perfectly well this is real," he said when he reached my side. "After all, he is engaged to Princess Rosa, and by marrying her, he will become the future king.

"Besides," he continued while John nodded with the stiff movement of a puppet, "our kingdom needs Don Juan. His unusual approach will give us an advantage I am not willing to lose. The dice of fortune are already rolling, and in two more days, our army will march to its victory. So now, Princess, you must leave. We have important matters to discuss, Don Juan and I. We have no time for your hysteria."

I bolted back and looked at John for help. But John, a self-conscious smile under the dark stubble that now shaded his face, was already addressing Father. Soon they were engaged in a heated discussion over some strategic details I couldn't follow. By the ease of their interchange, it was obvious they had had this conversation before.

I backed away from them, lost in misery. I had failed. Father would never listen. As for John, where did he think he was? Discussing a basketball game with his friends? That was about right. By the way he talked, he could be back in Davis on a Sunday evening sitting around a table at Al's. How could he be such a fool? Didn't he know that this time the game he was so lightly discussing was not a game at all, but war? How could I make him understand?

"Hold it!" A voice blasted in my ear, while something hard like iron yanked at my arm and dragged me back. The next thing I knew, I was on the ground, looking onto the red-bearded face of Don Gonzalo.

Behind me, I could hear the clashing of swords and the rapid breathing of people fighting. I didn't have to look to understand. I had just missed being cut into pieces by two of the soldiers fencing. How could I have been so mindless as to walk in their path? I was definitely losing my soldier's touch. Rejecting Don Gonzalo's hand, I climbed to my feet.

"My apologies, my lady," Don Gonzalo said, bowing to me.

I curtsied to him. "You don't have to apologize, Sir. You have saved my life, and I am most grateful."

Don Gonzalo smiled. "My pleasure, Princess. But next time I hope you will remember my lessons and not walk into the middle of a sword fight." This time his voice was firm and stern, as it had been so long ago when I was one of his pages.

I smiled back. "I will, Sir." And after thanking him again, I turned to go.

"Princess." Once more his voice was formal, the voice of a knight addressing a lady.

I looked back.

"It would be safer, Princess, if you would allow me to escort her ladyship to the castle."

At his words, I felt my cheeks burning. How could he dare to insult me like that? I had made a mistake, that was true, but he should know better than anyone that I was a warrior, not a damsel in distress, and didn't need his help. I was going to tell him so when an idea formed in my mind. Don Gonzalo was close to Father and John. Maybe through him I could get a better understanding of their plans or even find a solution to my present impasse.

I smiled. "I accept your offer, Sir, with great pleasure."

As soon as we had left the fields behind, I started my probing. "Don Gonzalo, I saw you before, fighting with Don Juan, and I was wondering, why did you let him win?"

Don Gonzalo didn't answer. Although I couldn't see his face—he was walking two steps behind me as protocol demanded—I knew he was embarrassed. After a short silence, I tried again. "What do you think of the present situation, Sir? Do you think there is still a chance that the differences between our kingdom and the Suavian kingdom could be solved in a peaceful way?"

"No, Princess." His voice was clear now, charged with excitement. "We will go to battle and get our revenge."

"Revenge?"

"As you know, Princess, Don Julián defeated us five years past. His army was smaller, and he wouldn't have stood a chance in open battle. But he avoided the confrontation and, again and again, launched surprise attacks on us. Before we could maneuver and retaliate, he was gone. It was a clever strategy, and eventually we had to surrender. Don Julián took from us the fertile lands of the upper river. Now our time has come at last to take them back. With Don Juan's remarkable approach to battle, we will be victorious. Unless . . ."

"Unless?" I repeated after waiting in vain for him to finish his sentence.

"Well, as the offended party, Don Julián may still choose to challenge Don Juan to duel before the battle. It is his right, and . . . that is why Don Juan must learn to fight with the sword."

I saw his point. Don Julián had been born a prince, a sword in his hands. John had seen his first only a month before—without counting the props I had used to teach him in California. If such a confrontation ever happened, John would lose his life and Father his advantage. Not that I believed in John's strategic abilities, but at the idea of a duel between John and Don Julián, a cold fear paralyzed me entirely. *I'm sorry, John*, I said to myself, *but you're going back to California on the next full moon. Even if I have to kidnap you.*

Unfortunately the moon would not be full for another four weeks, and by then it might be too late. I needed time. Father had made up his mind. No good asking him to delay his plan. But maybe Don Julián would be more receptive. Why shouldn't he postpone going to battle if I promised him what he wanted? And as far as I knew, what he wanted was my sister Rosa. Wasn't the fact that he had declared war on us to get her back proof enough that he still cared for her?

Knowing how volatile Rosa's affections were, I felt confident that with John gone, she would be willing to marry Don Julián. There would be no war then. Tío Ramiro would have to recognize my genius and reward my efforts by taking me back to California with him.

So once more I left my father's castle. Dressed in my old page's gear, I left through the gatehouse in broad daylight. On foot, holding Flecha by the reins, I was just another soldier among the hundreds, and nobody questioned my leaving.

I headed east across the plains, and by early afternoon reached the outskirts of Mount Pindo. Before turning north to avoid the impossible climb, I took a last look at the river. The mist that usually hung over the waters had lifted, leaving behind only shreds of cotton fog and a glimpse of the distant shore—the shore that was Suavia, the enemy kingdom.

The ominous laugh of a crow came from above. Black as night, it flew over my head and, flapping its wings to a halt, perched on the naked branch of a fallen oak. Letting out a screeching call, it stared at me with dark unblinking eyes. And for a brief moment, the time it took me to wheel Flecha around, I had the disturbing impression that through its eyes the ancient gods of the Xarens were watching.

THREE DAYS LATER, I REACHED THE CLOSEST FORD. THE RIVER WAS narrower there and supposedly shallow enough to cross—at least now, in the summer, when the water ran low. But it certainly didn't look safe to me as I watched the foam forming on the swirling rapids. I was about to turn and continue upriver to a safer crossing when my father's words flashed through my mind. "Two more days," he had said. His troops would be leaving the castle by now. If I wanted to reach Don Julián before they did, I didn't have time to find an easier place.

Gently, I pressed Flecha's flanks. Flecha snorted and shook her head. Again I dug in my heels, and this time she jumped forward and cantered into the stream.

By the middle of the river, the water was up to my knees. *Why didn't I take swimming lessons when I had the chance in California?* I wondered as I tried to keep a fretting Flecha from fleeing.

"Easy, Flecha! Easy! We are almost there," I said aloud to calm my fears.

Flecha plunged ahead until, dripping wet in water and sweat, we climbed the muddy bank of the Suavian kingdom.

Wild with relief, I bent forward and patted her neck. "We did it, Flecha, we did it."

I was still talking when, out of nowhere, the soldiers came.

FIFTEEN

The King

They appeared so suddenly that for a moment I thought the trees themselves had become alive and were aiming their branches at me. Breathing in my fear, I pulled at the reins, while Flecha snorted and frantically pranced at the air with her front legs.

My arms around her neck, I threw my weight forward, fighting to remain in the saddle. For a moment, Flecha stood still. Then she shook her head and, with a wild snort, sprang forward; her hair, wet from the crossing, slid between my fingers like silk. With a heavy splash, I fell backward into the river.

When I emerged dripping wet from the waters and crawled ashore, the soldiers were still there, and Flecha was gone.

Their arrows ready, the men moved closer. They were dressed in black with a golden sun, the emblem of Alvar, emblazoned on the front of their tunics. My quest was almost over, I realized with a shiver. These were Don Julián's men.

Setting my feet firmly on the muddy bank, I pushed my hair away from my eyes and stared at them. "I am Princess Andrea de Montemaior. I order you to take me to your king."

Without a word, two of the men advanced toward me. While one of them yanked my arms behind my back, the other reached for my face. I kicked and punched and screamed for help, but it was no use. Soon my hands were tied and my mouth and eyes covered in foul-smelling rags. Iron fingers gripped my arms and pushed me forward, up the steep slope. I could no longer see.

After a short discussion carried in hushed tones, I was ordered to walk. The firm grip of a hand on my arm gave me no choice. In total darkness, I stumbled forward. I walked thus for a long time through what seemed to be woods, as invisible briars scratched my arms and legs. Later, ages later, from somewhere above our heads, a voice called "Halt!" Someone from our group shouted a word, the password I assumed, and we trudged on.

Soon the smell of bonfires and roasting meat and the sound of harsh voices and roaring laughter surrounded me. Certain that we had reached the enemy camp and that soon I would see Don Julián, my heart swelled with hope. But not for long. After a quick exchange between my captors and a new voice, I was thrown to the ground, my ankles forced together and bound. Then coarse fingers pulled away the rags that covered my eyes and mouth. While I blinked, blinded by the sudden light, I heard heavy footsteps retreating. When my eyes finally adapted and I looked around, I was alone inside a tent. By the soft light that entered through the thick canvas, I realized it was early evening. A dark shape holding a spear stood motionless in front of the opening.

I dragged myself to the middle post and propped myself against it. My head was throbbing, and my body hurt and itched all over. For the first time ever, I wished I were in my own room back in my father's castle. My wonderful plan seemed too foolish now to even consider. And yet it would have worked, I was sure, if only I would have reached Don Julián. Why hadn't these stupid soldiers taken me to him?

As my eyes swept over my torn clothes and leather boots caked in mud, the obvious answer snapped to my mind. They had not believed me. I couldn't blame them, really. I didn't look anything like a princess. And there was nothing I could do about that now that Flecha had run away with my spare clothes, including my best gown I had planned to wear to impress the king.

At the thought of my mare lost in a foreign land, I moaned. How was she going to find her way back? Flecha needed me. I couldn't just give up. I had to get out.

I wiggled my hands, trying to unbind them. The rope bit hard into my wrists bringing tears to my eyes. If only I had a knife. But of course the soldiers had seized it when they had captured me by the river. At least I still had the pouch on my belt with my beautiful watch inside. The soldiers, probably thinking the pouch too small to hide a weapon, had not bothered to take it from me. I considered myself lucky; had they found the watch, they would have thought me a witch and killed me on the spot. Well, the watch was not going to help me now. What I needed was something sharp. Suddenly I remembered my arrow.

I could use it to cut the rope. But hard as I tried, I couldn't reach it. My back against the pole, I slid to the ground. Maybe it is better this way, I told myself. Even if I managed to leave the camp unnoticed, where would I go without a mount? Besides, I had come to talk with Don Julián, and I hadn't yet done so.

So I waited and waited, but except for a soldier carrying a bowl of stew, nobody came. Without a word he left the food on the floor and, after untying my hands, watched me as I ate. Much later, someone threw a blanket at me. Then the night fell.

I WOKE UP AT THE SOUND OF HOOVES. "AT EASE!" A DEEP authoritarian voice said and then added sharply, "Does she know?" After a short answer I couldn't hear, the newcomer continued. "We cannot take any risks. She has to stay now. Bring her to me!"

Hurried footsteps approached my tent, and a soldier came in. After cutting the rope that bound my ankles, he dragged me to my feet and ordered me out. Shivering in the cold air, I stumbled on my uncertain legs along a line of tents covered in dew until we reached a bigger one with the king's standard above. Upon saluting the guards who flanked the entrance, the soldier lifted the door flap and pushed me inside.

"Kneel!" he ordered.

My head raised in defiance, I stepped forward. "I am Princess Andrea de Montemaior. I will kneel to no one," I said to the shadows inside.

The rasping sound of a quill against paper that came from the back of the tent stopped brusquely, and silence froze around me like a living presence.

I blinked repeatedly until the shapes coalesced into forms. Looking through my squinting eyes, I saw a man dressed in black sitting behind a trestle table covered with books and papers. His dark face was tense and sharp as if chiseled in stone, and deep creases ran along his forehead. He didn't look at all like the gentle lover I remembered staring longingly into Rosa's eyes. And yet despite his plain soldier clothes and his disheveled hair, there was such arrogance in the way he was looking at me that even before he spoke, I knew without a doubt he was the king.

His eyes two burning points of fire aimed at mine, Don Julián rose from his chair. As if following an order I had not heard, the soldier by my side got up and left. The king moved around the table and came toward me.

"Who are you and what do you want?" he said, his voice sharp and cold as a naked blade. "You have two minutes to convince me you are worth my time."

His tone was not the soft pleading one I remembered from when he was making love to my sister, but cold and unfriendly. A voice you obey. It took all my will to resist the urge to comply.

"I have already told you. I am Princess Andrea of the House of Montemaior. I have come to you as a messenger. Unless you treat me with the respect I deserve, I refuse to talk."

Don Julián stared at me with his dark impenetrable eyes. Then he unsheathed his sword and, with a swift movement of his arm, cut the rope that tied my hands.

"You may proceed now, Princess," he said with a quick bow, his voice so cold and unyielding that I shivered.

Fighting the desire to rub my wrists, as I did not want to give him the satisfaction of showing weakness, I searched my mind for the speech I had so carefully prepared for the occasion. But Don Julián was staring at me so openly, so shamelessly, that suddenly I became painfully aware of my appearance. Aware that in my page outfit, now dirty and wrinkled after three nights of sleeping in it, not to mention my recent fall in the river, I looked anything but royal.

"Sire," I started, my voice surprisingly calm, "I have come to offer you a way to win back Princess Rosa without a battle. If you agree to postpone the confrontation with my father, I will help you get to her so you can again win her favor. I give you my word that Don Juan will be . . . gone by then."

"You came to offer me Princess Rosa back?" Don Julián repeated without bothering to disguise his amusement. "And what made you think I would want her now, Princess?"

"Because you are in love with her."

Don Julián started laughing. But there was no merriment in his laugh. It was a false, contrived, and somehow sad noise, so unexpected it made me wonder about his sanity. Finally he stopped, and looking at me as if I were the crazy one, he asked, "Have you ever heard of a marriage of convenience, Princess?"

And as the meaning of his question that was not a question sunk in, I started shaking. "But then . . ." I stopped. What I wanted to say but couldn't was that then the war was inevitable; that because of me, people would die. Again, like the day at the arch when I had seen the huge wave of water roaring toward me, I was paralyzed by fear. And this time John was not there to rescue me.

"Even if I loved Princess Rosa, it is too late now to make amends," I heard Don Julián saying through the cloud of cotton my head had become. "Personal feelings, Princess, are a luxury kings cannot afford. By breaking the engagement, Don Andrés gave me no option. The safety of my kingdom is at stake. If I do not respond to the affront, our enemies will judge us weak and will attack. I am afraid, Princess, that to accept your offer under these circumstances is totally out of the question."

Still I said nothing.

"Now if that is all, Princess, I must ask you to accept my hospitality. My men will escort you to Alvar." Turning away from me, he started toward the door.

At the mention of Alvar, another voice came to my mind. "I am Don Alfonso de Alvar," his brother had told me when we met on the tree, the day of the Spring Ball.

"Wait, Sire. May I have a word with Don Alfonso? He . . . he will understand."

Don Julián stopped, and his right hand reached for his sword as he turned. Certain that he was going to attack me, I snapped open the golden arrow that held my braid around my head, and jumping to one side, I looked up ready to confront him. But the hair hanging loose over my face blinded me. By the time I had pushed it away and could see again, the king was standing in front of me at arm's reach. His hands were empty.

"Why do you want to see Don Alfonso?" Don Julián demanded, his dark eyes searching mine.

"I . . . we . . . I mean Don Alfonso and I, we met before."

"That explains many things," the king said enigmatically. For a moment he hesitated. "If you want to see him, it is fine with me. I was going to send you to the castle anyway. Not as a prisoner, of course, but to ensure your safety. Our country-side is not safe for a princess alone." His eyes lingered on my hands as he finished, "Not even for one so well-prepared."

My face red in shame, I returned the arrow to my hair while the king called to the guards.

"Take Princess Andrea to Alvar," he commanded as they entered. "She will be staying there until further orders. In the meantime, she will be allowed to visit Don Alfonso freely. Just keep me informed of everything they say."

With a sharp bow in my direction, he moved back to the table and resumed his writing.

What an arrogant fool, I thought as the soldiers pushed me forward. And in my anger, I understood why my father was so intent on defeating him. He deserved it.

SIXTEEN

Prisoner

After riding all day and well into the night, the woods opened into a clearing to reveal the Castle of Alvar. As if growing from the rocks themselves, it loomed ahead of us, imposing and majestic over the lone mountain that supported it.

By then, the enthusiasm I had felt when leaving my father's castle, the frustration at my defeat, and even my anger at Don Julián had subsided to a waning memory. Exhausted and barely able to stay on my horse, I climbed the steep slope that led to the gate, while Lua the copper moon retreated behind the castle walls as if she, too, were being taken prisoner.

As soon as we reached the courtyard, a soldier came over and, after helping me to dismount, escorted me inside the castle. But instead of throwing me into the dungeon as I expected, he led me upstairs to the second floor of the keep and down an empty corridor, until finally we stopped in front of a massive door. The soldier placed his torch into a bracket on the wall, retrieved a rusty iron key from his belt, and opened a door. With a bow, he moved back and motioned me inside.

I walked in and found myself in a large chamber with rich tapestries hanging on the walls. Through the only window, half covered with heavy burgundy curtains, the light of Athos the golden moon was struggling to come in. Underneath the sweet smell of thyme that came from the rush at my feet, mold and dust still lingered in the air as if the room had been closed for a long time. Why should anyone bother to prepare such a room for a prisoner? A bouquet of roses resting on the trunk at the foot of the bed, red as blood against the black canopy, only added to my confusion.

Behind me, the door slammed. I jumped, startled by the hollow sound, and dragging my feet painfully forward, I crawled onto the bed. With the metallic click of the key turning in the lock still in my ears, I fell asleep.

A WOMAN'S VOICE BROKE INTO MY DREAMS. I TRIED TO IGNORE IT, but again and again her words called to me in my sleep. Two of them—"Don Alfonso"—lagged in my mind long enough to wake me up.

"Don Alfonso insists on seeing you, my lady," a maid was saying.

Don Alfonso. Alvar. Don Julián. The ride to the castle. Awakened by the painful memory of my capture, I jumped out of bed.

"Let him in," I said to the old servant staring at me from the other side of the bed. I couldn't make Don Alfonso wait. After all, I was his prisoner.

The maid shook her head. "First my lady, you should change into more appropriate clothing," she said as her sharp eyes swept over me. Contempt showing in the sharp tone of her voice, she added, "In anticipation of your wishes, I have taken the liberty of preparing a bath. If her ladyship would like to come with me, I will assist her."

Although I found her disapproving stare deeply offensive, I knew she was right—I did need a bath badly. Trying to look as dignified as possible in my beaten uniform, I followed her through a side door hidden behind one of the tapestries that opened into the servant's room.

While the maid helped me to undress, I tried to strike a conversation with her. A futile attempt. Disappointed, I gave up, and abandoning myself to the forgotten pleasure of the warm water, I submitted to her meticulous scrubbings in silence.

Back in my room, she helped me into the gown I had chosen from several she had placed on the bed. The dress, an old-fashioned blue muslin robe, was not exactly to my taste, but even I had to admit it was an improvement over my dirty and sweaty uniform.

Smiling at my reflection in the mirror, I thanked her for her help.

The maid didn't return my smile. "King's orders," she said and left.

Almost immediately I heard a knock at the door, and Don Alfonso, escorted by two soldiers, came in. He was as smartly dressed as he had been the day of the ball. This time, though, he was not wearing a uniform, but civilian clothes with no emblem on them.

"Welcome to Suavia, Princess," he said with an elaborate bow.

I curtsied back. "Thank you, my lord."

As we talked, the soldiers had closed the door and, arms ready, had taken positions at both sides. Don Alfonso did not seem to notice. Smiling widely, he asked after my health.

I ignored his question, and trying to keep the anger from my voice, I pointed at the guards. "You can dismiss your men, Sir. I have no weapons."

Don Alfonso stared bluntly at me. "I'm afraid they would not obey me, Princess." And as if in answer to the open question my face must have shown, he finished, "Yes, my dear lady. I am a prisoner, too."

"You, a prisoner? But . . . why?"

Don Alfonso offered me his arm. "You must be tired, Princess. Come sit by the window," he said smiling, though his even voice and his dark eyes did not.

"I gather your family is doing well, Princess," Don Alfonso said as we sat by the window.

"My family?" Why should he care about my family?

Don Alfonso's gaze moved to the door where the soldiers stood and then back to me. Falling to one knee, he took my hand in his and in a pressing voice whispered, "Your family, Princess, is precious to me."

As clearly as if he had said it, the name Margarida formed in my mind. And I knew why he was not with his brother fighting against our kingdom.

"My family is fine, Sir," I said in a voice I barely recognized.

Don Alfonso smiled and returned to his seat.

Dizzy with the implications of my discovery, I looked up. "Does Don Julián know?"

At the mention of his brother's name, his face turned red. "My brother is a fool who thinks only of glory. I tried to talk to him, to make him understand that war is not the only way to resolve the situation. And what did he do? He made me his prisoner. Me, his own brother."

"I know. I tried to reason with him as well. And he laughed at me. He told me his personal feelings couldn't interfere with—"

"Feelings? What does Don Julián know about feelings?" Don Alfonso had jumped to his feet, and ignoring the fact that the soldiers were listening, his voice exploded in the room with the violence of a trapped wolf. "As far as I know, he doesn't have any."

"But he loved Rosa. At least he—"

Don Alfonso laughed. "Loved Rosa? My dear Princess, where have you been? Love was never the issue for him. To win the contest was. And that he won, no one would argue. He won her hand by sword and blood. He defeated all his opponents without getting so much as a scratch. He is indeed a brave and fearless warrior. But strength and valor are not enough to make a great king. Sometimes words are needed, and words, Princess, are my brother's enemy. They always have been. And his knights are no better either. They stood behind him as one when he rejected my proposal. Their blind devotion to him gives me no hope. They thrive on blood, rejoicing in the thrill of the battle. For them, any reason to make war is welcome. Any excuse."

With long angry strides, Don Alfonso paced the room. I had the impression he had forgotten about me and the soldiers who, still by the door, had not missed a word. I did not know what to think. For all his annoying rhetoric and self-assurance, Don Alfonso was right. Hadn't I also tried to reason with Father and John to no avail? I remembered the excitement in their voices as they planned the war, the eagerness in Don Gonzalo's when he talked about revenge, and I had to agree with Don Alfonso: War was their goal; Rosa, their excuse.

"I am sorry, Princess. I lost my temper." Don Alfonso resumed his seat by the window. A wild shine in his eyes the only sign of his recent outburst, he was again smiling.

"You don't have to apologize, Sir. I think you are right. My father, Don Juan . . . they are not fighting for Rosa either, but for their own pleasure. They are all the same. Except for you. You are . . ."

"Different? Yes. I am different. I think fighting is a primitive impulse. Diplomacy is the mature way of solving problems. But what does it matter what I think? It is Don Julián who is King." Closing his hand into a fist, he hit the windowsill with sudden fury. "If only my brother would find his door and be gone."

The door! At the mention of the door, my mind started racing. Don Julián was looking for a way to go to the other world. Don Alfonso had told me so the very day I had crossed to California. Why hadn't I thought about it before? That was the solution I had been looking for. I would offer Don Julián access to the door if he were to apologize to Father and stop the war. This time he would agree. I was positive he would. If only I could talk to him. But how?

Eager to be alone to think, I asked Don Alfonso to leave, using the excuse that I was not feeling well. With many apologies and wishes for my good health, he complied.

As soon as Don Alfonso and his guards left, I looked around my room for inspiration. The door was locked and guarded, but the window—I ran to the window and pushed it open. The room was hanging over a cliff—imposing rocks that no human or animal could ever climb. That explained why I had been given such fancy accommodations. How thoughtful of Don Julián. Well, the match was not over yet. Only time would determine the winner.

My back to the window, I swept the walls with my eyes, searching for a way out. But the room, in all its sober beauty, was a prison, and my hands were bare. Of all my belongings, only my golden arrow and the pouch I had hidden under the pillows before taking the bath were left. I took the pouch out now, and leaning against the pillows, I undid the string and poured the contents on the bed. Some coins, a piece of rope, and, shining brightly against the blackness of the velvet cover, my precious watch. Slowly I ran my fingers over its glittering surface. So beautiful and useless. Dangerous, too. In this superstitious and backward world of mine, they would burn me as a witch if they ever found it on me. Oh, how I wished to be back in California once more with my cousin Kelsey. And John. The old John, of course, not this delirious puppet he had become under the spell of my sister Rosa. As usual, thinking of Rosa unleashed a sudden burst of anger in me. Closing my hand on the watch, I threw it against the covers. For a moment the rays of the sun reflected from the glass. And as I closed my eyes, blinded by the sudden glare, I had an idea, a crazy idea that grew and grew out of my despair until it became a plan.

Later that evening when the maid came to bring me my supper, I was ready. With my best smile, I asked her to exchange clothes with me. She refused. And so I had to do it the hard way. Quickly I produced my arrow, and pressing it against her throat until I drew blood, I repeated my wish that she'd undress. This time she obeyed.

Once she was finished, I bound her hands behind her back and her mouth with one of the pillowcases and changed into her clothes. Then I removed her gag, and holding the arrow against her chest to discourage her from screaming, I asked her the directions to Don Alfonso's quarters. Her eyes flashing in anger, she did not reply.

"Don Alfonso is your master and needs my help. You must tell me how to find him."

"King Don Julián is my only master," she whispered fiercely, "and you are his prisoner."

Her loyalty to her king was indeed impressive. Or maybe she had realized I was bluffing. Because the truth was, I could never kill her in cold blood. *If that is what it took to be a soldier,* I thought, *Father had been right all along. I could never be one.*

I covered her mouth again, and after fetching my watch from the pouch, I returned to her side. Holding it in front of me, I swung it slowly, making sure the maid saw the golden moon already half-hidden behind the dial. The golden moon that in our world symbolized Athos—the constant moon, the moon that never waned, from which, according to legend, the king takes all power.

For a moment longer, I stayed still. Then I covered the watch with my cupped hands and walked to the window. Raising my arms in what I expected to be a dramatic gesture, I lifted the watch above my head.

"By the power of the sun, I conjure thee," I intoned in hushed tones as I tilted the watch so the rays of the setting sun would reflect on the glass. Then I covered the watch with both my hands and lowered it to my chest. "The soul of your king has been taken. I hold in my hands the power to destroy it." Turning my back to the room, I opened the window, and arms outstretched, I held the watch over the cliff.

I heard a muffled scream and the rattling sound of a chair being dragged over the boards. I jumped back and, with quick steps, closed in on the maid, who was frantically shaking her head. The watch safe on my wrist, I uncovered her mouth. "The last corridor to the right, after the stairs," she spat at me, her eyes full of hate. "Then the second door on your left."

Disturbed by the sheer intensity of her stare, I hesitated—what I had just done felt terribly wrong. But my hesitation did not last. Yes, to tie up the maid and play to her superstitious nature was wrong, but I had not chosen to be here, either. If someone was to blame, it was certainly Don Julián, not I. So I gagged her again as gently as I dared, grabbed the bowl with the uneaten food, and left the room.

My eyes on the floor, my face and hair hidden under an ample shawl, I walked past the soldier guarding the door, and forcing myself to drag my feet to control my urge to run, I headed toward Don Alfonso's quarters. Once again I was lucky. Only one soldier was on guard. Holding tightly to the dinner bowl I had taken to justify my visit, I walked up to the door.

Suddenly alert, the soldier blocked my way with his spear. "Why are you back, woman? Don Alfonso has already eaten."

With a swift movement, I threw the porridge at his eyes. Before he could react, I had yanked the spear from his hands and knocked him unconscious with the bowl. Once I had tied his hands with his own belt and covered his mouth with the maid's apron, I unlocked the door.

Sitting by the window, Don Alfonso was reading. "I won't be needing anything else," he said without lifting his eyes from the book. "You may leave now."

"Don Alfonso. It's me, Andrea."

Don Alfonso looked up, his handsome face frozen in surprise.

"Would you please come, Sir? I need your help."

Always the gentleman, Don Alfonso rose to his feet and bowed. "Princess Andrea. What are you doing here?"

In a low whisper, I urged him to hurry. He came over then with a stiff walk. But when he reached my side and saw the man lying against the wall, his voice rose in alarm. "What have you done, Princess? Why have you killed him?"

"I have not killed anyone. He is only unconscious. So would you stop asking stupid questions and help?"

Tugging at his arms, I pulled him to the soldier. Don Alfonso didn't argue. He bent down, and while I grabbed the man's feet, he lifted his upper body and, with surprising dexterity, led the way back into the room. But as soon as the soldier was inside and the door closed, he went back to his complaining.

"I don't understand, Princess. Why did you do this?"

I sighed. I had imagined Don Alfonso would be thrilled with my rescue operation. Instead he seemed genuinely upset at me. Why had I bothered to go to him? I should have left on my own. But now it was too late. Worried that he would call the guard if I didn't convince him of the validity of my actions, I took a deep breath and plunged on with my explanation. "Because we must talk with Don Julián immediately. I have a plan. A plan to stop this war. I have found the door."

"I see you have found my door—"

"Not yours. The door to the other world. Remember? The one your brother is looking for." To make my point, I rolled up my sleeve and showed him the watch. Don Alfonso stepped back, fear flashing in his eyes. "You said your brother would do anything to go to the other world. Does anything include negotiating a peace treaty with Father?"

Don Alfonso stared at me for a long time. Then when I was sure he was going to declare me insane and call for the soldiers, he smiled. "Yes, I suppose it does. For access to the other world, my brother would most likely stop the war and leave. And I will marry Princess Margarida."

"What?"

"To make the peace last, we need an alliance between your House and Alvar. That I marry your sister seems the obvious solution. Don Andrés will—"

Having Don Alfonso as my brother-in-law was not exactly my idea of a happy ending, but now was not the time to argue. "Fine," I said. "Now we must hurry."

Don Alfonso was not convinced. "Why didn't you tell me of your plan this afternoon? We could have sent a letter to my brother, instead of . . ." At the look of disgust on his face as he pointed to the soldier lying on the floor, I finally lost my temper. Raising my voice until his was silenced, I told him of my plan in a quick angry gust of words.

"I hate violence as much as you do, Sir. But there was no other way. And yes, you will write a letter to Don Julián—we may need it to trick the guards into letting us leave. But we must carry it ourselves. This matter is too important to leave the letter in the hands of a messenger who may or may not deliver it. Anyway, it is too late for me now. I have kidnapped a maid and knocked out a soldier. I am not going to sit around and wait for your temperamental brother to send me to a real prison.

"As for you, Sir, I'm sorry if I disturbed your evening. I thought you would like to come with me. I see now I was wrong and I apologize. If you would be so kind as to tell me how to get to the stables, I will be gone presently."

"But of course I'm coming with you, Princess," Don Alfonso said as he bowed to me in his annoying manner. "What kind of a gentleman do you think I am if you believe I could allow a beautiful lady like yourself to go alone?"

I was going to tell him that I did not need his protection, that I had managed to do very well by myself until then, thank you very much. But the truth was, I would be happy to have him at my side, as he knew the castle and the way back to the river better than I did. So I swallowed my pride and graciously curtsied to him. "Your company is greatly appreciated, my lord," I said. As he smiled, I urged him impatiently. "Now, Sir, would you please change into the soldier's uniform? We don't have much time."

Without further argument, Don Alfonso complied. Once he was ready, he wrote a letter to Don Julián, and after he had sealed it with the signet on his ring, we rushed through the corridors and into the courtyard.

The page at the stables let Don Alfonso get a little too close. Soon the boy was unconscious and tied on the floor, and I was wearing his clothes.

Don Alfonso, in the meantime, had saddled two horses. We mounted them and rode away across the empty baileys until we reached the gatehouse.

The sun had been gone for a while now, and in the soft golden light of Athos, we were only shadows. But when the guard called to us with his compulsory "Who goes there?" that would determine our fate, my blood was pounding in my ears so loudly that I could barely hear the impatient thunder of the horses' hooves.

Ahead of me, Don Alfonso, anonymous under the soldier's helmet, waved the sealed letters at the sentries, shouting his urgent mission to the night shadows. There was a moment of silence, then with a screeching sound of rusty iron, a line of light appeared under the gate. Without a look back, we plunged ahead through the open mouth, down the steep hill that led to freedom.

IT WAS ALREADY MORNING WHEN WE REACHED THE CAMP WHERE my ill-fated conversation with Don Julián had taken place. Dressed as Suavian men, we were virtually invisible among the soldiers coming and going between the fields and the encampment. The guards let us through without challenge.

After leaving the horses—alas, not my dear Flecha this time—grazing in the enclosure, we proceeded to the king's tent. Two soldiers stood at attention on both sides of the entrance.

"We have a message for the king!" Don Alfonso shouted in his most imperious voice as soon as we reached them.

He was still talking when the flap of the tent was lifted from the inside, and a man appeared in the opening. He was dressed in black as he had been the day I had last met him, and the crown, symbol of his power, shone on his head. But when I raised my eyes, readying myself to confront his cold stare, my heart stopped beating. Because the man who was standing in front of me wearing the king's clothes was not Don Julián.

SEVENTEEN

The Bridge

My feet rooted to the ground, I stared at the man who was not Don Julián. Over the crossed spears of the sentries, our eyes met. *Who are you?* I screamed at him without words. But the man had already turned his attention to my companion. A flash of surprise gleaming in his eyes, his hand jerked to his sword. "At ease!" he shouted to his men.

As the soldiers stepped aside, the knight moved forward and, unsheathing his sword, dropped to one knee and presented the hilt to Don Alfonso. "My lord," he said with a curious mixture of respect and embarrassment.

Don Alfonso gasped. "Don Fernando?" He hesitated, then demanded, "Where is the king?"

"He is . . ." Don Fernando hesitated. "Please, Sir, come into the tent so we may discuss the matter in private."

Don Alfonso nodded and, with a wave of his hand, motioned me inside.

I didn't move. "Who is he?" I asked instead.

"Don Fernando is one of my brother's captains. Please, go in. It's safe."

Willing my legs forward, I walked past Don Fernando and yanked the flap open. The tent was empty. As my last hope of finding Don Julián vanished, the burst of energy that had sustained me through the night left me, and I started shaking. Stumbling forward, I dragged myself to the solitary chair standing behind the trestle table just as I remembered it from my last meeting and collapsed on it. Where could Don Julián be? Had he already crossed the river and engaged my father's army in combat? Or had he challenged John to a duel and killed him? But if so, why had he bothered to leave someone behind to impersonate him?

Through the confused rumble of my thoughts, I could hear the voices of Don Alfonso and Don Fernando arguing. Don Alfonso was pressing Don Fernando to take us to the king. Don Fernando, always polite, refused. "You must wait here, my lord. When the king comes back, he will explain."

"We cannot wait. New developments have occurred that he must attend to at once. I order you to take us to him immediately."

Don Fernando shook his head. "It wouldn't be wise, my lord."

"That is for me to decide!" Don Alfonso insisted. Turning toward the door, he called the guards.

I trembled at his bravado. Had he forgotten we were only fugitives? That soon men would arrive from the castle with news of our escape?

The soldiers came in.

"I am Don Alfonso de Alvar, and I order you to take me to the king."

The men looked at Don Alfonso and then at Don Fernando.

Don Fernando nodded. "Do as he says," he said brusquely. And one would have thought by the way he said it that he had just signed his own death sentence. Or ours.

Escorted by two soldiers, we left the camp. Once more I was unarmed, as Don Fernando had demanded we surrender our weapons. To my surprise Don Alfonso had agreed without protest. I had refused at first, not willing to give up my newly acquired freedom, but alone against a whole encampment, what choice did I have?

Under the scorching sun of the summer day, we headed north until we reached the riverbank. Then turning west, we continued downstream, cutting our way through the thick underbrush that flanked the river. Luckily the willows and poplars that grew close to the water provided us with welcome relief from the increasing heat.

By noon, at my request we stopped to eat. Don Alfonso, who had been unusually silent all morning, didn't touch his food. When I asked him what was bothering him, he answered cryptically, "I'd rather not tell you, Princess. If I am right, you will know soon enough," and refused to elaborate further.

Shortly after we resumed our march, the river bent away from us deep into my kingdom. We left the comfortable shade of the trees and cut straight across an open meadow. Soon I was struggling up a steep hill that defined the lowlands, trying to avoid the sharp thorns of the briars that were deceivingly inviting with their bright flowers.

The path we were following was barely a path at all, which made me think that Don Julián, wherever he was, did not want to be found. Too tired to care anymore about what his reasons could be, I concentrated on walking, a painful task that required all my attention because the slippers I was wearing—the page's shoes had been too big for me to borrow—were so worn out that my feet were soon covered with blisters. Only my pride prevented me from screaming every time I hit a pebble.

So it was that I had my eyes on the ground when we reached the summit, and I did not realize Don Alfonso had stopped until I bumped into him. Don Alfonso did not apologize. In fact he didn't even turn around. Annoyed at his inconsiderate behavior, I was about to complain, when something in his expression stopped me. Following his stare, I looked down. All my pains were suddenly forgotten, and I gasped in awe.

Below us the river had again come into view. As it wrapped itself around the mountain like a silver snake, the sun's rays reflecting from its surface gave the eerie impression that it was alive. Still, it was not the incredible beauty of the river that took my breath away, but something much more unexpected.

Farther to the left across the serpent's neck, a bridge was growing. Three arches in bright granite stones were already finished. Over the fourth one, which already reached into my kingdom, several workers were setting square rocks onto a wooden scaffold, while along the right side of the bridge, men were lined up and pulling at the ropes that dragged the blocks.

For a time, nobody in our group moved. Finally the angry voice of Don Alfonso broke the silence. "The wedding gift," he said. "Just as I feared." Then he turned toward the soldiers. "Let's go!" he commanded, as if he were in charge. Not bothering to see whether the guards or I followed, he rushed down the hill.

"What do you mean by the wedding gift?" I cried after him.

"The bridge was supposed to be a wedding gift for Princess Rosa," Don Alfonso said. "By crossing the river here, the distance between your castle and mine would be considerably reduced. And your sister, his bride, would be able to visit her kingdom often."

"So he did care for her after all!"

This time Don Alfonso did stop. "Don't be fooled, Princess. What my brother really cares about is his bridge. As you can see, wedding or war, he has managed to stay true to his real love.

"But now the bridge will bring only destruction. Once it is finished Don Julián will take your castle by surprise and then attack Don Andrés's troops from behind. Why should he accept our proposition now when his victory is at hand and he can demand access to the door as his reward?"

Without waiting for my answer, he resumed his walking. I stumbled after him while his words echoed in my mind, making me uneasy. Was Don Julián's love for his bridge so very different from my own desire to return to California?

I had almost reached the bottom of the mountain when the ground shook under my feet and a deafening noise came from the direction of the bridge. Looking up I saw that part of the scaffolding that had framed the fourth arch had collapsed.

"Perfect timing!" Don Alfonso shouted as wood and stones splashed into the river. "Just the thing to put my brother in a good mood."

"At least this accident will delay him for a while," I said when the blare finally subsided.

Don Alfonso shook his head. "Not really. The arch is almost finished. I'm afraid . . . Now what?" he asked, a piercing cry splitting the silence once more.

Again I looked toward the bridge. A worker hanging precariously from the broken structure was screaming for help. Just as I looked, the man lost his grip and fell into the water.

Moments later, his head appeared close to the pillars. With awkward movements of his arms, he struggled to stay afloat.

"He can't swim," I mumbled, and my stomach sank.

"Of course he can't," Don Alfonso said matter-of-factly.

Of course. How could I have forgotten we were not in California, but in my own backward world where nobody can swim?

Don Alfonso pulled at my arm. "Come on, Princess, there is nothing we can do. And the sooner we face Don Julián, the better."

I was about to turn when a sudden movement on the third arch caught my attention. A man dressed in the black uniform of the Suavian soldiers was pushing his way through a group of workers. Soon he had reached the edge of the bridge, and after unbuckling the belt that held his sword, he dropped it to the ground. Then he climbed over the railings, dived into the river with a clean jump, and started swimming toward the drowning man. When he got near him, the soldier disappeared under the water and, avoiding the thrashing arms of the worker, emerged behind him. Before I realized what was happening, the soldier had knocked the man unconscious and, holding the limp body with one arm, was heading toward the shore.

Several boats were already closing in on them when, again, Don Alfonso urged me to move. Reluctantly tearing my eyes from the river, I obeyed.

As soon as we left the protection of the trees and entered the open space before the bridge, two men broke from the line of soldiers blocking further access to the river. Their bows ready, they advanced toward us. But upon recognizing my companion, they lowered their weapons and at his request escorted us through.

We were still climbing down the steep slope that led to the water when the boats arrived. At the stern of the second one sat the soldier, impressively still, his black uniform gleaming in the unforgiving sun. Just as the boat reached the riverbank, he bent over the hulk and, ignoring the hands extended to help him, jumped ashore. As if coming from a single throat, a wild roar of elation broke from the multitude to welcome him. It was only then, as the man lifted his arm in an authoritarian gesture to command silence, that I finally understood our search for the king had ended.

From my position halfway to the water, I stared as Don Julián, kneeling by the body of the worker the soldiers had transferred to the shore, checked his breathing. Soon he was up again and, after shouting orders to his men, started walking toward the bridge in long hurried strides. With his long disheveled hair on his shoulders and his drenched clothes hanging closely to his muscular body, he was indeed a fearful sight.

Just then, one of the soldiers in our escort left the group and walked down to intercept him. Don Julián looked up past the man toward the place where we were standing, and for a split of a second, his eyes locked onto mine. As if hit by a bolt of lightning, I stumbled back into Don Alfonso's arms.

Don Alfonso held me back. "Do not panic, Princess," he whispered. "We must be convincing now if we want to stop the war." Pushing me aside, he moved forward and respectfully knelt to his king.

Certain that my legs would fail me if I tried to walk, I remained still, staring defiantly at the king. But my stare was totally lost on him. Don Julián was already addressing my companion, his face hardened into a mask of anger. "Why have you disobeyed my orders?" he was saying in the stern voice I remembered from our last encounter. "Why have you brought Princess Andrea here?"

"I didn't bring her, Sire. She came of her own free will."

Don Julián ignored his remark. "I was right not to trust you. What demon has possessed you that you have turned your back on your own people? By showing Princess Andrea the bridge, you have revealed our plans to the enemy. I have no choice now. You both must die." And the hate in his eyes was so unmistakable that I shivered.

Back on his feet, Don Alfonso faced the king. "Death, death. Is that all you think about, Brother?" he said, his voice full of scorn. "You could at least listen to us before passing your judgment. We have come a long way and deserve to be heard."

For a moment their eyes locked in a silent struggle of wills. Finally Don Julián nodded. "I will listen," he said coldly. "But first I must assess the damage to the bridge. In the meantime, you will be escorted to my tent."

That did it. I had not escaped from the castle and risked my life to be taken prisoner once more. I had had enough of his arrogant behavior. Avoiding the soldier already closing on me, I jumped in front of the king. "I demand to come with you, Sire. If I am going to die for this bridge, I claim the right to see it first."

Don Julián stared at me—his eyes, two arrows of fire, aiming at mine. But this time I was ready and unflinchingly held his stare. Brusquely Don Julián bowed to me. "As you wish," he said. And without waiting for my answer, he turned and preceded me up the slope, while Don Alfonso, surrounded by soldiers, remained behind.

Lost in the memory of another bridge, a red bridge dressed in clouds hanging over the San Francisco Bay, I climbed after the king. For a while, the soft grass of the shore was gentle on my feet, but as soon as I reached the bridge, the overheated stones burned my skin through my torn slippers. I gasped, and grasping the balustrade with both hands, I lifted my weight from the ground and turned my head toward the river to hide my pain. Down below, I could see the green waters of the river breaking into waves as they hit the pillars, while farther to my left, pieces of wood from the broken scaffold drifted slowly down the stream.

"Princess?"

The king had stopped by the rail and was staring at me with an unreadable expression. I flushed under his inquisitive eyes, and biting my lips to stop myself from crying, I hurried to join him. Don Julián resumed his walking along the left side of the bridge. As he advanced, his men, scattered around the abandoned blocks, looked to the ground and kneeled to their king.

We had almost reached the fourth arch when cries of alarm broke from the shore. Before I could understand what they were saying, Don Julián turned and threw himself at me, sending me against the railing. Struggling for balance, I tried to push him away. But my hands slipped over his wet clothes, which left a sticky substance on my hands—strangely warm. Just then with a heavy crack, the wooden rail broke under my weight. Our bodies still entangled, we fell from the bridge.

Soon the cold waters of the river closed over me. I came up gasping for air, and then went under and up again. As I sank for the second time someone grabbed me under the arms and dragged me to a wooden plank. Breathing in deep gulps of air, I turned around to confront the king. But the king, I realized with a shudder, was not a threat anymore. Barely able to keep afloat, he lay by my side in a pool of blood.

Trying not to draw conclusions about what I was seeing, I reached for him. Briefly our eyes met. When his eyes swept over me without showing any sign of recognition, I shivered again. I was more afraid of him then than ever before, but for a totally different reason.

Over my head arrows flew. I could hear the hissing as they sought their targets, the screams of the wounded after they found them, and the splashes of the water as the bodies fell. On the slope of the mountain I had recently climbed down with Don Alfonso, I could see the archers partially hidden behind the trees, aiming their bows. But who the attackers were was a mystery to me. Their colors were not my father's.

Not that I cared. I was too busy with my own problems. By my side, Don Julián was unconscious. I was holding him with my right hand, but my arm was getting numb, and I knew I couldn't do it for much longer. Wasn't anyone going to help? It was their king after all. But none of the men floating around me answered my cries. Face down, they drifted downriver, beyond help, beyond cares. Then, when I had lost all hope of being rescued, I saw an empty boat emerging from the shadow of one of the arches. I kicked the water, propelling the plank forward with my feet. And the boat came closer and closer until it hit the board. One hand on the hull, the other around Don Julián's waist, I led the boat toward some rapids where I knew I could reach bottom. Standing precariously over the slippery rocks, I hauled Don Julián into the craft and climbed after him.

I lay on my back, conscious only of my chest heaving painfully with each breath. Dark clouds billowed over my head, bringing an acrid odor to my nostrils. And then I was sitting against the bow, and the boat was rocking under me, and the bridge—the bridge was on fire. Long red flames embraced the wooden railings with their blazing tongues raised to the sky. Behind the dark clouds of smoke that had already turned the day into night, Athos the golden moon was rising.

Down by the shore, the Suavian soldiers were still fighting. *Who was in charge*, I wondered, *now that they had lost their king?* There could only be one answer. If Don Alfonso were alive, he would have had to take command. It was too late for dreams of peace now. Our plan had failed.

Crying without tears, I grabbed the oars and, for the first time in my life, started rowing. Luckily, the current aided me and in spite of my awkward tries, we progressed rapidly down river, away from the deafening clamor of the battle.

It was not until the river took a sharp bend and hid the bridge from me that I allowed myself to stop. After securing the oars inside the boat, I crawled toward the king. Don Julián, his left shoulder pierced by an arrow, was lying on his back in the same position I had left him. I didn't try to remove the shaft from his body, as I knew that without the proper care, he would bleed to death. Instead, I felt for his pulse. It was so slow and uncertain that I almost missed it.

"At least he has stopped bleeding," I said aloud to reassure myself. But I remembered the blood running down his shirt as we struggled on the bridge, and how the water had turned red around his body as I held him. I wondered whether he had any blood left.

I shivered. Don Julián, his eyes closed, his tattered clothes drenched with water and blood, didn't look impressive any-more. He didn't look like the arrogant king I had grown to hate, but like a man weary after a long hunt. Besides, regardless of who he was or what I thought of him, I felt bound to him now because I had to reluctantly admit that he had saved my life.

But what could I do? I was not a doctor. As if in the memory of a dream, I heard in my mind a voice saying "doctor." It was a male voice and very, very familiar. Suddenly I remembered. Tío Ramiro had said my mother had been a physician in her world. If it was true, she might be able to help Don Julián.

My mother and I were not exactly close. I resented her too much to trust her, but the fact remained that Don Julián was dying and that she was his only hope. Pushing back the panic that threatened to paralyze my will, I returned to the bench. Plunging the oars into the water, I started rowing toward my parents' castle.

EIGHTEEN

Mother

I rowed into the night, alone with my fears, the unconscious king a dark shape before the stern. I rowed away from the battle, but I could still hear the hissing of the arrows and the screams of the soldiers. I rowed and the splash of the oars splitting the water reminded me of the bodies falling from the bridge. Over and over I rowed, staring blankly at the water until my mind was empty.

Later, much later, the copper reflection of Lua on the water brought me back. It was a perfect half moon. *Three more weeks until the full moon,* I thought. And the memories returned. I remembered the world beyond the arch where I had met John. I remembered John and Rosa walking away from me in the bailey. And I remembered Father discussing the war with John.

At my feet Don Julián, who was still unconscious, moaned and jerked his arms. Don Julián, the enemy king. Careful not to rock the boat, I put the oars inside and crawled toward him. As I held his arms so he wouldn't hurt himself, it dawned on me that my father's victory was at hand. If he attacked now, before the Suavian army had time to recover from the loss of its king and today's almost sure defeat, he would certainly win.

"Our House will win," I said aloud. But the words only added to my distress. Disturbed by the unfamiliar feeling, I closed my eyes. When I opened them again, Don Julián was looking at me. "My people," he muttered trying to sit up. "What happened?"

"Please, Sire, don't move." *Or you'll bleed to death,* I thought but did not say. Avoiding his eyes so he wouldn't read the despair in mine, I rested his body against the stern. Then I took the goatskin I had been carrying on my belt when I fell from the bridge and gave him some water.

"Thank you, Princess," he whispered. His eyes were so close now, I could see my face in his pupils. To escape his blunt stare I moved away, leaning over the side to get more water. When I turned back, Don Julián, a knife in his hand, was sitting against the stern.

I froze. I had made many mistakes in my life, but this one topped them all. What kind of soldier forgets to take his prisoner's weapons? I surely deserved to die. As water from the inverted goatskin spilled over my legs, I waited for Don Julián to make his move. Slowly, very slowly, the king lifted his hand and, hilt up, presented his knife to me. He was surrendering.

I sighed in relief and extended my arm, only to drop it again. Don Julián had saved my life by pushing me away from the arrow—the arrow that had pierced his shoulder. That he would be my prisoner because of his bravery did not seem right.

"No, Sire. I will not—"

The sudden clank of the knife hitting the wooden planks covered my words. Don Julián, his eyes closed, was struggling for balance. By the time I reached him, he was unconscious again.

I laid his body on the boards, and praying that he would not die on me, I returned to the seat and resumed my rowing. All night, as the boat drifted downriver, I battled with my conscience. By the time the familiar shape of Mount Pindo emerged through the mist, I had reached a decision: I would not hand Don Julián over to Father.

Dawn was breaking upstream over the green canopy of trees when the towers of my parents' castle came into view. Over the keep, the tallest tower, there was no flag: The king was not in the castle. Taking that for a good omen, I steered the boat toward the riverbank. Then as soon as the hull touched bottom, I jumped into the shallow waters and dragged it ashore.

Bending over the hull, I took leave of Don Julián. "I am going to get help, Sire." Don Julián did not move, and when I touched him, I realized he was burning with fever. I did not want to leave him alone, so totally defenseless. And yet what else could I do? Praying silently to the ancient gods of the Xarens for their protection, I turned away and started the steady ascent toward the castle.

Once again I climbed the ramparts, my dirty clothes blending with the ivy, my hands and feet searching for the holes and grips on the weatherworn stones. When I reached the top, I crawled onto the walkway through one of the battlement crenellations. No one was in sight, which suited me fine. And yet the absence of sentries bothered me. If Don Julián had finished the bridge and attacked the castle, he would have found a poor resistance. I should have been happy knowing the danger was over. But it wasn't so simple. Men had died. I had seen them die, and that had changed everything.

I took a deep breath and concentrated on the moment. When I was sure no one was guarding the closest tower, I stole inside and ran down the spiral stairway, across the baileys, and into the garden. On the second level of the keep, the windows into Mother's chambers were closed. On my right, over the eastern wall, I could see the sun rising. I did not have a moment to lose. Mother's ladies-in-waiting would soon be sweeping into her room, and my chance to talk to her alone would be ruined.

With the ease of long practice, I climbed the tree whose upper branches hung just outside Mother's window—a maple tree, heavy with leaves that tickled my skin as I peered through a crack into the shadows of the room. As far as I could see, no one was there. To force the window open with my arrow took only a moment. Then I leaned forward and jumped inside, landing on bent knees.

Back on my feet, I ran toward Mother's red canopy bed and pushed the curtains open. My hand in midair, I stopped. With her eyes closed and her face clean of make-up, Mother looked so different from the fiery and commanding queen of my memory that I hesitated. Suddenly shy of touching her in her sleep, I only whispered, "Wake up, Mother. Wake up."

Mother opened her eyes. "Princess Andrea? What are you doing here?"

"Mother, I have come to ask for your help. I—"

But Mother was not listening. Her back propped up against the pillows, she stared at my clothes in alarm. "What happened, Princess? Why are you bleeding?"

"I am not. It is . . ." To my embarrassment I broke off, almost in tears. "Mother, you have to help him. He is dying."

"Who, Andrea? Who is dying?" By the fear trembling in her eyes, I knew she was thinking of Father.

"It is not . . . it is . . . Don Julián."

A look of utter shock in her face, Mother threw back her covers and started for the door. Quickly I blocked her way. "Please, Mother, don't call the guards. Don Julián is wounded. You have to help him."

"Help Don Julián? And why should I do that, Princess?"

"Because Tío said you were . . . are a doctor. And because if he lives, I have a plan, a plan to stop this war. But nobody must know I am back. And nobody must learn Don Julián is here."

"You are not making any sense."

Clinging to her arm, I pulled her back. "Please, Mother, I will do whatever you ask from now on. I will behave like a princess. I will be perfect, just like Margarida. I promise, Mother. But please, please, do as I ask."

Mother looked into my eyes for what seemed forever. Finally she nodded. "All right, Princess. As this obviously means a lot to you, I will see him. But remember, I am not agreeing to anything else."

"I understand. But please hurry. Let me help you to get dressed."

Mother glanced at my hands, caked with mud and blood, and at my ragged and filthy uniform, and the familiar expression—a mixture of disgust and annoyance—returned to her face.

Waving her hand toward the table where a jug full of water for the morning ablutions awaited, she ordered me to wash up. By the time I was finished, Mother was already dressed in a long black gown I had never seen before.

"I'll go now and fetch Don Julián," she said, "but first I'll wake up Don Ramiro and send him to you. Wait here until he comes. Then do as he says. He will take you somewhere safe."

Without waiting for my answer, she walked to the door and left. Exhausted, I collapsed on one of Mother's reclining chairs, and trying not to think of her wrath when she found the stains on its beloved red velvet, I closed my eyes. The next moment, Tío was shaking my shoulders. "Come on, Andrea. You have to get up."

Rubbing the sleep from my eyes, I stumbled after him, out of the room and down the silent corridors, until we reached the last door at the end of the hall. Wide awake now, I stared at the closed room—the mystery room I used to call it when I was a child—the only one in the entire castle that had resisted my attempts to break in. I waited, trembling in anticipation at the marvels soon to be unraveled before my eyes, while Tío fidgeted with the key. Finally with a heavy crack, the door opened.

Once more the reality didn't measure up to my dreams. The room was just a plain-looking room with bare walls and a bed, a table and chair, and a cedar trunk as its only furniture. An iron pot was hanging above the fire burning on the hearth.

"Who needs a fire in the middle of the summer?" I wondered aloud.

"We need it to boil water," Tío said sharply. Then he opened the low door that opened into the servant's room, and pointing to a frock that was lying on the bed—the plain brown type worn by maids—he told me to go in there and change.

When I returned, Tío was pushing the bed toward the window. Without bothering to ask him why, as I did not want to risk getting another of his enigmatic answers, I helped him in silence.

We had just finished setting the chair against the same wall when I heard heavy footsteps outside. As the door swung wide open, Mother's voice filled the room. "Leave him on the bed. And if you value your life, forget you ever saw him."

I pressed myself flat against the wall, my eyes on the floor so as not to be recognized. I waited. As the steps got closer, I saw boots, soldiers' boots, and the trim of Mother's dress covered in mud. Then I heard the noise of a body being dropped on the bed and my mother's majestic voice ordering them to leave.

Once the door closed behind the soldiers, I ran to the bed. Mother was already there, holding Don Julián's wrist.

"Mother, is he . . .?" I bent as I spoke, reaching for his other arm. But before I could touch him, Tío Ramiro pulled me back.

Mother did not seem to notice. Her eyes still on Don Julián, she let go of his hand and put two fingers to his neck. For an interminable moment, no one spoke. Finally Mother looked up. "He's alive," she said to Tío, "but barely so. We must hurry. Get Princess Andrea to sit by me and bare her left arm."

I jumped back. "Why?"

"Because Don Julián needs blood," Mother said matter-of-factly. "As we don't know his blood type, and since you are O, you are the perfect choice."

How do you know? I wanted to ask, but Tío Ramiro had already taken me to the chair and was rolling back the sleeve of my dress. Then Mother came over. I felt a sharp pain in my arm and my blood started pouring into the tube hanging between my arm and Don Julián's. After a while my eyelids felt heavy, and I drifted to sleep.

When I woke up, my sister Margarida was smiling at me. "Drink this," she said as she helped me to do so. "It will make you feel better."

Silhouetted against the window, I saw Mother bending over the bed. Behind her, Tío Ramiro, standing by the trunk covered now with a white cloth, was handing her a sharp metal object. The whole scene had a dream-like quality, and yet it seemed vaguely familiar. I knew I had seen all this before—the table, the instruments. Of course—on the TV, in my uncle's world.

"Needle, gauze!" Mother was saying and then, just as I slipped again into sleep, she whispered, "Hold it, Raymond! We are losing him!"

SLOWLY I OPENED MY EYES. I COULD TELL I WAS LYING IN BED, BUT where the bed was I didn't know. The room was not mine. Although it was still day, the long shadows crawling on the wooden floor already announced the sunset.

"How are you, Princess?"

I turned toward the voice. By the side of the bed my mother was looking at me, her eyes full of concern, a pale smile on her strained face. "Mother?" I said, and at the sound of my voice, my memories returned. Wide awake, I sat up and searched the room for the bed where Don Julián had been. But the bed was gone. And the window was in the wrong place, too. Of course, this was the maid's room where I had changed before.

"Don Julián. Where is he?"

"Don Julián is in the other room, Princess. And yes, he's all right. At least he's alive, and that is more than I would have guessed last night."

I fell back against the pillows and closed my eyes.

"Although the arrow didn't pierce any major organ," Mother continued, "he had lost a lot of blood. Actually he needed more blood than you could give, so I had to call Princess Margarida. I didn't want to bring her into this, but I had no choice."

I looked up. "Thank you, Mother."

"You are welcome, Princess. As you see, I have kept my word. Now it is your turn. I will listen to you as promised. But first I want you to know I have already written a letter to Don Andrés, telling him you are safe and that Don Julián is our prisoner. I was only waiting for you to wake up to send it to him."

"But you cannot do that, Mother. Don Julián is not my prisoner. He saved my life. He stepped in front of me to protect me from the arrows. And then when we fell into the river, I would have drowned without his help. Don't you see, Mother, that is why I couldn't let him die. That is why I brought him to you."

Mother stared at me for a long time. "You did the right thing," she said at last.

It was the first time, ever, that Mother had approved of me. I felt warm inside, and the pressure of tears built up behind my eyes. I pushed them back. "But Mother, if you tell Father that Don Julián is here, I have saved him for nothing. For my debt to him to be repaid, he must go back to his kingdom as a free man."

Mother frowned. "Princess Andrea, to let Don Julián go would be a terrible mistake. I don't think you understand how much he means to his people. Under his command, his men will die to the last, and the losses to our troops will be on our conscience. But if Don Julián remains our prisoner, with Don García's help the war will be over soon and the victory will be ours."

"Don García?" What had Don García, my sister Sabela's forbidden captain, to do with the war?

Mother nodded. "Yes, Don García. He is the one responsible for the attack on the bridge. A pigeon came this morning with a message for Princess Sabela. Apparently it was not the first. But this time she shared the news with me. According to the letter, Don García heard of the impending war and came from the east with his troops. He was spying on Don Julián's camp when he discovered the bridge. They attacked and destroyed it. Now he is on his way to join Don Andrés's army. The battle seems imminent."

Just as I was asking, "Did the letter mention whether Don Alfonso was among the dead?" the door into the next room opened, and my sister Margarida appeared in the doorway.

Mother, who had her back to the door and had not seen her yet, answered my question. "No, it didn't. Why do you ask, Princess?"

Margarida, her face as pale as the moon of my uncle's world, stumbled inside. Mother turned toward the noise.

"Don Julián is awake, Mother," Margarida said with a curtsy.

"Tell His Majesty I'm coming," Mother said, as if she were referring to a king. It took me a moment to realize this was actually the case.

Already at the door, she looked back at me. "Princess Andrea, we will finish this conversation later."

Letting out a sigh of relief, I fell back against the pillows. Mother had not sent the letter to Father yet. At least for the moment, Don Julián was safe.

I was almost finished with my toilette when I heard the door open. My hand still on the brush stuck in my tangled hair, I looked back from the mirror and saw Mother leaning on the threshold. Against the black of her dress, her face, usually unreadable, seemed weary to the point of exhaustion, and wrinkles I had never noticed had formed around her eyes. I frowned. But before I could ask the reason for her concern, her eyes met mine. Immediately her back straightened, and her face hardened once more into a mask.

"If you are ready, Princess Andrea, you must come with me."

I nodded and, dropping the brush, jumped to my feet.

Mother did not move. "Just a moment, Princess. There is

something I must tell you first. I know you didn't mean this to happen. But things don't always turn out the way we think they will. I want you to come and see, so you understand that your actions may have consequences you had not anticipated, and that for those, too, you will be held responsible. Come now, Princess, and see for yourself."

Her words wrapped around my shoulders like a cloak of impending doom, I followed Mother through the open door.

NINETEEN

The Time Reader

The room had been rearranged once more, and any signs of the morning's activity had been removed. To my right, Don Julián, his eyes closed, his face as pale as one of the marble statues carved on the tombstones that flank the chapel walls, was lying still under the gray woolen blanket. I shivered, and my feet, heavy with fear, refused to move further. But Mother, already at the king's side, motioned me forward.

I stumbled inside, barely breathing, while Mother bent over the bed and grabbed the sheet that hid the king's body. I closed my eyes, certain that she was about to pull it over his face. When I opened them again, the sheet was down at his waist and Mother was removing the bandage that wrapped his naked torso.

Don't, Mother! Please don't. I don't need to see. I know what I have done. Let him rest, I wanted to say. But my tongue was frozen and made no sound. Mother went on unwrapping until the entire bandage was in her hand, and the king's swollen open flesh came into view.

I moved back, averting my eyes from the wound. But Mother came over and, grabbing my arm, forced me forward. "Look!" she said in a hushed voice. "You must look and remember. This is what war is about. This is what men do to each other. You were too young to know. But I . . . I have seen too many young men, strong and healthy, leave and never come back. Dead in a battlefield for a stupid fight words could have solved. What a waste! But men don't learn. They care only about their honor. Then it is up to us women to fix the mess they have made."

It was then I saw the blood welling between the swollen lips of the gaping hole before streaming down the skin in a thin red line. My whole body aching with relief, I gasped. "He's alive."

Mother stared at me. "Of course he is alive, Princess. I have kept him alive as I promised you, even when I know that it is hopeless, that as soon as he can walk he will rush again to get himself killed. Because that is the way of men. That is why I don't want you to be a knight. Ever. I don't want you to end up like this." She paused for a moment, lost in thought. Then very softly, as if talking to herself, she continued, "As you may well have if . . ." Again her voice rose. "Princess, if you promise you will never leave the castle again, I will listen to your story. I guess I owe Don Julián that much for saving your life."

"I will, Mother. I will stay in the castle. I promise. I didn't want the war to happen, either. You see, Mother, the other day on the bridge, before the attack, we were trying to talk Don Julián into apologizing to Father. But—"

"Wait, Princess. Bring me some water first. I will dress his wound while we talk."

I rushed to the table, poured some water from the jug into a basin, and brought it to the bed. Mother dampened a clean cloth in the container and started to wash his wound. But as soon as she touched him, Don Julián moaned and raised his right arm to push Mother's hands away.

Mother moved back. "Would you hold him still, Princess?"

I walked to the other side of the bed and, trying hard not to look at the bloody opening, grabbed Don Julián's arm. Mother resumed her washing. "What do you mean by 'we'?" she asked as if there had been no interruption.

"Don Alfonso and I. Don Alfonso doesn't approve of this war either. He's willing to marry Margarida so our Houses will be united—"

"Princess Andrea, hold his arm please." Carried away by my speech, I had let go of Don Julián who, still unconscious, was again fighting Mother. Annoyed at being found at fault, I did as told, while Mother stared at me, her eyes lost in thought.

"Why would Don Julián accept your offer?" she finally asked, returning to her washing.

"Because he wants to go to the other world."

Mother's hands stopped in midair, and her body tightened. Then she turned, dropped the red-stained bandage on the floor, and grabbed a fresh one. "And Don Alfonso wants to marry Princess Margarida. Why?" she asked as she carefully dried the lips of the wound.

"I . . . I don't know."

Mother looked up and held my eyes with her bright blue ones until I felt myself blushing. "I see," she said. "And did Don Julián agree?"

"No, he didn't. But he didn't refuse, either. I mean, they attacked before we could ask him. But he will. I am sure that he will. Please, Mother, don't tell Father that Don Julián is here. Not yet. Not until I talk with him."

Mother did not answer. Carefully she wrapped a linen bandage around the wound. Then she covered Don Julián with the blanket, and after rearranging the pillows, she walked to the table. Pouring some water into another basin, she started to wash her hands.

"Princess Andrea," she told me as I joined her, "the most important thing now is that the wound doesn't open. That is why he must stay still. He will need constant supervision. You will take care of him during the day. Princess Margarida, your uncle, and I will take turns at night."

Walking back to the bed, she knelt by the trunk and opened it. When she turned back to me, she was holding two leather bags in her hands. "You have been to my world, Princess," she said, setting them on the table, "so you understand there is a high risk of infection in a wound. Luckily I have always kept some antibiotics even though it meant disobeying your father's direct order." Opening one of the purses, she showed me a white pill. "He must take one every six hours," she explained. Then she opened the other purse. The pills this time were red. "These are for the pain. Give them to him four or five times a day, or whenever you see he needs them. Of course don't ask, he will never admit to pain. Men!"

She said "Men" with such contempt that I smiled. Mother returned the smile, and taking my hands into hers, she looked into my eyes. "Why did you run away, Princess Andrea?"

"Because I wanted to stop the war."

"And before?"

"Because I don't fit in here, Mother. I belong in your world. Coming back with John was an accident. And when Rosa took him from me, I—"

Mother gasped. "Do you care for John, Princess?"

"Yes! No! I mean I did, but now . . ." Confused, I stopped. *John*, I thought, but his face was only a blur. *John,* my mind repeated, and there was no pain. Suddenly I felt free, totally free, the way a caterpillar must feel when it emerges from its cocoon and realizes it has wings. Elated in my newfound freedom, I promised myself I would never love again.

"I owe you an apology, Princess," Mother was saying. "I didn't realize you cared for him." In a lower voice as if talking to herself, she continued, "At the time, when John asked Don Andrés's permission to court Princess Rosa, it did seem the perfect solution to save John. And your father was so certain Don Julián only wanted to marry Rosa to get hold of our kingdom that I believed it, too. Only later, after Don Julián had declared war on us, did I question the reasons behind your father's decision. You see, Princess, when the war broke out, Don Andrés was thrilled, as if he had been expecting it all along, as if he had accepted John's proposal only to have an excuse to fight Don Julián."

"Excuses. That is what Don Alfonso thinks, too. He thinks men are always looking for excuses to fight."

"Then I suppose I will have something to discuss with Don Alfonso when he comes to marry Princess Margarida."

"Will you help me then, Mother? Will you let Don Julián go?"

Mother nodded. "But only if he agrees to talk with your father."

At her words, my feet started dancing. My manners forgotten, I threw my arms around her shoulders and hugged her wildly. "He will, Mother. I know he will."

Mother stroked my hair. "I hope you are right, Princess," she whispered, her body warm against mine. "I hope you are right."

But as she talked, I remembered the disdain in Don Julián's voice as he dismissed my offer of peace, the look of hate in his eyes as he condemned us to death, and a shiver of fear shot down my spine, shaking my confidence. Would Don Julián really give up revenge for a world he had never seen, or was I fooling myself again with false hopes?

THREE DAYS LATER, I WAS STILL WONDERING. BUT AFTER SO MANY hours of watching Don Julián drifting in and out of consciousness and talking in his delirium with people who were not there, I had almost lost hope that he would ever recover. Then on the morning of that third day, he asked, "May I have a word with you, Princess?" Looking up, I saw him staring at me with his dark feverish eyes, and my heart started racing and my mind went blank.

The next thing I remembered, I was on my feet, my legs trembling under the skirts of my gown, my head bent into a low curtsy, and my voice, strange and foreign, saying, "As you wish, Your Majesty."

Turning toward the window, I rested the bed linen I had been cutting into bandages on the window seat. Bright red over white, a drop of blood was rolling over the folded cloth. Only then I felt the pain, a sharp pain in my finger where the scissors had dug into my flesh. Without thinking, I took it to my lips to stop the bleeding and rushed toward the bed. The salty taste of blood was still in my mouth when I reached the king's side.

"Doña Jimena has explained to me my present situation," Don Julián said. "I understand that I owe my life to you. I am most grateful, Princess."

"You are welcome, Sire. But it is I who must thank you, as you saved mine first."

Don Julián frowned.

"On the bridge, Sire. You protected me from the arrows."

"Oh that," he said, his eyes staring blankly into the distance. "That was indeed an irresponsible act, abandoning my men in battle."

Although I had not expected that saving my life would be his first priority, I found his abruptness annoying. "Whether you meant it or not, Sire, you saved my life," I told him sharply, and my anger must have shown in my voice because Don Julián looked up at me, and his puzzled expression quickly changed to embarrassment.

"I apologize, Princess. I didn't mean it that way. As you probably know by now, I am not good with words. Don't get me wrong. I am glad you are alive, but I was not expecting to get an arrow in me. I just forgot I was not wearing my mail. So please do not feel you owe me anything."

He smiled at me then, and although I wasn't sure whether he meant what he had said or was just humoring me, I smiled back.

"Are we at peace now, Princess?"

"Yes, Sire."

Thinking the conversation was over, I was going to return to my seat, when I remembered my mother's instructions. I walked to the table then, and with my back to the king to conceal the pills, I smashed one of each in the bottom of a metal cup; after adding some water, I offered them to him. Don Julián thanked me and lifted the cup to his lips. His hand was shaking so badly that water splashed all over the covers.

"Please, Sire, let me help."

Without arguing, Don Julián surrendered the cup to me and, his eyes searching mine without shame, he drank.

I was helping him to lie back when the sleeve of my dress

slid to my elbow and momentarily uncovered my wrist. There, perfectly visible, my watch was reflecting the sun's rays. With a sharp movement of my arm, I pulled the sleeve down. But it was too late. The look of amazement in Don Julián's eyes left me no doubt. He had seen it. He extended his right hand. "May I have a look?"

There was such eagerness in his voice that, before I could think of any excuse, I had taken off my watch and was handing it to him. "It is a time reader," I told him, as if that would explain everything.

Don Julián examined the watch for a long time. "It is from the other world," he said at last, and it was not a question. A light of wonder I had never seen burned in his eyes, making him look extremely young and vulnerable.

"Have you been there, Princess? Have you found the door?"

"Yes, Sire. I . . ." I hesitated. Mother had ordered me not to disturb him. She had explicitly forbidden me to tell him about my plan, insisting that Don Julián was not strong enough to reach a clear decision. On the other hand, I intuitively felt that right then, caught in his intense desire to go to the other world, Don Julián might be susceptible to my offer. Hastily I continued, "Sire, the other day at the bridge, I was going to tell you about the other world, to tell you that you could go there if you agree to stop the war."

"I see. My honor for my dream. A tempting offer, Princess. A very clever one indeed."

"Do you agree then? Are you willing to negotiate with Father?"

Don Julián shook his head. "Don't you think, Princess, that now it is a little too late? Why should Don Andrés accept any demands from me when I am his prisoner?"

"But you are not his prisoner!"

Don Julián eyed me suspiciously. "Princess, I am in your father's castle. I cannot move without your help. And judging from Doña Jimena's description of my wound, I will probably die anyway. What—"

"But, Sire, Father doesn't know you are here. If you agree to settle your dispute with him without fighting, you are free to go back to your kingdom."

Don Julián sat up, his eyes bearing into me with such intensity that I blushed. "Would you let me go, Princess? Why?"

"Because I want this war to end. And having you meet with Father and sign a peace agreement is the only way."

For a moment Don Julián remained silent, then he shook his head. "I cannot do that, Princess. As much as I would like to go to the other world, I am the king. I cannot leave my people with Don Andrés knowing of my absence. What would stop him from taking my kingdom while I am gone?"

"You would have his word, Sire."

Don Julián said nothing.

Suddenly I remembered. "Would you trust my father, Sire, if our Houses were united by marriage?"

Don Julián looked up. "Marriage? I told you before, Princess, I do not want to marry your sister. Besides, even if I agreed, Don Andrés would never consent. He believes I was trying to get his kingdom by marrying Princess Rosa."

"Weren't you?" A flash of anger crossed his eyes, but still he said nothing. "Anyway, Sire, I was not talking about you, but Don Alfonso."

Grabbing the covers with his right hand, Don Julián bent forward. "You will marry Don Alfonso?" he said, and as he spoke all blood seemed to drain from his face. "That would be perfect. You are only the fourth daughter. Your husband could not have any realistic claim on Don Andrés's kingdom. It would be a good bargain for your father—"

It was then that, to my eternal shame, I hit him in the face with all the strength of my wrath. I hit a defenseless man who had saved my life, who was my only chance to stop the war, and who I had promised Mother to take care of. And as if that were not bad enough, as I moved back from the bed, horrified at what I had done, I saw my mother standing by the door watching me.

TWENTY

A Ghost from the Past

For a long interminable moment, Mother stared at me, her eyes full of contempt. Then without a word she moved to the bed, and as I retreated from her in shame, she bent over and grabbed Don Julián's wrist with her long ringed fingers. The king, I noticed, had fallen back from the force of my blow and was lying still against the pillows. I didn't have to get closer to know he was unconscious.

Finally Mother's shoulders relaxed. Letting go of Don Julián's hand, she turned to me and, in a low strained voice, ordered me to bring her a wet towel.

"This is useless," she said after pressing it against Don Julián's face for a while. "He needs ice."

But of course, we didn't have any ice here. Instead Mother asked me to crush some pills in a cup and mix them with water. Holding Don Julián's head gently on her left arm, she forced the liquid in his mouth. At last Don Julián stirred and opened his eyes. Mother shot a glance in my direction and, with a slight wave of her hand, ordered me out of the room.

Only too soon, Mother joined me. "Don Julián sleeps now," she said, and her voice was stern. "You must not disturb him. Is that clear?"

"Yes, Mother." Eyes averted, I waited for her to leave. But Mother wasn't finished with me yet.

"Don Julián has excused your behavior," she continued in the same harsh tone. "But I haven't. We both know, Princess, that in his present condition Don Julián could never have posed a threat to you. So pray tell me what happened. But do not expect my sympathy, Princess. Today you have shamed your family."

I knew Mother was right. I should not have hit Don Julián. She was also wrong. Don Julián had offended me first by dismissing me as the useless fourth daughter of my father. Too proud to admit either, I bit my lip until I tasted blood and said nothing.

Mother sighed. "All right, Princess. I cannot force you to speak. Still, I hold you responsible for your appalling behavior and order you to remain by Don Julián's side until he wakes up. And when he wakes up, you shall apologize to him."

I did not want to apologize to Don Julián. I did not want to see him ever again because I did not want to confront his stare. There was something very disturbing in the way he had looked at me just then, just before I hit him. But I couldn't tell Mother this, because I had no words for it. So instead I nodded and followed Mother back to Don Julián's room.

ALL AFTERNOON I WAITED BY THE KING'S BED, FEARING THE moment I'd have to speak to him and wishing it to be over. But Don Julián didn't wake up, and eventually my anger at him subsided.

Soon after sunset, Mother came back. "You are lucky, Princess," she said after examining him. "Don Julián is stable. But you are not excused. You will not leave his side until you get his pardon."

The room grew darker. From time to time, the king jerked his arms and moaned in his sleep. He had done this often before. But this time, I felt responsible. I felt it was my fault that he was hurting. Not knowing what else to do to assuage my guilt, I sat by his side and held his arms against the covers so he would not touch his wound.

I did not mean to fall asleep, but I think I did because when I opened my eyes again, I could see that the candle I had lit when Mother left was already half gone. Careful not to disturb him, I lifted my head from the bed to check on the king. Half-propped against the headboard, Don Julián was watching me.

Frozen in surprise, I stared at him, and he stared back at me with his dark insolent eyes that never yielded. Then he bent forward and, taking my right hand into his, raised it to his lips.

Still I did not move. I could not move. I could not talk, either. And I was glad it was dark in the room as I could feel my face burning.

Don Julián let go of my hand and lay back once more against the pillows. "I apologize, Princess, if I have offended you," he said, and his voice was clear but also sad—or was it tired? "It was not my intention. Your offer took me by surprise. But now that I have had time to reconsider, I see the wisdom of your proposal. I accept it. If you are still interested, Princess, I will write to Don Andrés in the morning."

I stared at him and still said nothing as thousands of questions tumbled over one another in my mind. Don Julián smiled, a sad smile that died on his lips. "Go now and get some rest, Princess."

"But . . . Mother . . . I mean, I am supposed to watch over you tonight until my sister comes."

"Do as I say, Princess. I have caused you enough distress already. And I wish to be alone."

I was not sure whether he was telling me to go out of kindness or of fear I'd lose my temper again. But as kings are supposed to be brave, I assumed the first and thanked him.

"By the way, Princess," he said, "I think it would be safer if a third party would be present tomorrow when I write. So it doesn't become too . . . personal?"

My face burning, I averted my eyes. Only when I reached the door did I gather enough courage to look back. Don Julián was staring at me in his usual shameless way. But the eyes that met my stare were not hard with pride, but dark with sorrow. And I knew that for once I had caught him unaware, and I had seen into his soul.

Wishing I hadn't, I turned again and left the room.

THE FOLLOWING MORNING, I OVERSLEPT. I WAS SUPPOSED TO TAKE over Don Julián's care from Margarida at sunrise, but the sun was already halfway up my window when I dragged myself out of bed. It was not until I saw my face in the mirror, black circles under my eyes, that I remembered the events of the previous evening and the incredible news that Don Julián had agreed to my plan. *Mother is going to be impressed*, I said to myself as I rushed through my toilette.

When I opened the door into Don Julián's room, Margarida was still there. Sitting by his side, she was quietly talking to him as she fed him from a bowl. Don Julián, his eyes intent on her face, was listening to her story and smiled from time to time. Margarida was talking about Don Alfonso, of how they had met at the Spring Ball.

"That is indeed a very romantic story," Don Julián said when she finished. Raising his eyes, he stared openly at me. "Don't you think so, Princess Andrea?"

He knew I was listening, I thought, blood rushing to my face. Muttering an awkward excuse for my previous silence, I stepped inside.

Margarida greeted me warmly. "Good morning, Andrea," she said, getting up. "I hope you don't mind, but I have been covering for you. Don Julián told me you didn't feel well last night, so I decided not to wake you up. Are you feeling better now?"

Trying to guess what else he had told her, I glanced at Don Julián. But his face was indecipherable. "Yes, I am better. Thank you for your help, Margarida."

"My pleasure."

Leaving the bowl on the floor, she bent toward Don Julián and pressed her palm against his forehead—the way Ama used to do to me when I was sick as a child and running a fever. Don Julián did not complain. And when Margarida offered him a cup, he did not try to take it from her, but drank from her hands as if he had done it all his life. Then he lay back against the pillows and closed his eyes.

When Margarida was finished, she came toward me. "Andrea, Don Julián has told me he has agreed to your plan and has asked me to bring him some paper and ink to write to Father. He was so insistent, I couldn't refuse. But I don't think it is a good idea . . ."

"Why not? You don't want to marry Don Alfonso?"

"No. I mean yes. It is not that, Andrea. What I mean is that Don Julián is not ready to meet with Father. He is too weak to leave the castle."

"I know, Margarida. But the meeting will not be for a couple of weeks. Don Julián will be all right by then."

Margarida sighed. "I hope you are right," she said and, after giving me a hug, turned to go. She was already at the door when I remembered Don Julián's request from the previous night.

"Margarida, please wait. Could you stay here while Don Julián writes to Father?"

Margarida shook her head. "I am sorry, sister, but if I don't go now, my dueña will get suspicious. I keep telling her I am with Mother, but one of these days she is going to check, and I will be in trouble. But if you want, I could ask Tío Ramiro. I am sure he will be glad to come."

I nodded. "Thank you, sister. You are the best."

After Margarida left, I asked Don Julián whether he needed anything. But he assured me that he was perfectly fine, that Princess Margarida had already dressed his wound, and that he was sure I had lots of things to attend to. Given my behavior of the previous day, I could not blame him for rejecting my help. Avoiding his eyes, I went to my usual place by the window and tried to look busy doing nothing.

It was with relief that I heard footsteps outside. I rushed to the door and let Tío Ramiro in. Tío didn't waste any time with me. After a brief greeting, he pushed me aside and walked up to the king.

"Your Majesty," he said as he knelt to him, "it will be an honor to serve you."

"The honor is mine," Don Julián said. His voice was again cold and reserved, the voice of the king. And when I looked at him, I realized he was not lying on the pillows anymore, but sitting against the headboard, his body tense with the effort, the knuckles of his hand white around the bedpost, and his eyes, dark and unreadable, intent on Tío's.

Tío Ramiro, his right knee still on the ground, returned his stare. "Before we proceed further, Sire, I owe you an apology."

"Apology accepted," Don Julián said. Then low, so low that I almost missed it, he added, "It has been a long time since that fateful day, Sir. Now, if we want to move forward, we must leave the past behind."

"That is a most generous offer, Your Majesty. But recent events seem to——"

"Silence!"

Sharp and cold like the northern wind, the word echoed against the bare walls, freezing the air in its wake.

"Princess Andrea. Don Ramiro and I have matters to discuss in private." The king had let go of the bedpost and, holding himself straight against the headboard, was staring at me with the distant arrogance of our first meeting. "I must ask you to leave now."

I gasped and felt a sharp pain in my chest, as if icicles were ripping my flesh. Pressing my hand against my ribs to ease the pain, I moved toward him.

"I will not go, Sire. I——"

Don Ramiro blocked my way. "Andrea, wait in the other room. No arguments."

Tears of frustration blurring my vision, I curtsied and left.

With angry strides, I paced the room—the room that had become my prison—and kicked the walls with my soft slippers that did nothing to mitigate the blows, yet I didn't feel any pain. After an indefinite time the door opened, and Tío came in. He was smiling.

"Andrea, would you come to Don Julián's room?" he asked, ignoring my furious demeanor. "I have to go now, and Don Julián must not be alone."

When I did not answer, he added, "It is done, Andrea. Don Julián has agreed to meet with your father to discuss the conditions for peace. But I'm afraid your father will need a lot of persuasion to believe the offer is genuine. That is why I have decided to deliver the letter in person and hope he will believe it was brought here to the castle to me because I am the arbitrator. Also, I must be the one to carry the answer back to Alvar so I can explain the situation to Don Alfonso and inform him of the place and time of Don Julián's return."

"Congratulations, Tío. I'm sure both of them will be overjoyed with the news."

"Andrea, what's the matter with you? Don Julián has accepted your plan. What more do you want?"

"An apology to begin with. An explanation perhaps. As you just said, Tío, it was my plan. Why couldn't I stay while you discussed it? Why did you dismiss me?"

"Andrea, please, grow up. Your plan has nothing to do with it. Don Julián was only trying to protect you when he asked you to leave." Turning brusquely, he closed the door behind him. "I know it's difficult for you to believe," he said coming toward me, "but the world didn't start the day you were born, and it doesn't revolve around you, either."

"And what exactly is that supposed to mean, Tío?"

"It means that you don't know all the facts. If you did, you would understand that Don Julián deserves your respect and not your hate."

"Why? Have you forgotten that Don Julián was the one who started the war? The one who made me a prisoner and sentenced me to death? Besides, I am not the only one with hate. Or haven't you noticed the look in Don Julián's eyes when you mention Father's name?"

Tío grabbed my arms. "Have you ever considered that Don Julián may have his reasons?"

"I don't care about his reasons. I've seen his actions. And as far as I am concerned, he's guilty."

Tío's grip on my arms tightened. "Andrea, please stop yelling and listen for a second." His face almost touching mine, he whispered, "Your father killed Don Julián's father. He stabbed him through the heart as Don Julián watched."

By the time I opened my eyes again, I was lying on the floor. Tío Ramiro was throwing water at my face.

"Easy, Andrea, easy," Tío Ramiro was saying, while around me the room continued to spin.

"What happened?"

His hands firm on mine, Tío helped me to sit up. "I'm sorry. I didn't mean to be so brusque."

"Brusque?"

Tío kneeled by my side and stared deep into my eyes. "About your father."

At his words, the fog lifted from my mind and I remembered. "Tell me it isn't true, Tío, what you said before about Father."

"Yes, Andrea. It is true."

I reached forward and, grabbing his arm, pulled myself up. "But it was in battle," I said, fighting the nausea crawling inside me. "It was in battle, so he had to . . . do it."

Tío shook his head. "No. It was not in battle." Again the room started spinning.

I felt the pressure of his arms under mine and heard his voice, merely a whisper in my head. "Come sit by the window. I will tell you how it happened."

Too distraught to argue, I let Tío help me to the window seat. Keeping my head down on my knees, I closed my eyes as the familiar voice with the foreign inflection of a distant world told the story Don Julián had tried to keep from me.

"Eight years ago, your kingdom and Don Julián's were on the verge of war over the lands of the upper river. To avoid the confrontation, Don Luis, Don Julián's father, challenged Don Andrés to hand-to-hand combat to decide to whom the lands should belong. Your father agreed.

"It was a long and even match, but finally your father lost his balance and fell on his back. Immediately Don Luis's blade was on his chest. For an indefinite time, they eyed each other in silence. Then Don Luis jerked his arm, and after briefly marking your father's cheek with his sword, he moved away, pardoning your father's life. But your father, blood dripping down his face, jumped to his feet and challenged Don Luis once more. Before Don Luis could do anything to protect himself, your father thrust his sword through his enemy's heart.

"From the circle of knights, Don Julián rushed to his father. By the time he reached him, Don Luis was already dead. Don Julián closed his father's eyes and laid him on the ground. Then taking the sword from the king's hands, he challenged Don Andrés to the death."

I looked up. Tío Ramiro was standing by the window, his eyes lost in the distance. "Tío?"

Tío Ramiro turned and stared at me with his pale blue eyes, the eyes of my mother and Kelsey, the eyes of my sister Rosa. "Yes?" he said, and I shivered because the anger was gone from his eyes, the truth of the story written in them. "But Tío, how can you be so sure that was the way it happened?"

Tío smiled, a sad smile that died on his lips before reaching his eyes. "Because I was there, Andrea. I was the arbitrator, the one who refused Don Julián his revenge. I ruled that the challenge had already been fulfilled and granted your father the lands in dispute. It was a difficult decision. A decision that has haunted me all these years. But in good conscience I could not have done otherwise, because although Don Julián was right, I couldn't let him fight."

"Why?"

"Because it would not have been a fair match. Don Julián was only twelve years old."

"That's why he attacked our kingdom and took the lands back five years ago," I whispered when I found my voice.

Tío nodded. "Exactly." Holding my head in his hands, he forced me to look into his eyes. "There has been enough blood between your Houses already, Andrea. The hate must stop." Dropping his arms, he walked away.

I stayed still, thinking of nothing and of everything, overwhelmed by feelings I could not understand. On the floor, concentric circles around the knots in the wood, like the open wings of butterflies, were looking at me as if asking my permission to fly. When I looked up again, Tío Ramiro was gone.

Dragging my feet on the boards, I went back to the king's room. Don Julián, his eyes closed, lay against the pillows. Glad I didn't have to talk with him, I approached his bed. But my relief soon turned to concern when I noticed how irregular his breathing was. I didn't have to touch him to know that, once more, he was burning with fever.

I stared at him for a moment, wishing for Mother to come. But it was still morning, and Mother was busy attending to her duties and would not be back until evening. I shrugged. Mother had taught me what to do.

I took a deep breath and walked to the table. Soon I was back by the bed with clean linens and a basin full of water. Tossing one of them into the basin, I twisted it until no more water dripped through my fingers and raised it to his forehead. But the moment I touched him, Don Julián opened his eyes and, pushing my hands away, pulled himself up. Looking through me with an empty stare, he whispered in a harsh hollow voice, "Father, I will avenge you, I promise," before falling back against the pillows.

I dropped the linen and jumped to my feet in such haste, I bumped against the basin and splashed water all over my skirts. Ignoring the water, I ran to the door. I had to talk to Tío Ramiro before he left the castle. I had to warn him that Don Julián had lied to us, that his heart was set on revenge. My hand already on the knob, I stopped. As soon as I opened that door, all chance of peace would be lost. Was I ready to give everything up? But, I argued in my mind, if I let Don Julián go, he would surely kill Father. Hesitant, I looked back. Don Julián was shaking so badly now, his bed was moving. How could I be certain under these circumstances that his words had not been the product of his fever?

Don Julián was talking again. But this time his babbling made no sense. Suddenly he called my name. As if under a spell, I let go of the knob and walked back to him. Clearly visible on his face, the marks my fingers had left were turning purple. I blushed at the memory of my outburst, and bending down, I picked up the towel and held it to his face. Shaking his head from side to side, Don Julián tried to push me away with his right hand. He was surprisingly strong in his delirium and to hold him still required all my energy. Finally, after an exhausting struggle, his muscles relaxed and he stopped fighting.

For hours I remained by his side, helping him fight the fever while memories of the past days flashed through my mind. I remembered the light of wonder in his eyes as he played with my watch. I remembered the pull of his hand as he helped me to the plank in the river and the weight of his body on mine when he was hit by the arrow. And with the memories, my hate for him grew thinner in my heart.

Later in the evening, when his fever broke and his breathing became more regular, I left the king's side and walked to the window. Out there, somewhere beyond the castle walls, Tío Ramiro was already riding to meet with Father. It was too late to stop him now. But it did not matter anymore, as my mind was made up. Whatever the consequences of my decision, I would not turn Don Julián over to Father. So that night when Mother came, I told her only about the fever.

"The fever should have been gone by now," Mother said. "But of course, Don Julián should have rested today instead of playing war games."

"I am sorry, Mother."

"Sorry does not change anything, Princess. From now on, he is going to rest whether he wants to or not." And after forcing a couple of red pills into his mouth, she made me promise to do the same every time he regained consciousness.

THREE MORE DAYS PASSED THIS WAY, SLOWLY FOR ME, A PRISONER in my own castle. By the end of the first day, I had memorized every stone of the wall, every pattern on the wooden floor and beams on the ceiling. By the end of the second, I knew by heart the shape of every tree that covered the only mountain I could see from the window. By the third one, I had cut enough linen into bandages to last through a siege. I had also decided that my mother and I did not share the same taste in books. The ones she had brought me were impossibly boring.

The problem was, I had too much time to think, and my thoughts were not pleasant. Memories of the archers aiming their arrows of death, of bodies floating on the river, and of the sticky feeling of blood on my hands as I pushed Don Julián away kept coming back as soon as I let my guard down.

I felt trapped in this room, trapped like a deer held against the steep walls of a ridge at the end of a hunt, with the enemy king as my only company and he only half alive. I missed my freedom.

In the morning of the fourth day, just as I finished dressing his wound, Don Julián opened his eyes. For a moment he looked at me with a vacant stare that slowly became focused. "Princess Andrea," he said, his voice clear.

I curtsied to him. "Your Majesty."

Keeping my eyes on the floor, I moved to the table. Taking the cup with the medicine in my hands, I returned to his side and offered it to him.

Don Julián shook his head. "No, Princess. I don't want to be drugged again."

"But you have to drink this, Sire, so your wound doesn't get infected."

Don Julián frowned.

"The medicine is from the other world. It will protect you."

He drank it then without arguing. Once he was finished, I took another cup. "This one is for the fever."

Gently but firmly, Don Julián grabbed my arm. "I don't have a fever."

"You need to rest, Sire, and this will help you."

"I have had enough rest, Princess. Let me be alive now, at least for a while."

"But Mother said—"

"And you always do as your mother asks, don't you, Princess?"

His voice was even, but there was laughter in his eyes and something else I could not read. Averting my face from his impish stare, I returned the untouched cup to the table.

"Have you really been there, Princess? In the other world?"

The other world. His words echoed in my mind, and I was back there again. Back in California, visiting the missions with Tío, riding with Kelsey in her red convertible . . . Been there?

"Yes, Sire. I have been there."

Don Julián bent forward. "And is it—this other world—is it worth a kingdom?"

Again I nodded. "It is."

Don Julián smiled and said nothing. Sitting against the pillows, he stared at me, his dark eyes probing mine. And because he said nothing, I smiled back and told him about the house by the beach and the white pale moon. I told him about bicycles and cars, about computers and TVs, and about candles that never burn out. And about the classes and the library and the basketball games.

I talked for a long time until I realized the earnestness in his eyes was not only excitement, but fever. Worried that when Mother came, she would realize I had disobeyed her orders, I gave him his medicine. Then I walked to the window so he wouldn't see my pain as I remembered that for me, that world was closed forever because I had promised my mother I would never leave the castle if she helped Don Julián.

The following day, I taught Don Julián how to read the
time on my watch while I answered his questions. His enthusiasm was so contagious, I found myself swept away with it. I
forgot where I was and who he was, and I was happier than I
had been in a long time. Until he asked, "Why did you come
back, Princess?" and the spell was broken.

"It was an accident," I whispered as I remembered the last
day at the beach, the storm, the rain pouring over my head as
John and I ran toward the arch, and the shimmering of the air
as we crossed the door.

Don Julián was talking again. "Is the . . . accident in any
way related to your coming to my camp on your own?"

"Maybe."

"When I talked with you that day, Princess," Don Julián
continued, ignoring my discomfort, "you seemed to have a
personal reason to stop the war, as if you felt somehow responsible for it. But why? It was Don Juan and not you who took
my bride away—Oh, of course! Don Juan! Don Juan is from
the other world, isn't he, Princess?"

"Yes. I met John—Don Juan—in the other world. I
brought him here by mistake. I was going to take him back. I
just needed time for the door to open again. But you laughed
at me. You . . . you didn't want to listen. You just wanted an
excuse to fight."

Don Julián stared at me for a long time in silence. "I apologize, Princess," he said at last. "I didn't want to offend you,
then or now. I just didn't know . . ."

His eyes lost in the distance, he let the sentence trail off.
When he spoke again, his voice was strained and hollow, and
his words came in halting breaths as if he were forcing them
out of a place they didn't want to leave.

"Things are not simple, Princess, especially for a king. Preparing for war is very costly in both money and time. I wanted time to build the bridge, to design a dam. An alliance with your House seemed like the perfect solution. Besides, it is not true what I told you the first time we met. About not caring for your sister. The truth is, I really believed I loved Princess Rosa when I proposed to her. Your sister, Princess, is very beautiful and I . . . I had never been in love before."

I considered his words. Who was I to judge him? What did I know about love? Hadn't I cried my heart out only two weeks past when I had learned of John's engagement to Rosa? And right now, I couldn't even recall his face.

"Do you believe me, Princess?"

"Yes, Sire. I believe you." But as I was saying it, I remembered how his eyes had shone with hate the day we had met by the river, and I could not keep myself from asking, "But if you wanted peace, why were you so intent on killing Don Alfonso and me when you met us by the river?"

"Because if you were ever to escape and tell Don Andrés about the bridge, my plan would have failed. I couldn't let that happen, Princess. The future of my kingdom depended on it."

"And you would have killed your own brother?"

"My brother is one. My people, many."

I looked away.

"I'm not a monster, Princess. I do love my brother. But—"

"No, you don't. If you did, you would have found another way to solve your differences. That day I saw hate in your eyes. You would have enjoyed killing Don Alfonso. Killing him with your own hands."

Don Julián returned my stare, his eyes cold and hard like frozen rain, reflecting nothing. "You are right," he said, and his voice was firm now. "That day I did hate my brother. I hope, Princess, that you will never understand why."

Without a word, I turned my back on him and walked to the window. Shadows were crawling over the ramparts, and the mountains beyond were barely visible. Another day was coming to an end. Inside me something else was ending too. Something I couldn't name. A chance at peace? We had come full circle, Don Julián and I. And now we were enemies again.

THAT NIGHT I DREAMED OF THE BATTLE AGAIN. THIS TIME DON Alfonso was the one bleeding in my arms, while Don Julián, his sword red with blood, was looming over us laughing. I woke up in a cold sweat, the images gone, but the laughter was still there. It was coming from Don Julián's room.

Still half asleep, I left my bed. My bare feet silent on the naked boards, I rushed to the door and pulled it open. In the flickering light of the candles, I saw Margarida and Don Julián standing by the window. My sister was holding Don Julián by the waist, while his arm rested on her shoulders. They were laughing as she helped him to walk. Feeling like an intruder at a party to which I had not been invited, I closed the door and returned to my bed.

Disconnected details, like pieces of a puzzle, were coming together in my mind. I remembered how Don Julián would take food from Margarida and not from me. How relaxed he was around her. How only the previous day he had asked her for more pain pills when he thought I wasn't listening.

My back against the pillows, I closed my eyes. But how could I go to sleep hearing their muffled laughter coming through the door, their whisperings loud enough to grasp a word here and there, but not to understand a complete sentence?

Getting up once more, I walked to the window. Dark clouds heavy with rain were covering the sky, and the ramparts were only a shapeless shadow. Suddenly a lightning bolt cleaved the darkness, and as the rolling sound of thunder died in the distance, Don Julián's voice echoed in my mind: "I really believed I loved Princess Rosa when I proposed to her, because I had never been in love before." Was he trying to say that now he understood he had never loved Rosa because he was really in love with my sister Margarida?

As I considered the consequences of this possibility, my heart sank. If Don Julián were to ask for Margarida's hand in marriage, there would be no peace. I was certain Father would never agree to marry his daughter to the man who, he believed, only wanted his kingdom.

Don Julián's closeness to Margarida hurt me in another way too: It made me feel lonely in the immense castle that was my home, but where I felt like an invisible guest. It was true I had voluntarily agreed to stay in hiding so that Don Julián could return to his kingdom and stop the war. But after all my troubles, Don Julián was still my enemy, and now he was taking away from me the only sister I cared for.

Pressing my forehead against the glass, I looked outside. The storm was in full force, and angry gusts of wind were sending blankets of rain against the castle. Even through the closed window, I could feel the water running down my face.

"ANDREA, ANDREA! WAKE UP!" A VOICE WAS CALLING. IN MY dream, my sister Margarida was bending over me, shaking my shoulders.

"Margarida, what are you doing here?" I asked her, for in my dream it was still night.

"Mother wants to talk to you."

The storm had moved away, and through the window, Athos the golden moon was visible again in the dark sky. I shivered. It was cold in the room, and my nightgown of fine silk and lace wasn't helping. Pressing my hands against the windowsill, I tried to get up, but my legs were numb, and I would have fallen if Margarida hadn't held me by the arms. "Are you all right?"

No, I wasn't all right. I wasn't dreaming either. I shook my head. "I'm fine. Just cold."

"Take this." Margarida took off her cloak and wrapped it around my shoulders. "Let's go now, Andrea. Mother is waiting."

I thanked Margarida with a nod, and still shivering under the heavy woolen mantle, I followed her through the low door into the room that was Don Julián's. But when I crossed the threshold and in the golden light of Athos streaming through the window saw his bed empty against the wall, the old fear awakened in me. Don Julián had escaped. A sense of impending doom grew like a wave at sea and then broke and drew away, its energy spent, leaving me shaking. All I could feel was relief.

"Come in, Princess Andrea. We don't have much time."

By the table across the room, beyond the stream of light of the golden moon, I saw Mother, a mere shadow in the flickering flames of the candles. Although her eyes were turned toward me, her fingers were busy arranging small packages in a leather bag. Next to her and facing me, a soldier was sitting. But something was wrong. The soldier was sitting in the presence of the queen, and when our eyes met, he didn't avert his as soldiers are supposed to, but returned my stare with the arrogance of someone used to being obeyed.

I gasped and, caught by surprise, did nothing to conceal my hate. For a moment Don Julián stared at me, his eyes bright with fever, shadows dancing on his face. Then brusquely, he turned his head. It was the first time he had ever averted his eyes from mine. I followed his gaze and my smile disappeared. The door to the corridor had silently opened, and the shape of a man materialized from its shadows.

"Tío Ramiro," I yelped, rushing to him, "Why are you back so soon? Has Father refused to meet with Don Julián?"

Mother moved toward me. "Princess Andrea, would you please calm down and listen? I'm afraid our plans have changed."

TWENTY-TWO

Upriver

"Don Andrés has agreed to talk to Don Julián," Mother explained. "But he has set the meeting for three days' time. If Don Julián is to attend, he must leave immediately. You, Princess, with Don Ramiro's help, will take him across the river to his kingdom as planned. The problem is that Don Alfonso will not be at the other shore to welcome him."

"Has he refused to collaborate?"

"No, Andrea." Tío Ramiro, who had been paying his respects to Don Julián, got up and moved toward us. "I came back as soon as I learned of the new date to make sure Don Julián could be at the meeting on time. I didn't have time to cross the river and meet with Don Alfonso. So he doesn't know Don Julián is with us, nor that he's the one who has called the meeting."

Mother nodded. "If we want our plan to succeed, Princess, we must find another way to alert Don Alfonso of Don Julián's coming so he can arrange his safe transport to the rendezvous place. Don Julián is in no condition to walk to Don Alfonso's camp."

"I will do it, Mother. I will get to Don Alfonso and give him the message."

Mother smiled, her eyes bright with pride, and my heart filled with joy at her approval. But before she could answer, the voice of the king, harsh like the roll of thunder, echoed against the stone walls. "I appreciate your offer, Princess, but I cannot accept it. I am certain my brother has no warm feelings for you at present, and your life will be forfeited as soon as you enter my kingdom."

Mother looked back. "And why, my lord, would that be?" she asked, her voice a mere whisper over the rush of her skirts.

"Your Majesty, from my brother's point of view, Princess Andrea betrayed us on the bridge. I am certain his orders will be to kill her on sight."

Now that was a stupid assumption if I ever heard one. "And why in all the kingdom would he think that?"

Don Julián stared at me, his dark fierce eyes ablaze with cold fire. "Because your behavior at the bridge, Princess, is suspicious to say the least. As soon as you discovered the bridge, your men attacked, and in the confusion that followed, you disappeared."

"If that is what you think, Sire, fine. You can walk all the way to the bridge for all I care."

Mother stepped in front of me. "That is enough, Princess!"

I recoiled against the wall, angry tears welling in my eyes at Mother's words, while Mother, switching without pause from her imperious maternal tone to her official manners, faced Don Julián. "I apologize for Princess Andrea's manners, Your Majesty. But I'm afraid you must accept her company even longer than I thought. I understand your concern about Andrea as Don Alfonso could well have drawn the wrong conclusion, and I agree she should not go alone to meet your brother. So I believe the only solution is that Princess Andrea and Don Ramiro remain with you until you reach your brother."

"With all due respect, Your Ladyship, I disagree. Princess Andrea must not come."

But Mother's mind was made up. "I'm sorry, Sire, but that is not negotiable." Before Don Julián could argue, she was back at my side. "Now, Princess, you must tell us the best way to leave the castle and get to the river without alerting the guard."

I shrugged. "And why should I know that?"

"Princess Andrea. You have been getting in and out of the castle whenever you felt like it for the past ten years. Please don't play the innocent with me now. Answer my question."

I shook my head. "Really, Mother, I don't know. We cannot climb the walls. I mean . . . Don Julián can't." Suddenly I stopped. I couldn't tell Mother my secret escape route. If I did so, she would make sure I would be stuck in the castle forever. Out of the corner of my eye, I could see Don Julián. Dressed as he was in soldier's clothing—blue pants and a blue tunic with the white stripe of our kingdom—and a smile dancing on his lips at my blunder, he could have been one of us. One of us! That was it. I looked up. "Mother, we could leave through the front gates as Don Ramiro's escorts."

For a moment Mother stared at me, her eyes deep in thought. "It is a good idea," she finally said. "I will give you a letter with the royal seal, granting you permission to leave the castle in case someone questions you. Now go to your room and get ready. Princess Margarida will bring you a soldier's uniform."

"Will you be careful, Andrea?" Margarida asked me later as she braided my hair.

"You know I'm always careful."

Margarida didn't laugh. "I mean it, Andrea. This is not a game. Don Julián . . ." Her fingers faltered for a moment before reprising the rhythm of the weaving. "Don Julián must meet with Father successfully or there will be war."

I could hear the concern in her voice, but whether her fear was for me or Don Julián, I couldn't tell. The taste of doubt was bitter in my mouth.

My muscles tense with anger, I got up. "Don Julián will be fine, don't you worry. If need comes, I will protect him with my life." Yanking the helmet from the table, I swirled around. "And now if you will excuse me, I must go."

Her voice, an urgent whisper, reached me at the door. "Andrea, wait. You haven't changed yet."

I turned. Margarida, a startled look in her hazel eyes, was pointing at my clothes. I looked down, and when I saw my flimsy nightgown still clinging to my body, I started laughing. My sister smiled. "Really, Andrea, you'll never change." And then she was laughing, too.

But when, once dressed, I crossed the door into Don Julián's room, the smile froze on my face.

In the flickering light of the candles, I could see Don Julián, his broad shoulders resting back against the chair, his dark eyes intent on Tío Ramiro who, one knee on the ground in the pleading pose of a vassal, was presenting a quill to him. And as I looked, rooted in place by the fear that I was witnessing the unraveling of my plan, Don Julián took the quill and, bending slightly forward, started drawing at the bottom of the paper.

I watched him, mesmerized, trying to collect my thoughts. What was he signing? But before I could ask, the rasping sound of the feather nib against paper stopped. Without a word, Tío

Ramiro took the paper from the table, placing another one where the first had been. Again Don Julián signed. Tío Ramiro proceeded to seal the papers with dripping wax. Mother, who had been standing behind the king's chair, moved to his side and, raising her hands to his shoulder, asked softly, "If I may, Sire?"

Don Julián nodded. "If you please, my lady."

As soon as Mother had unbound the sling, Don Julián reached for the table and stamped the warm wax with the coat of arms of the House of Alvar engraved on the signet ring of the middle finger of his left hand.

Tío stepped forward and took the papers. Holding his left arm against his chest with his right hand, Don Julián leaned back against the chair and closed his eyes. Without a word, Mother wrapped the sling under the king's arm and tied it over his shoulder.

Brushing past me, Margarida walked into the room and headed toward the bed, covered now with the white piles of bandages and the dark shapes of leather bags. Her touch broke the spell that had paralyzed me in the threshold.

"Why another letter, Mother? Have Don Julián's requests to Father changed?"

Mother turned. "The letter, Princess, is no concern of yours."

As she talked, Don Julián bent forward. Shadows dancing on his face, pale as wax against his dark hair, he stared at me with a mixture of frustration and amusement. "The letter, Princess, doesn't change anything. It is just the written account of my conditions for peace that follow exactly on the lines of your proposal."

"And the second one?"

Don Julián smiled, but his eyes were dark. "The second one, Princess, is for my people. It names my brother Don

Alfonso as King of Suavia to avoid confrontations among my lords were I to die before reaching Don Andrés."

Mother nodded to the king. Then, her eyes on mine, she stepped toward me. "Don Julián has done so at my request, and I am most grateful. As you know, Princess, we cannot risk writing a letter to Don Alfonso explaining the situation. It could fall into Don Andrés's hands. So we just hope that a copy of Don Julián's conditions for peace and his resignation will be enough to keep you and Don Ramiro safe. At least Don Alfonso will understand that Don Julián was alive on today's date and willing to talk to Don Andrés. Don Andrés, on his part, will have to accept Don Alfonso as king and negotiate with him, if . . . necessary, because he is bound by his word to meet with the King of Suavia."

And Margarida will marry Don Alfonso, I thought, and a wave of relief swept over my body. Mother, misreading my smile, dragged me to the window. "Princess Andrea, I know you don't care for Don Julián, that for you he's only the enemy. But you must understand that from now on, it is your obligation to keep him alive, and if you do anything to jeopardize his safety, I will never consider you my daughter again. Have I made myself clear?"

"Yes, Mother."

Of course, I knew it was in my best interests to keep Don Julián alive, that if he died on the journey and his men were to find us with the body of their beloved king in our hands, they would probably kill us before we had time to explain. But the truth was, I did not believe for a moment that Don Julián's life was at risk. I was going to tell Mother that I found her concern for our safety deeply exaggerated, when I heard the dull metal-

lic sound of a latch against wood. I turned just in time to see
Tío Ramiro leaving.

I frowned.

"He will bring the horses to the garden," Mother answered
my silent question. "We will meet him there." Then she turned
to my sister. "Princess Margarida, would you please precede us
to make sure nobody is in the hall?"

Margarida grabbed the bags already packed on the bed. After
handing me one of the packs, she curtsied to Mother and again to
Don Julián and left. I was about to follow her when Mother called
after me, "Princess Andrea, where do you think you are going?"

What had I done now? But as I was soon to realize, this
time it was not what I had done, but what I had not done. I was
supposed to help her bring the king to the garden.

Of course Don Julián insisted he did not need help, but
Mother told him that if he did not cooperate, she would have
to sedate him, and then it would be more difficult for us to
drag him down the stairs. He finally gave in, and while Mother
held him by the waist, he put his right arm over my shoulder
and rose to his feet. His touch was surprisingly light, which
confirmed my belief that Mother's concern for him was exaggerated, until I realized Don Julián was leaning more heavily on
her. That did not make any sense, because I was on his right
side, and putting pressure on his left shoulder must have hurt
him. And I knew then that he was avoiding me on purpose, and
that my hard feelings for him were returned.

Thus we stole along the gloomy empty corridors and down
the stairs of the eastern tower of the keep until we reached the
door that led to the garden. Margarida sprang from the shadows as we reached the bottom and held the door open for us

into the dark moonless night that precedes dawn in my world when Lua is waning.

Once we were outside, Mother started toward one of the wooden benches barely visible along the main path, but Don Julián, letting go of my shoulders, moved back against the wall. Mother released her hold and looked up into the king's face the way she looks at me when I'm being stubborn.

Don Julián returned her stare. "My lady, before I take leave, I want to thank you for the faith you have shown in me."

For a brief moment, Mother smiled. "Your Majesty," she said, her voice a mere whisper, "I hope your freedom will bring peace to our kingdoms. But even if releasing you today means the river turns red with blood and my people curse my name as they fall under the swords of your men, I couldn't do differently."

I frowned. What was she talking about? Mother had helped Don Julián—quite reluctantly in fact, if I remembered cor- rectly—only because I had begged her to do so. Who was she trying to fool with her big words? But Mother, ignoring my puzzled stares, continued in the same tone. "When Princess Andrea brought you to the castle, Sire, I helped you only because it was my duty. But knowing you has given me hope that peace is still possible. It pains me immensely to see you leave before your life is . . . before it's time."

Could that be true? Did Mother really trust Don Julián? Apart from his frantic outburst when, still delirious, he had promised to avenge his father, Don Julián had not given us any reason to mistrust him. And yet . . .

To be alone with my thoughts, I moved away from the king toward the trees that flanked the path. The grass, still wet with rain, was soft under my feet, and the air had the musky smell of damp soil. As I walked, drops of water dripping from the

branches ran down my face, bringing to my lips the nearly forgotten taste of freedom.

Don Julián's words came to me as clearly as if he were standing by my side. "Doña Jimena, I am in debt to you forever. I owe
you my life, my freedom, and my kingdom. And on my honor, I
swear I will use all my power so you will not have to shed a single tear as a consequence of your present kindness."

And so all is well that ends well, I thought. Don Julián will
stop the war, and Father will let John go. And I had no choice
but to remain in my world because I had promised Mother. But
before I could dwell further on my gloomy future, Don Julián's
voice reached me again.

"Thank you for everything, Princess," he was saying. "I have
no words to express my gratitude to you. I do hope my brother knows how lucky he is."

I turned. Don Julián, a shadow against the wall, had bent
his head to kiss Margarida's hand. And although I could not see
their faces, their closeness was enough to make me sick. What
my sister answered to the king's advances I never knew, for the
clatter of hooves covered her words. By the time I returned to
their side, Tío was already there holding three horses by the
reins, and Don Julián and Margarida had parted.

"Be careful, Princess," Mother told me while Tío helped
Don Julián to his mount. "Follow the plan and for once, do not
get yourself in trouble."

"I won't, Mother, I promise." With a deep curtsy to her and
a hug to Margarida, I climbed on my horse and, wheeling it
around, followed Tío's toward the castle gate.

As I expected, the guards did not argue when Tío Ramiro
ordered them to lower the drawbridge for us, and without
delay we crossed the moat.

We galloped east, at first, to not raise suspicions. But as soon as the gateway disappeared in the darkness of the moonless night, we turned right and headed for the river. Stranded ashore on the muddy bank where I had left it, the boat awaited us. We dismounted then, and while I tethered the horses—so Margarida would find them in the morning—Tío helped Don Julián into the boat. I took off my boots and, after throwing them over the stern, entered the water—bitter cold against my ankles—and pushed the boat while Tío steered it into the stream. When the water reached my knees, I hauled myself over the stern, grabbed one of the oars, and started rowing.

It was harder than I remembered, because now the current was working against us. Even in the cool air of early dawn, my tunic was soon drenched in sweat. Things got only worse when the sun, crawling from its hiding place, hit the water with its breath of fire, and the humid heat of the summer day surrounded us like an oppressive blanket.

I was glad when, at high noon, Tío decided to stop. Hidden under the shadows of the alders and poplars that flanked the shore, we ate some bread and dried meat. Then we lay down at the bottom of the boat to rest. I wanted to take turns sleeping, but Don Julián, who had slept all morning, insisted he would watch over us. I resisted his offer. After all, he was our enemy. But Tío Ramiro, visibly upset by my remarks, ordered me to be quiet in not-so-friendly terms.

Despite my indignation at being addressed so rudely, I must have fallen asleep immediately, because the next thing I remembered was Tío calling my name. For a moment I imagined I was back in California in the little study in Tio's house, and I smiled. But Tío did not return my smile, and soon his stern look plus the dull aches all over my body brought me back to our gruesome reality: lost between two armies intent on destroying each other.

Upstream, over the eastern horizon, Athos the golden moon was already rising. *The sun will be setting soon*, I thought, sitting up. But the moment I moved, my muscles burst into flames of pain, and I had to bite my lips not to scream. Yearning for the impossible luxury of a shower, I was about to jump ashore when Tío called after me. "Andrea, before you go, would you mind giving Don Julián his medicine?"

I did mind, but knowing better than to argue with Tío, I dragged myself toward the stern, and taking two pills from the leather pouch where Mother had packed them, I dropped them into Don Julián's hand. Don Julián, undeterred by my brusque manners, smiled at me. "May I have some water, Princess?" he asked just as I turned to go.

I shook my head in disbelief. Why was he asking? The goatskins were closer to him than they were to me. And my body was so sore from rowing, that moving hurt as if needles were piercing my muscles. I was certain that right then he could not feel any worse than I did. Besides, if it had not been for him and his stupid pride, I would probably be in California, or at least riding Flecha over the meadows, not to mention that because of him Flecha was stranded in enemy country and I was stuck in this impossibly small boat. Before I could stop myself, I was yelling at him, "Why don't you get the water yourself?"

So intense was my anger, I forgot where I was and stamped my feet against the planks, sending the boat into a frantic rocking, which threw me against the hull. By the time I crawled back to my knees, Tío was helping Don Julián to drink, their silence screaming in my mind louder than any word could. I jumped into the shallow waters and climbed ashore.

Wading into the stream, I rejoiced in the coolness of the water. But the memory of my outburst kept playing back in my mind until it became painfully obvious to me that my behavior had indeed been childish. My anger spent, I was flooded with shame. But when I returned to the boat, ready to apologize to the king, Tío was dressing Don Julián's wound. Not wanting to interrupt, I moved to the prow. My back to them, I nibbled at some biscuits I found by the bench and bided my time.

"Andrea."

I turned. Tío Ramiro, a finger on his lips, was pointing at the rope that bound the boat to the shore. Behind him I could see Don Julián, eyes closed, wrapped once more under a blanket. No time now for apologies. I nodded to Tío, and eager to please him, I untied the boat. Then as fast as my stiff muscles allowed, I resumed my seat and, grabbing an oar in my blistered hands, started rowing.

But Tío Ramiro did not let me forget my blunder. "Andrea, your attitude toward Don Julián is intolerable," he said, his voice reminding me of the time long ago when I had sat for his lecture. "I thought we had reached an agreement, but obviously I was mistaken. I don't know why you think his being at your mercy gives you the right to humiliate him. Have you forgotten that the first duty that comes with power is respect? You may be a princess by birth, but that doesn't make you a lady. As for Don Julián, even under these demanding circumstances, he has proved again and again that he is a king, by birth and by action."

Downstream, along the western horizon, the last rays of the sun had dyed the sky in russet and purple shades. Yet not even the perfect beauty of the evening could stop Tío's nagging. "I don't think you understand that Don Julián is a brilliant man, not only as a king, but as an engineer as well. In this backward world of yours, what he was doing—building the bridge—is far advanced beyond what anybody else has ever done.

"I'm ashamed of you, Andrea. I'm sick of your hate. I'm sick of your father's stubbornness and of the barbarian ways of this world. I cannot wait to leave. But as it is, I am still here. And while I'm here, I will not tolerate your childish outbursts."

Childish outbursts. Right. How could he dare to judge me? He and Mother and even Margarida. Why were they all so intent on telling me how to behave toward Don Julián? Couldn't they at least remember that I was the one who had saved his life and give me credit for it?

Besides, if they really thought me so useless, why did I even bother to help them? I might as well jump into the river and disappear in the forest. That would teach them to appreciate me. I dropped the oar and seriously considered following my whim. And then, just as the boat veered to the right in response to my missed beat, a sudden burst of light—the glint of sun against metal—caught my eye. I gasped, and jerking my head back, I looked again.

"What is it, Andrea?"

"A soldier, Tío. Over there, on top of the hill."

Tío touched my elbow. "Let's go! He must not see us!"

Tío Ramiro was right. Although the white stripe on his blue tunic claimed the soldier as Father's man, he was as dangerous to our mission as one of Alvar's. My fingers tightened once more around the oar, I stroked the water and, under Tío's lead, rowed toward the shore.

TWENTY-THREE

Into Enemy Land

"What is he doing there?" I asked Tío Ramiro as soon as the branches of the trees had hidden us from the soldier.

"He's probably watching the bridge. From where he stands, he must have a clear view of the river beyond the upcoming bend. According to your report, that is where the bridge is."

The fact that my father had left sentries to make sure no one crossed over the river was less surprising than the fact that we had not considered that possibility.

I sulked. "What are we going to do now?"

"Haven't you heard anything I have been telling you? First we must wake Don Julián so he can join us in the discussion."

To prove to my uncle how unwanted his criticism was, I bent over the sleeping king and gently shook his shoulder. With the swiftness of a wild cat, Don Julián turned and pushed himself up on his right arm.

"Sire."

Don Julián looked up. For an indefinite moment he stared at me, his eyes dark and cold like mountain lakes, reflecting mine. Then as I was about to turn away, his pupils yielded under my gaze and he smiled.

Holding me aside, Tío kneeled by the king. "We must talk, Sire. The river is under surveillance."

"Don Andrés's men?"

"I'm afraid so. We just saw one up the hill, watching over the river. We cannot pass by him unnoticed."

"I see." Don Julián shifted his weight and rested his back against the side of the boat, his gaze lost in the distance.

"But we cannot go back," I said over Tío's shoulder. "We cannot cross the river farther down; it is much too wide. So we must get to the soldier and take him prisoner before he can alert Father."

Tío Ramiro rolled his eyes, "Would that be all, Andrea?"

"It is an excellent plan, Princess," Don Julián said, "if we knew for certain we are dealing with a solitary soldier. But as I don't believe that is the case, and we don't know where the others are—"

"But it is the only way. I—"

"It is out of the question," my uncle cut in. "I have never hit a man in my life, and I'm not going to start now."

Don Julián nodded. "As for me, Princess, I cannot fight either. Doña Jimena wouldn't approve."

"I will do it then," I said, getting up. But my uncle grabbed my arm and pulled me down.

"We appreciate your offer, Princess," Don Julián said, "but there may be another way."

Without letting go of my arm, Tío turned to him. "Your Majesty?"

"I was wondering whether you still have the letter Doña Jimena gave to us."

"Yes, Sire, I do. But the letter says—"

"What it says is irrelevant. We may safely assume the sentinels cannot read. You will read it to them."

Tío Ramiro frowned. "And it will say . . ."

"That Don Andrés orders them to join him at once. Of course, you will have to improvise some story about robbers stealing your horse to explain your unexpected arrival." Don Julián paused for a moment, and after glancing critically at Tío, he continued. "In your present condition, I don't think you will have any problem convincing them."

Tío laughed. "I guess you are right. I could certainly use a bath and new clothes. But at least I don't have a hole in my shoulder."

"Touché." Don Julián smiled. "Do you agree then?"

"I do, Sire. I think it's worth trying." Then turning to me, "Andrea, do you think you can take the boat to the other shore on your own?"

"No, she can't," Don Julián answered for me. "The current is strong in the middle. She will need my help to steer the boat."

"Then, Your Majesty, I cannot leave. Because if you row, Sire, your wound will open again and . . . what is the use of taking you to your men if you die before reaching them?"

Don Julián nodded. "Princess Andrea will row."

Tío got up and bowed to the king. "It would be a great honor to see you in my world, Sire."

"The honor will be mine," Don Julián said. And although he was sitting, he seemed to be looming high over my uncle.

"Remember that Don Julián is hurting, Andrea," Tío whispered in my ear as he hugged me. "So please take care of him. Let me be as proud of you as I've always been."

Without waiting for my answer, he jumped overboard and disappeared through the hanging branches of the weeping willows.

AFTER TÍO RAMIRO LEFT, I HAD THE STRANGE IMPRESSION THAT the boat had grown smaller or that the king had moved closer. I knew, of course, that nothing had changed. Except for the fact that now, without Tío between us, I had to deal with Don Julián directly and first of all apologize to him for my previous outburst. And I was not ready. To bide my time, I looked at the shore where the willows were still weeping under the golden light of Athos and then back to the river that touched both kingdoms. But finally, like iron is drawn to a magnet, my eyes returned to the king.

Don Julián, sitting still against the stern, was watching the shore with the deep concentration of a hound about to pounce on its prey. Except for his left arm folded at his chest and the sling under his elbow, nothing in him spoke of illness. And the doubt returned. Was he really hurting as Tío had said, or was he just being arrogant when he had asked me for water?

"Does your wound hurt, Sire?" I heard someone asking, and although I knew it had to be me, the voice was not mine.

Don Julián turned and stared at me. "Not at all, Princess," he said. "I just like the attention." But for a brief moment he had hesitated, and in spite of my desire to believe him, I knew he was lying.

"You must tell me the truth, Sire," the alien voice said.

Don Julián looked away, and for a while only the splatter of water against the hull filled the silence. Then just as I was about to apologize for my intrusion, he turned again to me and whispered, "Yes," as if it was the most difficult word he had ever said. "Yes, Princess. It does hurt."

"I'm . . . sorry."

"Do not be, Princess. I am used to it. Besides, I'm getting better."

"But when you take the pills, it does not hurt anymore, does it?"

Don Julián frowned. "Do we agree that this is the last question I will answer on the subject?"

I nodded.

"The truth, Princess, is that it hurts all the time. When I take the medicine, the pain becomes . . . tolerable." He paused for a moment and bent toward me. "But why do you want to know? Are you planning to get yourself an arrow?"

"No. I mean . . . It is just that . . . " I hesitated. I could not tell him I had asked because I was sick and tired of waiting on him, because I wasn't even sure it was the truth anymore.

"I do not know why you are asking, Princess. But I assure you, you must not worry about me. Tomorrow I will be with my men, and in two days I will meet with Don Andrés. Your plan will succeed."

"It is not only my plan I'm worried about."

Don Julián smiled. "Is it not? Are you sure you are not doing all this so your name will be sung by the troubadours as the beautiful princess who halted a great war?"

As I looked away to hide my smile, the clear neigh of a horse came from the shore, relieving me of the need to answer. Soon the beat of hooves followed. My uncle has done his part well. The soldiers were leaving. I moved to untie the boat.

"Princess," Don Julián's voice stopped me, "remember. We must wait."

He was right. It was I who had told them the path followed the river for a while before heading inland. And so we had agreed to wait to give Tío and the soldiers time to leave the shore. *Half an hour would do*, I said to myself, looking at my watch. Above the golden moon half visible at the left of the blue dial, the two hands were together, pointing up. It was midnight: time for Don Julián to take his medicine. I took two pills from one of the leather bags lying at my feet and offered them to him.

Don Julián did not move. He was looking at my hands, at my tanned hands covered with blisters. They were not the white soft hands of a coddled princess, I knew he was thinking. Not the hands of my sister Margarida and definitely not Rosa's. Ashamed, I pulled them back and, trying at least to hide my broken nails from his piercing stare, closed them tightly.

"You should take care of your blisters, Princess," Don Julián said, and although I looked for criticism in his voice, I could hear only concern. Bending forward, he opened my hand and took the white pill from it. This time he did not have to ask. Reaching down, I grabbed the goatskin and helped him to drink. Then I offered him the red pill.

Don Julián shook his head. "No, Princess. I would rather not have it now."

"But you said before—"

"When I take it, I cannot think straight. And we are not safe yet. I promise I will have one as soon as we get to the other side."

I was returning the pill to the pouch when Don Julián added casually, "Princess, if you don't mind, I think it would be safer if I carry them on me."

I thought for a moment. His request made sense. Nobody should see the pills because they were from my uncle's world. If given the chance, Don Julián's men would search the bags, but they wouldn't dare touch their king. In silence I handed the pouch to him. For a moment he held it in his right hand as if considering what to do. Then he looked at me. "I'm afraid, Princess, that I need your help," he said, pointing at his immobilized arm.

I nodded, and kneeling by his side, I tied the strings to his belt. My fingers were clumsy, and it took me forever to finish the knots, not only because my blisters hurt whenever they touched the leather, but also because being so close to Don Julián made me feel uneasy. Which was indeed strange after all the time we had spent together in the boat, not to mention the interminable days in the castle. But something was different now. My hate, I realized, was gone.

When I finished, Don Julián kissed my hand. Unable to hold his stare, I looked away. And as I did, my eyes rested on my watch. In a sudden impulse, I took it off and offered it to him. "You should keep the time reader, Sire, so you know when to take your medicine."

Don Julián didn't argue. "Thank you, Princess."

He stayed still while I hid it in his pouch. Then he moved back and leaned against the boat, his eyes on the shore.

I returned to my seat and, bending over the river, submerged my hands in the cool water. After I had rubbed some salve on the blisters and wrapped a bandage around them, I untied the boat. Fighting the tears that welled up in my eyes when I grabbed the oars, I steered the boat into the stream. Soon the hill where I had seen the soldier came again into view and glided away as the river took a sharp bend north.

The pain in my hands had faded to a dull ache, when Don Julián, who had been sitting still at my feet, jerked himself up. Holding to the stern with his right hand, his face tense with the effort, he was staring upriver with the lost look of a zombie. Under us the boat rocked.

I stopped my rowing and looked back. I recognized the place. It was from this very spot that I had taken a last glance at the battle the day Don García's men had attacked. Only the bridge remained. The shining stones that had taken my breath away the first time I had seen them had turned black with the smoke, and the wooden rail was gone. As I looked at the broken remains, a great sadness overcame me. Regardless of its purpose, the bridge had been a beautiful thing, and now it was gone.

Slowly, we reached the bridge and continued farther upriver. The bridge was only a dark speck in the distance when Don Julián told me it was time to cross. I nodded and, following his directions, steered the boat toward the distant shore of Alvar.

As Don Julián had predicted, the current got stronger midriver, and although I was rowing with all my might, we were drifting downstream. I was wishing Tío Ramiro were there when I heard a blunt noise under the hull. I knew we had hit a rock. Although it was not a big blow, it was so unexpected that I dropped the oars. The boat began swirling out of control.

Before I could react, Don Julián sprang to his feet. Pushing me aside, he took the oars and straightened the boat with skillful strokes. Then he motioned me back. Handing me one of the oars, he asked me to help him get the boat ashore.

I nodded, ashamed of my weakness, and resumed my rowing.

As soon as the hull touched bottom, Don Julián jumped into the shallow waters and tied the boat to the naked roots of an old poplar tree. Without looking back, he clambered up the steep slope and started walking upstream through the thick shrubbery flanking the river.

I scrambled to my feet and, tossing the bags over my shoulders, climbed after him. But the bags were heavy, the ground slippery, and I lost my footing and fell splattering into the mud. By the time I got up again, Don Julián was gone.

Dirty and angry, I dragged myself out of the mud and up the slope, following the trail Don Julián had left. At the beginning, the path—a narrow trail of trampled leaves and broken twigs—ran along the river, but after a short while, the bushes on my right thinned and the path bent inland. And when I turned as well, I found myself looking into a clearing, an open expanse of grass and heather glowing softly in the golden light of Athos. The king was nowhere in sight.

More surprised than worried, I glanced to the distant trees that closed the field, wondering if the king was already there. But Don Julián had not had enough time to reach the trees, unless he had run. And Don Julián could not run.

It was only then that the significance of the entire incident struck me. According to Mother, Don Julián was too weak to walk. Yet he had helped me to row. Something was wrong. Had he lied to us? But why? And where was he now?

In the middle of the opening, a rocky outcropping projected long shadows on the dense scrub. As I moved closer, I saw the dark figure of a man half-hidden behind one of the boulders. I ran to him as fast as my weary legs allowed, but the king didn't move.

"Are you all right, Sire?"

Don Julián turned. "You're dismissed, Princess."

"But, Sire—"

"As you have just demonstrated, Princess Andrea, you are of no help to me. In fact, your arrogance and inexperience will only jeopardize my mission. We are in my kingdom now, and you must obey my orders."

He had spoken with the authoritarian voice of our first encounters, reverting to the king I hated so much. Astounded at the virulence of his unexpected attack, I stared at him.

"Haven't I made myself clear, Princess?" Don Julián continued, his voice a cold whisper. "I refuse to suffer your contemptuous behavior any longer. I order you to leave."

At his words, from somewhere inside my fear, came the memory of the promise he had made when delirious in the castle, the promise to avenge his father. He had meant it. Don Julián had never intended to negotiate with Father. He had only used that claim as an excuse to get to his kingdom. And now that he had gotten his wish, he would turn on us. Blinded by rage and tears, I bit my tongue to stop my crying and ran away from him.

I ran across the heather, through the brushwood, and down the slippery slope into the water until I reached the boat and climbed inside. Only then, I saw the blood. Red rusty stains over the oar, on the seat, and on the floor, a dark cloud of insects gorging on it. For a moment I just stared, my mind refusing to understand. Then, as the now familiar scent hit my nostrils, a wave of nausea overcame me, and bending over the river, I was sick. And when there was nothing left in my stomach, I climbed to the shore again and started back toward the opening. Excuses were over. Neither my hate for the king nor his disdain for me would change the fact that if I left him now, I would be as responsible for his death as if I had killed him myself.

I found Don Julián sitting under the boulder where I had last seen him. I noticed he had taken his shirt off and was trying to cut the bandage with a knife. Both the knife and his hand were red with blood. Strain and frustration showing on his face, he was biting his lower lip so hard that it was bleeding.

I curtsied to him, still afraid of his anger, and pretending a confidence I did not feel, I asked, "May I help, Sire?" as if he had never insulted me, as if I had never left.

Don Julián dropped his knife, startled. He could not totally hide the pain in his eyes. Distressed by his silence and thinking that my losing control of the boat was the reason for his contempt for me, I started to apologize. But Don Julián did not let me finish. "It is I who has to apologize, Princess, for my clumsy attempt to make you leave. Although I did it so you would be safe, I hate myself for what I said."

"Then, Sire, you didn't mean it?"

"Of course not. But if you believed me, why did you come back?"

"The boat is covered in blood," I jested. "I didn't want to get dirty."

Don Julián smiled. "In that case it's better you don't get near me until I'm finished."

Ignoring his request, I knelt by his side and helped him undress his wound. When I realized that the blood was still coming, a wave of panic grew inside me.

"You shouldn't have rowed, Sire," I told him to cover my fears.

"You are probably right. But there are so many things I should not have done that one more does not make much of a difference." Then, as I pulled off the last of the bandages and the blood poured out like a stream from his shoulder, he fell back against the rock, unconscious.

I laid his body on the grass, and taking a linen cloth from the bag open at his feet, I pressed it against his wound. When it turned red, I grabbed another one and then another. Only after the bleeding stopped did I dare to look at the king. His pulse was irregular, but at least his breathing was steady. After taking two red pills from the pouch hanging from his belt, I smashed them in a cup, added some water, and forced them into his mouth. I washed his wound, wrapping a bandage tightly around his shoulder.

I dressed him with his own shirt, the one he had been wearing at the bridge. Now that we were in his kingdom, he did not need to pretend he was one of us. Once I was finished, I covered him with a blanket, and my back to the boulder, I stood watch.

DAWN WAS BREAKING OVER THE DISTANT TREES WHEN I WOKE UP. Don Julián, his eyes closed, was breathing slowly at my feet. Bending over him, I touched his forehead. It was burning. But when I checked his bandage, I saw with relief that it was only slightly stained. After forcing some water through his parched lips, I collected the dirty bandages and started for the river.

On my right, the sun crawled out of hiding. It was the last day before the meeting with Father. Don Julián was barely alive. In two days' time he would still not be well enough to talk with Father. My plan had failed.

Unless . . . My mind started racing. I still had the letter with the conditions for peace signed by Don Julián. All I had to do was to find Don Alfonso and give the letter to him. Then Don Alfonso would show it to Father, and my worries would be over. I jumped to my feet. Don Julián would know where to find Don Alfonso. I would ask him and then . . . But there was a big flaw in my plan: Don Julián could never make it to Don Alfonso's camp. He would bleed to death if I moved him now.

"I will have to go alone."

Startled by my voice, a couple of ducks looked up, their unblinking eyes searching the shore for danger, and then they went back to preening their feathers.

"I will have to go alone," I repeated. But the idea of leaving Don Julián sent a fear beyond reason into my heart. My back to the tree, I let myself slide to the ground. Above the steady sound of rushing water, I heard the cracking noise of a twig breaking, then the sound of wings taking flight. And as I turned, a familiar voice whispered in my ear. "Good morning, Princess. As always, it's a pleasure to see you."

Almost touching mine, Don Alfonso's face was looking down at me. Although his lips were drawn into a smile, the sharp point of his sword against my throat belied his words.

TWENTY-FOUR

The New King

"Where are your soldiers this time, Princess Andrea? Are they waiting for your signal to cross the river?" Always the gentleman, Don Alfonso's voice was firm and pleasant. But his eyes, cold with hate, were not asking. And by the pressure of his blade on my skin and the shadows of the men I could guess were behind him, I knew I was in no position to provoke him.

Don Alfonso moved back. "Why did you return? The truth, Princess, or your man will die."

"No!"

They had found him then. They had found their king but had not recognized him. Just my luck. If I did not stop them, these stupid soldiers would kill their own king and blame me for it.

Lunging to my feet, I turned toward the clearing where I had left Don Julián. But before I could move further, a black wall of Suavian soldiers had closed in on me. Again Don Alfonso's sword grazed my neck.

"Easy now or I'll kill you both," Don Alfonso said. I knew by his voice that he had moved to a place beyond reason, and he meant it.

Forcing the anger from my eyes, I stared at him. "You must listen first, Sir. Peace is still possible."

Don Alfonso laughed. "Peace? How do you dare talk of peace with the blood of my brother still on your hands? You should have thought about it before, Princess. Before your men killed my brother." His voice was cold now, tense like the string of a bow under an archer's hand. And just as dangerous. "Don Julián was a great man, and he died because of you. His death will forever divide our kingdoms."

"Last time we talked, Sir, you didn't have such a high opinion of your brother. Besides—"

Don Alfonso snarled. "You may well get the credit for my change of mind, Princess, if that makes you happy, as your treason was the cause."

"—Besides, Don Julián is not dead."

"You would say anything to save your life, wouldn't you? But this time it will not work."

His sword was cutting my skin, and as I tried to move away, my back hit the tree. There was no place to go. "Don Julián is alive," I repeated. "He's here with me." But the time for talk had passed. Don Alfonso moved his hand slightly, and the blade came down like a burning fire onto my chest.

"Let her go."

The king's voice, harsh like thunder, exploded in my head. And when it died, as suddenly as it had started, the pressure of the blade was gone. But not the pain.

Bright points flashing before my eyes, I reached for the front of my tunic, a warm and sticky liquid dripping through my fingers. "Do you believe me now?" I screamed, half-blind with pain and fear.

Don Alfonso, his handsome features frozen in hate, returned my stare unflinchingly. "Our conversation is not over, Princess," he said in a cold whisper. But I noticed with relief that his men were no longer pointing their arrows at me. As the surprise in their faces turned to awe, they dropped their weapons and kneeled to their king.

Over the bent heads of the men, Don Julián's eyes met mine and held them with the arrogant stare I had grown to know so well, but when he spoke, his words were for his brother. "Don Alfonso, bring Princess Andrea to me."

With the tip of his sword, Don Alfonso motioned me forward. I did not need the encouragement. I remembered all too clearly how the blood had poured from Don Julián's wound the previous night. I also knew what would happen to me if he collapsed before he could talk to his brother. Ignoring my own pain, I ran to the king's side.

Don Julián nodded at me. "Princess," he said and then turned to Don Alfonso. "You must listen to Princess Andrea. She will . . ."

I jumped forward, arms outstretched, and grabbed his body as he stumbled. His eyes closed, his breathing coming in halting gasps, he rested his head against my shoulder and moaned in pain as if he were beyond care. And once more, the cold of a metal blade was on me.

"Don Julián is wounded, Sir," I said without turning. "To kill me will not change anything."

The blade moved away. "What happened?" Don Alfonso asked. His hands, already bare, were helping to lay the king on the ground. Don Julián did not fight, but opened his eyes and whispered, "Do not harm her. It's an order."

Don Alfonso nodded, but before he could answer, a cry of alarm broke through the silence. Beyond the line of the trees, I saw the dark shapes of men. By the white stripes that flashed here and there across the shadows and the glint of the sun against metal, I knew they were soldiers. My father's soldiers.

Yet it could not be. Tío had said Father had agreed to suspend all hostilities until he had met with Don Julián. What were his men doing in Suavia then? Had he broken his word?

Certain that only a word of command lay between me and death, I waited for the arrows to come. Instead, an imperative voice called the soldiers to a halt. The imposing figure of my father moved forward, sword in hand, into the clearing.

"Don Julián!" he shouted. "You summoned me to your kingdom with the promise of peace. But you failed to mention that my daughter's life would be the price. You were wrong to assume I would let my love for her stand in the way of my duty. I will not negotiate with you under these circumstances. The truce is over, as your life will be before sunset today. But the life of your men will be spared if you return Princess Andrea to me."

I gasped at the absurdity of Father's assumption. Don Julián's voice, clear and steady, rang out. "Don Andrés, I hear in your words the fear for your daughter, and I excuse your anger. But your fear is misplaced. Princess Andrea is our guest, not our prisoner. She is free to go. And my offer for peace still stands. You are right to say my life is in your hands, but we both know that if you kill me today, our kingdoms will go to war and many more lives will be lost. I only ask that you meet with me. If my proposal fails to convince you, my life will still be yours."

"Agreed," Father said after a slight hesitation. "But first you must set my daughter free."

"That was always my intention," Don Julián replied. And turning to me, he ordered, "Leave us now, Princess Andrea. Don Andrés awaits." His voice, cold and impersonal, hit me like a slap in the face.

"No!" I shouted and the air felt thick in my lungs, as if I were breathing through mud.

Don Julián stared at me. "Goodbye, Princess," he whispered, softly now. But his eyes ablaze in his pale face were asking me to stay.

"Sire. I cannot go. Mother . . ."

The unfinished sentence trailed between us. Mother had ordered me to bring Don Julián safe to his men. And right now he was far from safe. I had to find a way to stay.

"You must go!"

A hand grabbed me from behind, and Don Alfonso's voice, tense and harsh, hissed in my ear, "Come on, Princess Andrea. Don Andrés is getting impatient. You must leave."

"I will take care of myself, Princess. I promise," Don Julián said, and as the shadow of a smile crossed his face, he added, "My brother will help."

"Goodbye, Your Majesty," I said with a deep curtsy.

"Goodbye, Princess. And . . . thank you."

I walked away, the ground swaying under my feet like the river had the night before, under the hull. As I passed by Don Julián's men, I could feel their eyes on me and hear the rushing of their feet as they got up, closing ranks to protect their king.

In front of me, across the clearing, Father was waiting. I knew that my case did not look good from his point of view.

Not only had I left the castle in time of war, but I had managed to be captured by the enemy as well. By the time I reached his side, my knees were trembling so violently, I hardly managed to kneel to him.

Without a word, Father helped me to get up and, drawing me closer to him, raised his hand to the front of my tunic. Blood remained on his fingers when he took them away. He looked at my clothes still covered with Don Julián's.

Pushing me aside, Father moved forward.

"Father! Wait!" I called after him. "It's not—"

But he wasn't listening.

"Don Julián!" he shouted. "You claim good will toward my daughter, and yet you have hurt her. Only a coward would do such a thing. To defend my honor, I challenge you to single combat until one party dies."

As he spoke, the wall of Suavian soldiers parted, and a figure dressed in black emerged through the opening. Raising his sword in formal salute, Don Alfonso stepped forward. "Don Andrés, your challenge has been heard and accepted." His voice, deep and firm, reached us across the opening. "To the death."

Father's hand moved to his sword. "The challenge was to the king," he said. And in his anger, the old scar on his right cheek started throbbing—the scar Don Alfonso's father had cut on his face so long ago.

Don Alfonso did not falter. "Your Majesty," he said, and there was confidence in his voice, "you are speaking to him." After returning his sword to his scabbard, he took a folded paper from his belt and handed it to a soldier who had materialized by his side.

I moved back as the man came forward with the paper in his hands and the night all around him. Father took the letter and started reading. But I couldn't hear his words, because in my head another voice was talking, the voice of another king. "The second one, Princess, is for my people," Don Julián had told me two nights past in the castle. "It names my brother Don Alfonso as king of Suavia to avoid confrontations among my lords, were I to die before reaching Don Andrés."

Inside me something broke into a thousand pieces, each of them hurting like a stabbing knife, and the pain was so intense I thought I would die. Barely able to stand, I stumbled toward the closest tree and, gasping for air, leaned against its rugged trunk.

I could still hear voices and see people moving, but they were just images and noises my brain could no longer process. Instead memories flew through me.

I saw Don Julián, his clothes red in blood, sentencing me to death.

I saw Mother's stern face as she announced, "If he dies, I will not recognize you as my daughter."

I saw Tío Ramiro standing by the arch. "Take care of him, Andrea," he was saying. "You are responsible for his life."

Suddenly I was on the boat again, and Don Julián was lying at my feet bleeding. Mother and Tío were looking at me from the bridge. I wanted to warn them that the bridge was on fire, but I had no voice. "You have failed, Andrea. Don Julián is dead," Mother was saying.

"No!" I shouted, but when I looked back at Don Julián to prove she was wrong, he was not there anymore. Instead I saw Mother and Tío sitting on velvet chairs.

"You have failed, Andrea," Mother repeated. "Don Julián is dead, and his death was in vain. You didn't stop the war."

"You should have tried harder," my uncle added.

At the sound of metal against metal, the images disappeared, and I found myself standing alone under the trees by the edge of the clearing. In front of me, inside the opening, the black soldiers from Suavia and the blue ones from our kingdom had come together into a circle. I noticed at once that they were unarmed.

Feeling strangely detached, as if somebody else were in charge of my actions, I moved toward the weapons the soldiers had placed into a pile, sampling the bows until I found one that fit my arm. A quiver with arrows slung on my back, I walked to the line of men and pushed my way into the circle.

In the middle of the field, two knights were fighting. The one in black was Don Alfonso. But his opponent, even though he was wearing the coat of arms of Montemaior embroidered on the white stripe of his long tunic, was not Father. He was taller, for one, and slimmer, and slightly awkward with the sword. A sinking feeling in my stomach told me it was John.

John who, letting out a cry of war, thrust his blade at Don Alfonso—and missed. Losing his balance, he fell on one knee while the king, ready to strike, jumped forward. With steady hands I raised my bow, and once again the arrow came alive in my hands. Then free like a bird, it flew through the air straight to its target: Don Alfonso's feet. The tip of his sword still on John's chest, Don Alfonso looked up, startled.

Another arrow already notched to the bow, I aimed again. This time at his heart.

TWENTY-FIVE

The Aftermath

"Father!" I called. "You promised to meet the King of Suavia. You cannot break your promise. Not because of me. Don Julián saved my life and was escorting me to you. Please, Father, tell Don Alfonso you are willing to talk. Tell him to stop fighting."

Out of the corner of my eye I saw Father, his hands open in the sign of peace, leave his place among his knights and enter the clearing. Blocking Don Alfonso's body with his own, he advanced toward me across the heather with long angry strides.

"I will listen to Don Alfonso, Princess Andrea. You have my word," he said as he reached my side, his eyes cold.

All my energy spent, I dropped my arms, fell to my knees, and surrendered my bow to him.

Father took it in his hands and summoned his men. "Escort Princess Andrea!" he ordered. Without another glance in my direction, he turned and started toward Don Alfonso.

Feeling exhausted and empty, as if all my strength had been in the bow Father had taken from me, I squatted on the ground. But even holding my head with my two hands, the world did not stop spinning.

"ANDREA!" A VOICE WAS CALLING.

I recognized the voice, the deep and mysterious voice that once had so unsettled me, and opened my eyes. I was under the branches of a poplar tree, its heart-shaped leaves swaying in changing patterns against the sky. Closer to me, so close I could see his light brown eyes that reminded me of honey, John was staring at me.

"John?" I tried to sit up. But as I moved, a sharp pain cut through my body. Looking down I saw a piece of cloth wrapped around my chest. I could not remember who had dressed my wound or when. But I did remember how I had gotten it—under Don Alfonso's sword. Don Alfonso the new king. And as the pain returned, that other pain I couldn't bear, my arm yielded under my weight and I fell back.

"Come on, Andrea! Get up!"

"Go away!"

"I'm afraid I can't. Your father wants to see you."

John was offering me his hand, the same hand I had wished so many times to hold in mine, but when I grabbed it, I did not feel any comfort.

"Don't make Don Andrés wait," he said as he pulled me to my feet. "You're in enough trouble already."

John started toward the path around the trees. "I told your guards to go," he said. "I wanted to have a word in private with you. About what you did before. I mean about your interrupting the duel. It was kind of annoying, really, as if you didn't trust my ability to win."

The truth is, I had no idea you were the one fighting when I set out to stop it, I wanted to say. But I said instead, "I'm sorry, John, but I've had enough excitement lately. Right now I'd rather have a little peace. And you see, if you had killed their king, the Suavian soldiers wouldn't be exactly in the right mood for peace talks."

"You've a point there," John agreed. "But it would have been neat to get my knighthood."

Knighthood! So that was why he had volunteered to fight in place of Father. It would have bothered me not so long ago to learn that my champion was more concerned with his knighthood than with my honor. But I had lost my innocence. I knew knights did not really fight for us ladies. If they did, they would have the courtesy of asking first whether we want their help.

"Actually," John was saying, "it might have looked like I was in trouble and, well, maybe I was. You see, for a moment I freaked out. So maybe it was just as well that you stopped the duel."

"You're welcome," I told him, knowing that this was as close to a thank you as I would ever get.

John looked back. "For what?"

I shrugged.

"Well, anyway, whatever your reasons, the truth is that your little number up on the field must have been pretty convincing. The war is over."

I did not feel relief at the news, nor joy. In fact I could not feel anything.

"Did Father sign the treaty?"

"Yes. Your father was so thrilled with Don Julián's resignation that he—"

"Resignation? What do you mean? Is Don Julián . . ." Rushing to him I grabbed his arm. "Please, John, tell me, was Don Julián at the meeting?"

John laughed. "Don Julián at the meeting? Of course not. But why do you ask, Andrea? You were with him. Don't you know he's dying?"

I stumbled back, while John, oblivious to my despair, continued. "You know, maybe you were right all along about me splitting. I guess I kind of miss my old life."

I suppose that under other circumstances I would have been delighted with the news, but as it happened, just then, we had reached the edge of the forest. Ahead of us, I could see the Suavian soldiers still gathered around the boulder, and all I could think was that I had to see Don Julián. Turning away from the path, I started walking across the undergrowth. I had not gone far when I felt a strong pull on my arms. "What are you doing, Andrea?" Holding me tight, John dragged me back to the trees.

Father, the scar on his right cheek clearly visible above his gray beard, was closing in on us. But this time, although he was as imposing a figure as ever, I was not scared of him. Nothing he could do to me now could be worse than the pain I was already feeling.

Father started right in on me as soon as John left, "I don't need to tell you that your challenging my authority in front of my men is an unforgettable act of insubordination. Were you one of them, I would have no choice but to sentence you to death today. Just be glad I didn't allow you to become a squire when you asked me to. As it is, you will return to Doña Jimena and remain with her until you marry. And any further attempt to leave the castle, and you will be held as a prisoner. Have I made myself clear, Princess?"

"Yes, Father."

Keeping my eyes on the grass so he could not see my total indifference, I curtsied to him.

"Come now, Princess. And don't forget that until we get to the castle you will be under my direct supervision."

I nodded. Not daring to steal a last glance toward the opening, I followed Father into the woods where the troops were waiting. Soon we were on our way.

EVEN IN MY SULKING MOOD, I COULD NOT HELP BUT NOTICE THAT the men were happy. A feeling of relief and excitement was in the air, in the way the knights and soldiers carried their arms and in the open way they laughed and addressed each other. Their happiness set me apart. The fact that I knew most of them by name did not make things any easier.

In front of me, Father was chattering with John. I knew John could not possibly follow his explanations—his Spanish could not have improved that much in the time I had been gone. But Father did not seem to mind.

"Don Julián's resignation is indeed good news for our kingdom," Father was saying. "What I don't understand is why Don Alfonso was so adamant about Don Julián being allowed to go to your world. Don Julián is not going anywhere if you ask me. The truth is, I was reluctant to give my consent. I even insisted on talking to him to get from his own lips the promise that he would abide by the treaty. But after I saw him, I did not argue anymore. Why bother? I doubt if he'll make it through the night."

His words hurt so much I could barely walk. But I swallowed my pain and kept my pace with them, while Father continued, "If he dies, I'm not going to grieve for him. You cannot imagine what a nightmare he has been for us all these years. Don Alfonso, on the other hand, is a gentleman. No problem there if we ever have to go to war again. Although I don't think we will. With Princess Margarida as his queen, we shall have a good grip on Suavia.

"By the way, Princess Andrea," he said, turning to me, "Do you think Princess Margarida will be upset about this marriage?" Father laughed. "Actually I wouldn't blame her if she would be. But she has no choice. She shall comply."

He laughed again, and his laughter became one with the sound of the water rushing through the ragged rocks I could see upstream, breaking the surface of the river with their sharp teeth.

Ahead of us the terrain rose into a steep slope of imposing boulders, and the trail veered right away from the river, winding itself around the mountain. A black line of Suavian soldiers came down the path carrying tents and supplies. I learned then that Don Alfonso had decided to camp by the river for the night. The contrast between the cheerfulness of our men and the serious faces of the Suavian soldiers was striking and did nothing to calm my fears.

We had just resumed our climbing when the dark clouds that had been gathering all afternoon finally broke, and the rain poured over us, turning the path to mud and slowing our advance. Aware that every step was taking me farther from Don Julián, my heart sank deeper and deeper into despair. I could not understand myself. My plan had worked, the war was over, and John was safe and willing to go back to California. And there I was, mourning for a man who only the week before had sentenced me to death. Victory, I discovered that day, can taste like tears.

A SMALL PARTY OF MEN WAS WAITING FOR US AT THE FORD. A MAN I recognized as Don García was coming toward us. He was wearing the white stripe of our kingdom across his brown tunic, which meant that Father had accepted him back into his service after his timely attack on the bridge.

With the wide swing of one more used to riding than walking, my sister Sabela's forbidden Captain darted through the heather-covered field that flanked the river and kneeled to Father. After a brief exchange between them, Father swung upon a horse, crossed the distance to the river, and entered the ford, with John close behind.

As the men dispersed around me to grab their mounts, Don García reappeared by my side, a horse in tow. With a bow, he offered me his free hand the way a courtier does to a lady. I took the horse because I had no choice, but his hand I ignored. I did not want anything from him. After all, it was his men who had wounded Don Julián at the bridge, he being the one who had given the orders for the attack. Already on the horse's back, I dug my heels into its flanks and headed for the river.

I had not been riding long when Don García caught up with me. Although it had stopped raining a while ago, my clothes were still damp and I was shivering. Without a word, Don García took off his cloak and offered it to me. Again I refused his offer.

"I don't blame you for being angry at us, Princess," he said, rewrapping his cloak around his shoulders. "To break the truce in a misplaced attempt at rescuing you was indeed a foolish act in which I had no part. In fact, from the beginning I was against Don Andrés's idea of following Don Alfonso."

I reined my horse in. "Following Don Alfonso?"

"Yes, Princess," Don García said and, wheeling around, faced me. "This morning when the scouts came to tell us that

Don Alfonso was leaving the camp with some of his men, Don Andrés suspected a trap and decided to follow him. I opposed his plan. I told him I trusted Don Julián completely. You see, Don Julián and I have known each other for many years. We trained together when we were children. I knew he would never break his word, but Don Andrés insisted and well, you know the rest. But believe me, I'm really glad the war is over."

Spurring his horse, he rode ahead, leaving me shaking and cold with no one to blame.

For the rest of the journey I rode alone, my thoughts swirling in my mind like autumn leaves in a gale. When we reached the encampment, Don García came over and led me to a small tent by the King's pavilion.

"I will bring you dry clothes and some food so you don't have to eat with us," he said as I stumbled inside. "I gather you would rather be alone."

He bowed to me after I thanked him. "Actually, Princess, it is I who must thank you. Your brave gesture has ended the war and made it possible for me to return to Montemaior."

"Are you coming back, Sir?"

"Yes, Princess. Don Andrés has decided to name Princess Sabela as his heiress and has agreed to our marriage."

It was only as I congratulated him that I realized I was really glad his exile was over. Don García had shown more concern and understanding for me these last few hours than either John or Father had during the entire ordeal.

Don García nodded. "By the way, Princess, there is something I don't understand. If Don Julián's men were escorting you to us, why didn't they provide you with clean clothes?"

I stared at him, my cheeks burning. But Don García only smiled and, without waiting for my answer, bowed to me and left.

Later, after I had changed into dry clothes and forced myself to eat, I lay down on the cot and tried to sleep. But as soon as I closed my eyes, the cold despair I had been fighting all day came back, tearing me apart.

I got up and peeked out of my tent. Farther down the lane, I could see a company of men gathered around a campfire, laughing and singing. How many times, back in my father's castle, had I watched them from the ramparts, yearning to join them? But this time their songs of heroic exploits and glorious battles spoke to me only of blood and pain. Disturbed by their careless merriment and my sorrow, I left my tent and walked away into the night.

TWENTY-SIX

The Making of a Lady

The morning found me by the river staring blankly at the distant shore that was now Don Alfonso's kingdom. I was trying to erase from my memory the vacant look in Don Julián's eyes as he had asked me to go, when a heavily accented voice called me out of my misery with a cheerful, "Good morning, Andrea."

"Tío Ramiro!" I cried. But at the memory of my failure to protect Don Julián, my voice died in my throat and I moved back.

"Come on, Andrea. You shouldn't let a little argument with your father upset you so," Tío said, misreading my hesitation. "I know it is not a pleasant experience, believe me. He was ready to courtmartial me yesterday when he learned I had taken the guards off the bridge without his permission. And by the way, I'm getting too old for these games. Next time Don Julián has a crazy idea like that, he'll have to pull it off all by himself."

"That's not funny, Tío. Don Julián is dead—or nearly so. Didn't Father tell you so?"

"Sure he did. But I know better—" He stopped in midsentence and, coming closer, held me by the shoulders. "What is it, Andrea? What happened?"

"It was my fault, Tío. I let him row. I lost control of the boat, and Don Julián had to help me row. When we reached the shore, his wound was reopened. Then Father came and I had to go."

Through my tears I saw Tio's face. His smile was gone, and a deep furrow had appeared between his eyebrows. "I see," he said.

"I didn't meant to, Tío. I really didn't."

"I know," he said, his voice gentler than I ever remembered it. "But that does not change the facts now, does it?"

I shook his arm. "Tío, we must go and help Don Julián. We are at peace now. We could go to Alvar. We have to."

Tío pried my fingers from his arm. "Sure, Andrea. We go to his castle, knock at the door, and say, 'Hello, we were just passing by, can we come in? And by the way, how is your wound?' Come on, Andrea, be reasonable."

Reasonable? Who was not being reasonable here? "You don't understand. Don Julián's wound is open. Without stitches, it will never heal."

Tío shook his head. "I do understand. I understand you feel guilty. But you must put things in perspective. There is nothing we can do for Don Julián now. And in the meantime, cheer up. We don't want your father to suspect something and start asking questions. I've told enough lies for the day."

"You! You! That's all you care about!"

"If your Father ever guessed we had Don Julián in his own castle and let him go, he'd have no mercy on us. Not even your mother would be safe from his wrath."

I moved away. Tío was right and yet . . . I felt the pressure of Tio's arms upon my shoulders. "Come on, Andrea. Let's go back. There is something I want you to see."

Farther ahead over the stream, letting out a piercing cry, a silver bird dove into the waters and flew away, a fish in its beak still twitching. Tío turned me around and looked deep into my eyes. "Trust me, Andrea. It'll make you feel better."

I very much doubted that, but if I were to return—and I had to, because I had given my word to Father—I would rather do it on my own before he could notice my absence and send his men after me. I was too stunned then to realize he had already done that—that my uncle's arrival had not been a coincidence. He was there following Father's orders to bring me back after the soldier assigned to watch over me had returned to the camp with news of my whereabouts.

But just then, I didn't know that. And when I looked up at Tío and asked him, "What do you want to show me?" I thought the choice was still mine.

"It's a surprise," my uncle said, gently pushing me away from the river, through the alder brush, and up the trail I had followed the previous night.

Soon the bright pennants of Father's army came into view, and the acrid smell of cooking fires and the sharp voices of men shouting orders reached us from the plateau of the campsite.

Tío dashed forward with long strides, but just as the trail started its steep ascent toward the encampment, he turned right. My heart leaped in my chest when I saw he was heading toward the enclosed field where the horses had been turned loose to graze.

We're riding back to Suavia after all, I thought. But before I could ask him, Tío stopped by the fence. "*Mira.* Look," he said, his voice almost drowned by the thunder-like noise of hundreds of hooves beating the turf.

For a moment I just stared, my gaze lost in the maze of horses that filled the enclosure, flashes of bay, tawny, and black-and-white bodies.

Tío pointed east. "By the oak tree."

I squinted my eyes, and against the brightness of the rising sun, I saw the slender shape of a horse, its golden mane flying in the breeze, already cantering forward. It was Flecha.

I gasped.

"Some soldiers found her downriver by the lower ford . . ."

I leaped over the fence and ran to her. It was not until I lost myself in her musky smell that I realized how much I had actually missed her.

LUA THE COPPER MOON WAS CLOSE TO ITS ZENITH WHEN, AFTER four days of riding, we finally glimpsed my Father's castle from the slopes of Mount Pindo.

"Easy, Flecha, easy." I drew her to a halt.

Sitting high on my saddle, I stared at the impressive fortress that I had once called home. But its view failed to reassure me. The castle did not feel like home to me now, but cold and foreign inside its mighty walls—the walls of a prison.

"Only three more days until the full moon," the familiar voice of my uncle whispered behind me.

Three more days for the door to open, I knew he was thinking, as it was the reason we had returned in such a hurry, leaving Don García behind in charge of dismissing the troops.

"I have had enough adventures," Tío had told Father. "I'm going back."

Father had agreed to return with him, apparently on my behalf. According to Tío, my father was worried about me and wanted to bring me under Mother's custody as soon as possible.

As for me, I did not care much one way or another. Still without news from Don Julián, I was torn inside with fear. Tío had labeled my feelings as guilt and had lectured me extensively about it. I had nodded to him, pretending to listen. But the pain had not gone away.

WE DID NOT SET UP CAMP THAT NIGHT, BUT PRESSED ON TOWARD the castle across plains bright as day in the soft light of the two moons—twin moons, we called them, in the days when Lua is waxing and rides the sky from dusk to dawn in the wake of her sister. And in the early hours of morning, we entered the courtyard. There, a cheerful crowd surrounded us, shouting greetings and blocking our advance.

Holding Flecha's bridle tight in my hands, I endured the excitement of the multitude with my best smile, but their joy found no echo in my heart.

Father addressed his people with a short speech of thanks and victory and then swung to the ground as the crowd parted to let him through. I jumped off my saddle and followed Father and his knights into the keep.

But when I entered the Great Hall and in the glittering light of hundreds of torches saw Mother dressed in gold sitting majestically on her throne, I froze. Mother had told me that if Don Julián were to die because of me, she would never recognize me as her daughter. For all I knew, Don Julián was dead by now, my negligence the cause. So when I reached her side, I stammered an awkward greeting from deep inside my throat and, averting my eyes, sank into a low curtsy.

"We are glad to have you back, Princess Andrea," Mother said, and her voice was warm. "Come and join us now. Your place by your sisters has been empty too long."

Just as I climbed up onto the dais of thrones, Father spoke. "Princess Andrea," he said, his voice so uncharacteristically gentle that I shivered, "I know these last weeks have been difficult for you and that you are exhausted. You have my leave. Go now and rest."

Not so long ago, I would have been offended by his paternalistic innuendo, but just then I was too distressed to feel anything but relief.

"Your wish is my command, Your Majesty," I said as was expected. And with a deep curtsy to both of them, I left the Hall.

IT WAS STRANGE TO BE BACK IN MY OWN ROOM, TO LOSE MYSELF IN Ama Bernarda's bosom and pretend I still needed her to take care of me. It was strange and familiar, like the memory of a pleasant dream.

I smiled at Ama, who was assessing me, her deep blue eyes bright with tears, her bony fingers probing my face, and said nothing. Finally Ama moved back and proceeded to strip off my soldier's uniform. But when she removed the linen bandage Tío had wrapped around my chest and saw the ugly cut under my neck where Don Alfonso had dug his sword, her cries broke into a wail.

I told her the wound was not deep and was almost healed by now, but Ama was too busy making up her own story—a long string of reproaches and accusations at the blood-thirsty tyrant, Don Julián, who had done such a terrible deed—and did not listen.

I moved away from her, and to escape the pain her words had awakened, I sank into the tub. The water was warm, and the smell of sandalwood, my favorite fragrance, almost sent me back to a time when to wear a dress for dinner was the worst of my worries.

My head underwater, I held my breath until my lungs were bursting. When I came out, Ama was still talking. "I cannot thank Don Alfonso enough for returning our dear princess to us," she was saying. "How could anyone want to hurt my dear child, I cannot understand. An evil mind Don Julián must have to kidnap you like that. But don't you worry, my princess, it is all over now. You see, now that Don Alfonso has forced him to resign, he cannot hurt you anymore."

I climbed out of the tub and grabbed the towel from the chair. Ama came after me. "I'm sorry, Princess. How insensitive of me to remind you of him. I promise I will never say his name again. As far as I am concerned, he is as good as dead. And grateful I am for it."

Still I said nothing. Ama shook her head and went on with her apologies while she helped me into my nightgown. Weary beyond endurance, I climbed into my bed and hid my head under the quilt.

That night, my nightmares returned. I dreamed again of blood all over my clothes and on the boat, of corpses floating down the river, of the bridge aflame.

Early the next morning, Mother came into my room. Before I had time to get up, she bent over my bed and took me in her arms. And because she had never done such a thing before, I knew how much she had worried about me. I also knew that she did not know.

I moved back from her. "Mother, there is something you must know—"

Mother raised her hand in a commanding plea for silence. "I do," she said in an even and clear voice—the Queen's voice. "Don Ramiro has told me what happened upriver."

"I didn't mean to."

"I understand, Princess. It was not your fault. Don Julián was not well enough to travel. His chances to reach his people were slim from the start. In fact, without your help, he would never have made it that far."

I frowned. Did she really mean that?

Mother grabbed my hands. "I'm proud of you, Princess Andrea. It took a lot of courage to go to Suavia and confront Don Alfonso and your father."

"But Mother, it was because I brought John into this world that the war started. And it was because of me that Don Julián was wounded on the bridge."

Mother took my face into her hands. "Stop blaming yourself! War existed before you were born, and it will long after your time in Xaren-Ra has passed. I don't know what would have happened without your interference. No one will ever know. But I do know nobody could have done more to help Don Julián."

I felt her eyes deep in mine, forcing her will into my mind, leaving a wave of peace in its wake. "Besides," she said, a faint smile on her lips, "brooding doesn't accomplish anything and will only make Don Andrés suspicious. So dry your tears, Princess, and come celebrate with us tonight. After all, it is thanks to you that the war is over."

Soon after Mother left, my sister Margarida came in. She was so radiant in her happiness, I felt ashamed of having ever suspected her of flirting with Don Julián. As far as Margarida was concerned, the world turned only for one reason: Don Alfonso.

Margarida helped me into my gown and then, as we had done so many times in the past when we did not want to be overheard, we went down to the orchard. Strolling under the apple trees, whose branches protected us from the heat of the sun, we discussed the recent events. Margarida asked me millions of questions about her beloved Don Alfonso. I tried to paint him as brave and dashing as she expected him to be, without stretching the truth too much.

We walked in silence for a while, the summer sun bright over our heads, my mind in shadows, until Margarida stopped. "Mother has told me about Don Julián," she said, her hazel eyes deep with sorrow. "I am really sorry, Andrea, that Don Julián didn't make it."

I jerked back, leaves and branches swirling before my eyes, the ground swaying under my feet, and a voice, a pressing voice in my ear holding me down. "Andrea, please, please, forgive me. I didn't mean it that way. I am sure Don Julián will get better." But when I looked into her face, her eyes avoided mine.

Wrapping her arms around my waist, Margarida pulled me to her, rocking me and gently stroking my hair. When I opened my eyes again, a tall figure was closing in on us. My vision blurred by tears, I didn't recognize him until, in a heavily accented Spanish, he greeted us. "*Buenos días*. Good day."

I wiped my eyes on my long sleeves, while Margarida curtsied to him. "*Buenos días, Don Juan*," she said. "We are honored by your presence."

John nodded, a faint smile on his lips at her obvious lie, but his eyes did not leave mine.

My sister took the hint. "I should be going now," she said and, after hugging me once more, turned to go.

John waited until Margarida was out of sight. Then his words, this time in English, came rushing forward in a long stream I could hardly follow. "Andrea, I'm going back to California. I've asked your father for permission to take Rosa with me. It wasn't easy, but finally he's given his consent. If she agrees."

I shrugged. "Congratulations." I wondered whether he knew that he had been Father's prisoner until Tío had pleaded for his freedom.

John shook his head. "Don't congratulate me, Andrea. Not yet, anyway. You see, the problem is Rosa doesn't want to come. That is why I'm here. I thought maybe you could tell her about California, how much you like it and all, so she will change her mind."

"I? But Rosa and I . . ." I did not finish. John was looking at me with such despair that I felt I had no choice. "All right. I'll talk with her. What do you want me to say?"

"You've been there, Andrea. You know what it's like. Just tell her the truth."

So that very morning I went searching for my sister Rosa—the same dear sister who had stolen my boyfriend—with the implausible mission of convincing her to go with him to my lost paradise. Most amazing still was the fact that I was not jealous of her. I could not even remember how it had felt to be jealous.

For two days, I told my sister about California and its wonders. But despite all my efforts, Rosa found the world I described dull and cold. Nothing that John or I said changed her mind.

On the third day, John and Rosa said their good-byes while I spied on them hidden behind a hedge in the garden. John cried a little and Rosa a lot. Between her tears, Rosa told her lover she would go to a convent, and that if he ever wanted to come back, she would be there waiting. Knowing my sister, I found it a little melodramatic. I had no doubt in my mind that she would be back with us in less than a month.

Later, when the sun had started to descend toward the ocean, I saw John and Tío Ramiro leave the castle. I knew that once I would have given anything to go with them, but I could not find my wish anymore. Somehow I was scared of my wishes. I had wished to go to my uncle's world and had brought war into my own. I had wished to date John, and I had almost gotten him killed. I had wished to be a warrior, and now I could not get rid of all the blood I had seen.

So this is what it means to grow up, I thought as they disappeared in the distance—to stop wishing. Without regret, I left my old hideout on the ramparts and went inside to my new life.

FOR MANY DAYS AFTER MY ARRIVAL IN THE CASTLE, I WAITED IN hope and fear for a messenger to bring news from Don Julián. But my waiting was in vain. Desperate to hear from him, I repeatedly asked Mother to send a courier to Alvar. Mother refused. "Don Andrés would become suspicious if we do, Princess Andrea," she explained. "If Don Julián is alive, he will escort Don Alfonso when he comes to be engaged to Princess Margarida in the fall. Until then, we can only wait."

Mother was right. As far as Father was concerned, Don Julián's well-being was of no importance now that he was not the king. Reluctantly I complied with her request and stopped asking. But no reasoning could stop my grieving.

In the meantime, Father had announced that Sabela was to be his heiress, and we had celebrated extensively her engagement to Don García. That is, all except my sister Rosa, who, defying my predictions, was still at the convent.

True to my word, I submitted to my new role in the family. With Rosa gone and Sabela by Father's side almost every day learning the intricacies of the affairs of the kingdom, I did not have time to be idle. My desire for adventure gone, I did not mind, but actually welcomed my palace obligations. Even my visits to Flecha dwindled. For the time being, I just wanted to be left alone. And to forget.

But my nightmares did not go away. I knew guilt at my failure to keep Don Julián safe was causing them, and that only seeing him again would make them disappear. So I watched in earnest as the flowers turned to fruit in the trees and the leaves lost their green, until finally the day arrived when Don Alfonso entered the Great Hall to claim his bride.

Finding it difficult to stay still, I searched for Don Julián among the king's retinue. But my hope soon turned to despair when, after examining the knights one by one, I had to admit to myself that Don Julián was not among them. Suddenly the immense hall full of people seemed as empty as a field of snow, and my heart, once warm with hope, froze inside me.

TWENTY-SEVEN

The Wall Shatters

As if trapped in a nightmare from which I couldn't wake up, I endured the engagement ceremony, grateful to my body for remembering what to do, because my mind had forgotten what to command.

During the course of the morning, I was close to Don Alfonso on several occasions, but the rigidity of the palace protocol had prevented me from talking to him. It was not until late in the afternoon, after the ball had already started, that I managed to maneuver my way through the line of dancers and at last found myself in front of him.

Don Alfonso, looking straight into my eyes, acknowledged my presence with a polite, "Princess Andrea." Then, as the dance started, he bowed to me.

"Where is Don Julián?" I asked him as I curtsied back. "Is he all right?"

Don Alfonso smiled. "Why do you want to know, Princess? Your plan has obviously worked. You don't need him anymore."

Afraid that soon the steps of the dance would take Don Alfonso away from me, I swallowed my pride and whispered, "Please, Sire."

Don Alfonso's smile widened. "Yes, Princess. He's all right. But why do you ask? Are you in love with my brother?"

Without losing his smile, Don Alfonso raised his right hand and swiftly blocked the fist I had aimed at his jaw. Still holding my hand in a tight grip, he swirled me under his arm in perfect synchronization with the other couples. Then just before we parted, he pushed a folded paper up my right sleeve, and with a nod, stepped over to his next partner.

It was hot in the room, and the noise like a wave made of music—of the rhythmic tapping of feet and the humming of human voices—crashed inside my head, making me dizzy. Mumbling an excuse to the red blur who had taken Don Alfonso's place, I stumbled away and out of the room.

When I returned to my senses, I was standing by the oak tree, my friendly childhood companion to my stolen glimpses over the adult world. But for my heavy panting, I had no recollection of having run to the garden.

My feet ankle-deep in fallen leaves, I leaned against the old trunk and, taking deep breaths into my starved lungs, recalled Don Alfonso's words. "Yes, Princess, he's all right."

I could feel my body shaking as relief poured into the empty place inside me where sorrow used to be. I closed my eyes. But his voice, his deep authoritarian voice, called me back. "Good evening, Princess."

I opened my eyes and saw the dark figure of a man against the dappled blanket of russet leaves. Don Julián. Don Julián looking at me with his insolent eyes, as if he had never left.

My body tight like a bow under an archer's hand, I jumped. Don Julián stared at me. "I didn't mean to scare you, Princess."

"You didn't, Sir."

Don Julián smiled. "So I see." Bowing slightly, he took my hand to his lips. Then again he looked at me, his dark deep eyes probing mine.

I retrieved my hand his fingers were burning and moved back. "Is anything wrong, Sir?"

For an instant longer, Don Julián looked at me in that curious way that made me shiver. Then, as if a door had closed in his mind, his eyes went blank.

"As you know, Princess, tonight I will follow Lua into the New World," he said. His voice had lost its warmth. "Before I leave, I want to thank you again for everything you did for me when I was . . . wounded." He paused then and searched my face, eagerly, almost desperately as if waiting for me to speak. But at the thought of him leaving, something inside me was breaking again, and I could not think of anything to say.

Don Julián looked away, and after taking off the watch I had given to him so long ago on the river, he handed it to me. "I will not be needing your time reader anymore, Princess." He turned to go.

"Wait, Sir, I . . ."

"Yes, Princess?"

Don't go, Sir. Please don't go, I wanted to say. But I did not know what to say to keep him from leaving. "Why didn't you come to the ceremony?" I said instead, not because I cared, but because it was the first thing that crossed my mind.

Don Julián eyed me sternly, and for a moment I thought he was not going to answer. "I didn't think we were ready to celebrate together, Don Andrés and I," he finally said. "Not yet anyway. Men have died on both sides. Somebody must be blamed. So they blame it on me because I was the one who started the war."

"Don Alfonso, on the other hand," I said, remembering Ama Bernarda's stories, "is being sung as a hero."

Don Julián smiled, a brief smile that did not touch his eyes. "You are right, Princess. My brother has always been the lucky one."

He had said that before, I knew. But when? Suddenly I remembered. "I hope my brother knows how lucky he is," he had said to my sister Margarida when they had parted in the garden. And the doubt returned. Was Don Julián in love with Margarida as I had suspected then? Not sure whether I could handle the truth, I changed the subject. "But you got your wish, Sir. You are going to the New World."

Don Julián smiled again, his mirthless smile. "Yes, Princess. I got my wish. And tonight I would rather . . . I would give anything to be my brother."

I gasped. So I was right! I had been right all along. Don Julián was in love with Margarida. And the pain was so intense, I had to bite my tongue to keep from crying.

Don Julián did not seem to notice. He was staring blankly at a place beyond me as if he, too, were lost in pain. "He got his lady," he said slowly, "while mine is . . . gone." Again he looked at me, his eyes dark and cold like burnt diamonds, searching mine.

"I'm sorry you couldn't get your lady, Sir."

"Sorry? You are . . . sorry?" he repeated, grabbing me by the arms so violently that he hurt me. I welcomed that pain, which made me forget that other one I could not name. "That's all you can say? Sorry? I don't want your pity, Princess. I want you to help me find her again."

"Never!" I shouted, trying unsuccessfully to free myself. "Do you want to stop the wedding and start another war? I will never help you."

As suddenly as he had grabbed me, Don Julián let go of my arms. "Stop the wedding? I do not want to break their engagement, Princess. Why should I? I want you to come with me."

He wants me to go with him? He does not care for Margarida? As his words exploded in my mind with the violence of a summer fire, my mind went blank. I said nothing.

"Would you come with me, Princess?"

I wanted to go so badly that my entire body hurt. And yet . . . I shook my head. "No, Sir. I cannot go with you."

Don Julián did not flinch. "So it is true," he said. "The woman I love is gone." Looming tall over me in his anger, he continued, "I loved her because she was different. She was independent and strong-willed and followed her own mind. And today I only see a beautiful princess dressed in gold and painted like a doll. And as useless as one."

"I'm not a doll!"

"Oh, but you are, Princess. Doña Jimena was right, you are indeed a comely princess now, not the spirited maiden I love."

How did he dare insult me when it was to save his life that I had given my word never to return to the other world?

Don Julián was still talking. "When I asked your mother permission to take you with me, Doña Jimena said you wouldn't want to leave. She said that you were a lady now and didn't care about the New World."

Not knowing whether to be pleased or upset, I stared at him. "Did Mother really say that?"

"Yes. I didn't believe her then, but I do now. And I'm sorry, for you and for me. Goodbye, Princess Andrea. The sun is going down, and there is nothing left for me to do here."

And turning his back on me, he walked away in a rustle of leaves.

My legs rooted to the ground, I remained still, looking at the place where Don Julián had been. And as his words settled in my mind, I came to realize that for the past few months I had been staring at a wall—a wall where reality had been playing itself somehow in a distorted way. But now that the wall had been shattered by Don Julián's angry words, the false images were gone, and I could not pretend anymore. I could not pretend that I was ever going to be happy as a lady in my world. Pretend that I didn't miss the freedom of California, the excitement of the classroom, or the spicy smell of the Coffee House. Pretend that it was the light that prevented me from sleeping every time Lua the copper moon was full.

And as the barriers I had unconsciously built around my feelings disappeared, I had to admit to myself that it had not been guilt over my failure to protect Don Julián that had made me wail in pain when I thought he might be dead, but something more disturbing. I finally understood that I cared for him in a way I had sworn to myself I would never care for anyone when I had fallen out of love with John. And still, it was different. With John I had been a willing victim. I had never wanted to love Don Julián. In fact, I had been so reluctant to do so, I had kept it a secret even from myself.

I moved my arms. Something cold—the perfect circle of my watch—was in my hand. And as I looked at the moon, now full, that from inside the glass seemed to be calling to me, the yearning to follow Don Julián was overwhelming. But it was not so simple. *Don Julián is wrong*, I thought with a pang of anger at the recollection of his words. I am not a useless doll. But he had been right about one thing: I had changed. I would not run away this time. I would never run away again. Resolutely I picked up the heavy train of my gown and returned to the castle.

Back in the Great Hall, the minstrels were still playing as they had been before I left, and the couples were still dancing, weaving intricate patterns as they swirled around each other across the floor. And no one among them seemed to have noticed the world had changed.

Keeping close to the walls, I made my way through the different groups of people talking and wandering around the Hall until I reached the eastern side. As I expected, Mother was sitting by one of the tall windows that opened into the garden. She was not alone, but talking to one of her ladies.

I knew I was not supposed to interrupt Mother under any circumstance, but if I were to make it to the arch tonight, I didn't have time for subtleties. Twisting my skirts in my hands, I walked up to them and, after the briefest of curtsies, said boldly, "Mother, I need to talk to you."

Mother finished her sentence. In a strained silence full of questions, she turned to her lady and nodded. And the lady was on her feet, deep in a curtsy, as Mother rose from her chair and swept past me toward the balcony.

Mother was already sitting under the trellis on the same bench where once—had it only been last spring?—Don Julián had offered a rose to my sister Rosa and promised her his eternal love. But the roses were gone now, and only the gnarled branches remained, bare of leaves, their skeletal fingers twisted around the frame waiting for the winter to come.

"Princess?"

I looked up. But the bitter taste the memories had brought to my mouth had taken my words away.

Mother returned my stare, the twinkle of a smile in her blue eyes. "Princess, is there anything I can do to thank you for rescuing me from yet another boring conversation with Lady Alicia?"

I shook my head. But then the words rushed out. "Yes, Mother. You can, you may . . . I mean, I want your permission to go back to California." Mother's eyes grew wide. "I know, Mother. I know I promised you I would never leave the castle, and yet I have to go, because . . . because I don't belong here.

"I have tried so hard. All these months, I have really tried to become the princess you always wanted me to be. And for a while, I even fooled myself into believing I had. But I was wrong. I was wrong, Mother! I'm not a lady, and no matter how long I stay in the castle, I will never become one. Please. Let me go." The last I said in a whisper.

Mother sat on the stone bench, a queen on her throne, looking at me as if she had never seen me before. And I blushed under her stare for what I hadn't said and she could sense. When I thought my heart would explode, she closed her eyes for a moment.

"I guess Don Julián was right," she said and smiled.

I jumped forward at the implications of her words. "Mother, did you send him to me?"

"No, Princess. I didn't send Don Julián to you. Well, not exactly. Don Julián came to say goodbye this morning. He asked about you. I told him that the war had changed you, that you had become a lady. 'But is she happy?' he persisted, and I had to admit that you weren't, that you were still distressed by your experience. So I told him you still needed time to heal. He insisted that you would never heal if you remained here, that you had to go to California. He was so adamant that when he asked my consent to talk with you, I agreed. Now I see that he was right. You do want to leave."

"I'm sorry, Mother. I . . ."

"I understand, Princess. You are who you are. Nobody, not even you, can change that. But I want you to remember that you are a lady, indeed. You could have run away tonight. Instead you came to me. Now Princess Andrea, if you want to go, you have my permission. But before you go, one more question, Princess. What are you going to tell Don Andrés?"

Tell Father? I had not planned to tell him anything. Father would never agree to let me go. He had warned me already he would banish me forever if I left again.

I shook my head. "I have no time, Mother. Lua will rise soon and—"

"I see. You have not changed after all," Mother said, and her voice was hard, but there was laughter in her eyes. "I guess you give me no choice: I will have to ask him to give you his permission myself." Pulling me to her, she hugged me tightly. "I'm going to miss you, Princess."

"I will miss you, too, Mother," I whispered back.

I was smiling as I rode on Flecha across the baileys toward the massive tower of the gatehouse. What was there for me to fear now? The gate was open, the drawbridge down, and the sentries, smartly dressed in blue and silver, seemed more like decorative figures than real soldiers. But when the guards saw me they came brusquely to attention, and crossing their shiny spears, they blocked my way.

"Hold it!" one of them said, his voice a hollow impersonal grunt under his helmet.

Flecha reared and neighed in anger. "Step aside," I yelled to be heard over the loud clank of metal against stone.

The men did not move. "You cannot leave the castle on

your own, Princess Andrea. King's orders."

"The orders have been canceled!" I insisted in my most authoritative tone.

The guards stood their ground. "I'm sorry, Princess," the same voice said, "but you must wait here until I get the king's confirmation."

Wait? I could not wait! To the west, the sun was already sinking into the ocean. If I wanted to make it to the New World tonight, I had to leave now.

As if reading my mind, Flecha lunged forward, and when the soldiers jumped to one side to avoid being crushed under her hooves, she dashed through the gate.

Followed by shouts of "Alert! To arms!" we galloped away.

By the time I reached the end of the drawbridge, I could already hear the sound of hooves behind me. The soldiers had not wasted any time. Having a host of Suavian soldiers garrisoned outside the castle walls probably had something to do with this. I had chosen the wrong day to leave the castle without the King's consent. I pressed Flecha's flanks, urging her forward.

My plan was to reach the limit of the forest before my pursuers caught up with me. Once there, I would turn west toward the Forbidden Lands, hoping the soldiers would lose my tracks, not expecting me to head that way. But the sound of thundering hooves alerted me that the soldiers were steadily gaining on me. I would never make it to the trees in time.

Despite my efforts, the soldiers closed on me. Soon I was surrounded. I reined in Flecha and turned to face their leader that, by the crossed spears embroidered on his blue surcoat, I realized was Don Gonzalo, my former instructor from my days as a page.

I nodded to him, and just as I placed my right hand over my heart to acknowledge I was surrendering, a piercing yelp of trumpets swept from the castle ramparts. Two short calls and then a pause before the call repeated itself. My heart jumped to my throat as I recognized the summons. Father was calling his men back.

As the sound died in the distance, Don Gonzalo raised his arm in salute and, wheeling his horse around, shouted a brief order at his men. As one, the soldiers turned and followed him back to the castle, their blue-and-white uniforms soon nothing but a speck of color against the dried brown of the autumn bracken.

With an exhilarating cry of triumph, I bent over Flecha. "We did it, Flecha! We did it again! We are free!"

Flecha neighed and pawed the air with her front hooves. And then at my command, she galloped west toward the secret path that led to the Cove of the Dead.

THE SUN HAD ALREADY DISAPPEARED INTO THE OCEAN WHEN WE came to the boulders where I had once hidden from Tío Ramiro. To reach the steps carved in the cliffs that would take me to the arch, I would have to walk from there.

One hand over Flecha's neck, the other holding my skirts, I slid to the ground.

"Goodbye, Flecha," I whispered as I stroked her gently.

Flecha did not move. Kicking the ground with her hind legs, she rubbed her muzzle against my hands looking for a treat.

"Easy, Flecha, easy. I have nothing for you. Eh! Wait a minute. What have you got? Give me that back. Now!"

After a frenzied fight, I retrieved from her mouth the paper she had stolen from my sleeve. It was only when I saw the stamp pressed on the red wax—the rising sun over the horizon, the seal of Alvar—that I remembered the note Don Alfonso had passed to me in the ballroom.

I stretched the paper, now all wrinkled and wet with saliva, against Flecha's saddle, and after breaking the seal, rushed through the unfamiliar handwriting. When I reached the signature, my hands jerked back as if they had touched fire. It was Don Julián's.

I blinked and waited for the words to stop swaying.

> *Princess Andrea,*
>
> *I am leaving tonight for the New World. I would be honored if you came with me.*
>
> *Doña Jimena has given her consent, although she insists you will not want to leave. But I cannot believe you have forgotten how much that world once meant to you.*
>
> *I will wait for you by the oak tree where you met my brother. I beg you to come. The thought of never seeing you again hurts me too much to even consider.*
>
> *Yours,*
> *Don Julián de Alvar*

As I read, Don Julián's strange behavior in the garden played back in my mind, taking on a new meaning. He must have assumed when he first saw me by the oak tree that I had agreed to go with him. His anger at my refusal made sense now.

Why hadn't Don Alfonso told me his brother was waiting for me? I guess he was having too much fun playing with my feelings. At the memory of Don Alfonso's mocking face, the desire to return to the castle and kill him with my bare hands was overwhelming. But I remembered my sister Margarida and her incomprehensible love for him and let it go.

I patted Flecha's flank again. "Go, Flecha, go."

Flecha stared at me, pleading with her big limpid eyes.

I shook my head. "I'm sorry, Flecha, but you can't come."

With a loud neigh of reproach, Flecha turned and cantered away.

I ran along the narrow ledge—loose gravel flying under my satin slippers, pebbles lashing at my spoiled feet—until the path came to an end.

Down below, the ocean had once more claimed the stretch of land that was the Cove of the Dead, and only the arch, a naked rock like an island dressed in foam, was still visible. From where I stood at the top of the cliffs, I could see the waves breaking against the mouth of the cave. I hesitated. The prospect of getting to the arch across the water was not a pleasant one, since I still could not swim. But waiting for the tide to recede was not an option. Lua would be rising any moment now, and I would lose my chance to cross if I did not make it to the cave soon.

My skirts tucked around my waist, I crawled over the boulder that blocked the trail. Turning my back to the ocean, I started down the crude steps carved into the wall. I climbed for what seemed forever until my feet touched the water. Shivering from both its frozen touch and my fear that I would never reach the sand in time, I kept on going, lowering hands and feet one at a time into the now slippery holes. Steadily the water rose, past my knees and up my hosiery.

I stopped then, afraid that my skirts, heavy with water, would drag me down. I was about to climb back when I realized my right foot was not on rock but on soft ground. Tentatively I lowered my left foot. Yes! It stayed level with the other: I had reached the bottom. Taking in a deep gulp of the moist salty air, I released my grasp of the wall and turned.

All I saw was water—dark-green angry water—roaring toward me. I yelped as a wave broke against my chest, sending me backward, a hapless doll against the rocks. I called Don Julián's name.

But the only answer was a bitter taste in my mouth from all the water I had swallowed along with my pride. The laughing cry of seagulls high above my head mocked my despair. As the water pulled back, I plunged ahead and to my right toward the arch.

The next wave hit me again in the chest, pushing me back, but the following one I waded through before it broke, and the one after.

I slowly made my way against the incoming tide until, at last, I reached the ragged rocks of the arch. I clung to them with both hands and feet to avoid being dragged by the under-current from the cave. And then, during a brief pause in swirling water, I leaped forward and rode the wave that was now roaring into the cave.

The force of the ocean was so overpowering I lost my balance, and the wave, wrapping itself like a blanket around my body, pushed me under, crushing my chest with its icy fist. I tried to break to the surface for air. But tossed about by the water, I had lost all sense of direction. Then just when I thought my lungs would burst, I felt the subtle change, the feeling that the water was getting thinner and the air warmer. Air! Air at last, pouring into my lungs. But the water that had held me before was gone, and I fell. I heard my voice screaming and a loud thump as something hard rose to receive me. Then noth-ing—a black empty nothing filled with pain.

Coughing and spitting, I pushed my body up. It hurt to move. I was still struggling to stand when two leather boots suddenly materialized in front of me. "Do you need help, my lady?"

I jumped to my feet, annoyed at being found in such an unbecoming position. Unexpectedly my left foot gave way, and I fell again.

Don Julián knelt by my side. As his head leveled with mine, our eyes met. "Princess Andrea! Are you all right?"

I yanked my dripping hair away from my eyes and nodded.

Again I tried to stand, but when I leaned on my left foot, a wave of pain shot up my leg. Bright points of light flashing before my eyes, I stumbled.

Don Julián's hands were already on my waist holding me. "What's wrong?" The concern in his voice seemed real.

"Nothing," I said, pulling myself away. But ignoring my protests, Don Julián lifted me in his arms and carried me to the back of the cave. As he propped me against the rocks, I understood how much he must have hated depending on us when he was wounded back in the castle. Tío Ramiro had been right. Under the circumstances, Don Julián's self-control had been remarkable.

"It's your ankle, isn't it?" Don Julián was asking.

"I think so, Sir."

Don Julián knelt by my side, "May I have a look?"

I pulled back. "No."

With the last trace of dignity I had left, I gathered my skirts and set them between us. Soaking wet as they were, they just hung there, pasted to my legs with all the grace of a dirty mop.

Don Julián smiled. "I'm afraid you have no choice, Princess. You need help, and I am the only one around. Unless, that is, you wish to spend the night here. But I would not recommend it, my lady. In your damp clothes, you would probably get sick." Again he smiled.

"Would you please stop laughing at me?"

Don Julián's gaze hardened. "Laughing at you?" he repeated, and there was a note of surprise in his voice. "I'm not laughing at you, Princess. Not at all. It's just that . . . I suppose you have a reason to be upset with me. I suppose I should apologize for what I said before in the garden, but the truth is that if my words were what brought you here, I would not change a single one."

"Are you saying that you lied to me?"

"No, Princess. That is not what I mean. I did not lie. Of course what I said was not true, or else you would not have come. But I believed it then. You seemed so different then, so distant, that I really thought you had changed and I . . . I could not stand the idea. I lost my temper. But do not worry, Princess, it will not happen again."

"But when you said that . . . Did you mean it when you said that . . ."

Don Julián smiled. "When I said that I love you? Yes, Princess. I am afraid that is true. I do love you."

Falling to one knee, he grabbed my hands and searched my face eagerly, the way he had before in the garden. "Don't you know, Princess, I have been in love with you from the moment I first saw you? From the moment you walked into my tent, broken and dirty, demanding to be treated as my equal?

"Don't you know I would have given you both moons that day, had you asked for them? I would have happily parted with my life, my kingdom, and my crown, just to see you smile. But all you asked of me was that I would marry your sister. And that, Princess, I could not do. I could not give you up—not yet—when I was still in shock at having found you."

I was shaking so hard by then, I could not answer. Don Julián stared, still for a moment, his eyes ablaze. Then again his eyes grew cold, as embers do in an untended hearth. Letting go of my hands, he pulled back.

"It's all right, Princess," he said, his voice formal now and distant, the voice of the king he once had been. "I understand. I understand I have no claim on you. And I promise I will never mention my feelings again."

"No, Sir, I . . ." I bent forward as he was getting up and raised my arms to stop him. Of their own will, my hands reached for his face. When I touched him, I felt his body tense as if he had expected a blow. Yet he did not move. For an indefinite time, I stood still, staring into his dark angry eyes. Then bending slightly, I kissed him.

Don Julián held me back. "Princess?" His eyes, wide open in surprise, were pleading.

"I don't want you to forget me, Sir," I whispered. "I love you."

His hands were already on my waist pulling me to him when, over the pounding of my heart, I heard the steps—hurried steps over the sand outside the cave. Don Julián set me back against the wall. Drawing his knife, he swept around and faced the entrance where the dark shape of a man was now standing.

"Welcome to my world," a familiar voice said.

Don Julián sheathed his knife and bowed. "Thank you, Sir."

Tío Ramiro did not return his bow, but stepped inside, his right arm stretched in front of him. Don Julián walked up to him and firmly shook the hand Tío was offering, the way people do in California.

As the tension left my chest, the pain returned. I bit my tongue to prevent a moan, and closing my eyes, I willed the pain to go away. When I opened them again, Tío was staring at me, his face set in a frown.

"Do your parents know you are here, young lady?"

"Of course they do," I said. *That is none of your business,* my tone translated.

A flash of pique crossed Tío's face. Don Julián spoke. "Princess Andrea has twisted her ankle. She needs help."

Tío knelt by my side and checked my foot and ankle. "It is not broken," he said, getting up. And as if that meant it did not hurt either, he took my arm. "Come on, Andrea. You're soaking wet. You must change before you catch a cold. Let's go home."

I shivered, noticing the cold for the first time. Leaning against Tío, I limped forward.

"I think it would be better if I carry her."

As Don Julián spoke, Tío Ramiro dropped his arm and, leaving me standing precariously on one foot, turned. "Are you sure, Sir?"

"Absolutely."

Don Julián was already by my side, his arms wrapped around my body. As his face touched mine, I shivered again.

"I have arranged for you to meet the professors in the engineering department, as we agreed," Tío said to Don Julián, leading the way toward the entrance.

Agreed? I thought, confused. When?

"Will they let me go through the program at my own pace?" Don Julián asked.

Between the pain in my ankle and the exhilarating feeling of being so close to Don Julián, my mind was not working properly. It had taken me all that time to realize they were speaking in English.

"But . . . wait a minute! When did you learn to speak English?"

Tío looked at Don Julián. "Haven't you told her?"

"Told me what?"

Don Julián smiled. "Don Ramiro came to Alvar last summer after the peace treaty was signed."

"What?"

"It was your idea, Andrea. You asked me to help Don Julián."

"Why didn't you tell me?"

"Because you would have insisted on coming and ruined our secret. Besides, your previous behavior toward Don Julián didn't exactly qualify you as welcome in his kingdom."

Tío was right. And yet he was not. But before I could make up my mind, we left the arch. As we came onto the beach, Don Julián stopped and set me gently on the sand. I stared after him, toward the east where the moon, tinted orange by the last rays of the setting sun, was rising. Don Julián turned to me. His hands again on my waist, he lifted me above his head and swirled me around. Against the piercing screams of the seagulls, I heard Tio's voice. "Obviously I was mistaken."

When Don Julián put me down, Tío was gone.

"Don't be angry at him, Princess," Don Julián said, a twinkle in his eyes. "Don Ramiro didn't know."

"What was he supposed to know?"

"That you cared for me, Princess."

We were so close then, I could see only his eyes, his dark mocking eyes, burning into mine. Inside his pupils, the pale moon of the New World was dancing.

"What is it, Princess? Do you still believe, as my brother claims, that I have no feelings?" Don Julián asked.

"You haven't given me any reason to believe otherwise, Sir,"
I teased him.

"You are right, Princess. I haven't. Yet."

Wrapping his arms around my waist, he pulled me to him.
As I closed my eyes, I felt the salty taste of the ocean on his lips.
Then, once more, I was gasping for air.

Around us, the New World stood still, waiting.

Acknowledgments

I want to express my gratitude:

To my children, Nicolás and Natalia, who have given me so much;

To Spain and its history, from which I borrowed freely;

To Sandy Asher, who saw the potential of the story when it was merely a seed;

To Dandi Mackall, who helped it grow;

To Mary Lanctot, my first reader;

To Don Swain and the writers of the Bucks County Writers Workshop for their critique and support;

To Peggy Tierney and Stephanie Burgevin at Tanglewood for believing so strongly in my story;

And to my parents and my sister María José, who sent me on my journey.

About the Author

Photo by Natalia Eldering-Ferreiro

Carmen Ferreiro-Esteban grew up in Galicia, northern Spain, and obtained her Ph.D. in biology from the Universidad Autónoma in Madrid. She later went on to spend several years working as a postdoctoral researcher at universities and government institutions in both Spain and the United States. She presently lives in Doylestown, Pennsylvania, with her two children and works as a freelance writer and translator. The author of four books on drugs and diseases, this is her first novel.

About this book, Carmen says, "*Two Moon Princess* is loosely based on personal experience. Like my protagonist Andrea, I arrived in California from Spain, the Old World. I have tried to capture in the book the sense of wonder I felt during those amazing first months in California and the shock of finding myself an alien in my own country when I went back."

To find out more about the author and this book, please visit www.carmenferreiroesteban.com.

For study guide questions on this book
and activities developed for all of our titles,
please visit Tanglewood's website at
www.tanglewoodbooks.com